> You have walked through "Hillcrest" and have seen the humble community. Thanks for listening to the old stories.
>   Your brother in Christ,
>   Paul Brown

FUNDY BAY

P. B. Russell

P. B. Russell

This book is dedicated to my daughters, Emily and Stephanie, for all their love and support through good times and bad, and for making me feel like a good Dad.

FUNDY BAY

CONTENTS

CHAPTER ONE 4
CHAPTER TWO 21
CHAPTER THREE 34
CHAPTER FOUR 60
CHAPTER FIVE 89
CHAPTER SIX 115
CHAPTER SEVEN 128
CHAPTER EIGHT 135
CHAPTER NINE 144
CHAPTER TEN 174

CHAPTER ONE
The Village's History

As my Great Uncle Power used to say, "Fundy Bay isn't the end of the world, but you can sure see it from there!" Undoubtedly it was similar to hundreds of other small coastal communities along the Bay of Fundy and Atlantic Ocean shorelines of the US and Canada, but to me, growing up there in the 1960s and 1970s, it offered a rich mosaic of fascinating characters, superstitions, and geographical wonders with an unlimited number of things to see and do. Then again, trying alongside my brother to set my neighbour's outhouse on fire was my idea of a fun time, so perhaps my frame of reference was a bit skewed.

I don't know if anyone knew exactly when Fundy Bay was first settled although 1838 was the date most often quoted. The local historian and church deacon, John Grady, recalled being told that the village was originally called Miller's Cove, since the majority of early settlers to the area were named Miller. That name stuck until 1865 when it was changed to Grady's Cove to reflect the predominance of the Grady family in the village. Apparently the name was changed again in 1879 when some enterprising individual, new to the area, convinced the elect of the community that the rather mediocre harbour would attract much more commercial activity if it was referred to as a bay and not a cove. At that time, the Grady family was fading in numbers and influence and was unable to maintain its place of honour in the village name. For a while it seemed that the community would never get a new name since each family presented strong arguments why their surname should be so honoured. Finally, the stalemate was broken when someone, in a last gasp of originality, suggested that since the community was located on the Bay of Fundy, why not choose the name "Fundy Bay" before some other village did. And that was that.

The 1850s and 1860s were a time of rapid expansion within the community. A post office was established in 1855. A United Baptist church was built in 1855 and opened in January 1856. A lighthouse was erected in 1859 on an elevated piece of land overlooking the harbour. A one room school was built in 1868 along the Porter Road.

During this time, the main occupations of those within the community were fishing, forestry, and farming, all on a modest scale.

Fundy Bay encompassed approximately two square miles on the Bay of Fundy coast of Nova Scotia, on the economically disadvantaged side of the gently sloping North Mountain ridge. The population of the area seemed to remain fairly steady at 220 to 230 persons year in and year out. However, of that number, approximately sixty percent were of the Crawford and Goomar clans, another twenty-five percent had Betts or Cobb as a surname, and the remaining fifteen percent mostly kept their doors locked.

Our family was only one of two in all of Fundy Bay with Beck as a last name. At any one time there were probably no more than a dozen different family names in all of Fundy Bay. This predominance by a select few families resulted from the fact the Crawfords, Goomars, Betts, and Cobbs freely and repeatedly intermarried, meaning that they were really all family or near family. This rampant intermarrying made relationships quite complex for the genealogists in the crowd. My good friend, Gord Cobb, often tried to make sense of the intertwined relationships which were created since his mother and father had been first cousins and his grandparents on his father's side had been first cousins, and second cousins to Gord's grandparents on his mother's side. We weren't sure, but we suspected that this made Gord his mother's uncle, twice removed.

In any event, these bonds didn't prevent the families from having their own rivalries and name calling contests, but generally these were settled by the time the next Crawford-Goomar wedding rolled around. These nuptials were moments to celebrate. Usually they were preceded by groom-to-be Goomar quitting grade eight once he had reached voting age, getting on the welfare roll, which in Fundy Bay was held in higher regard than steady employment, and acquiring a barely holding together noisy car to transport his lovely teenage bride-to-be to their pre-owned but new-to-them mobile trailer which they hauled in the woods next to Ma and Pa Goomar. The proud parents did not seem to mind subdividing their property in this way with their son and daughter in law (nee niece) and served as able babysitters to their latest granddaughter, who we all had to admit had performed her flower girl duties admirably while preceding her Mom up the aisle.

In the 1960s and 1970s, during the time of my childhood, Fundy Bay was a typical, small, WASPy, rural town stuck in time, ignorant of the fact that the era in which they were living had long since passed in the far away urban centres. Truth was, you had to travel over one hundred miles to get to the nearest city, Halifax, which was also the capital of the province. In fact, Halifax was simply referred to as "the city". In the 1960s, a trip like that would take you four hours one way, a pilgrimage that few Fundy Bayers would ever make. Hell, many of the residents had gone their entire life without ever leaving the local county.

Anyone who did not live in Fundy Bay or in any of the neighbouring coastal villages was considered to be "from outside". The typical Fundy Bayer had no idea of or concern for the goings-on in urban centres or in other countries; after all, it really didn't affect them. If someone from outside ventured into the community and started up a conversation about the fighting in Ireland, the famine in Africa, the earthquake in California, or the results of the last national election, they'd get very little uptake. We knew which party won the last election, but somehow when you got past all the rhetoric, the promised changes never made their way to Fundy Bay. People would usually take the time to vote, making their way to the house which had been chosen as the polling station while discussing how lucky the homeowner was to be raking in some easy cash.

Most necessities could be purchased at the local store, and those that couldn't could be delivered or picked up by one of the neighbours making his monthly trip to town. No need to go to a bank since you needed all your cash just to make ends meet and for Saturday night's poker game. This isolation was not all that hard to understand: many of the villagers were illiterate, so the daily newspaper offered little attraction other than for the comic strips. Few people could afford a television, and those industrious persons who could were the very ones with no time to watch it. Even fewer people owned a reliable vehicle, and those that did rarely took the time to get it registered or apply for a driver's license since it was used mostly for local trips anyway, hauling traps or hay.

Other than indoor plumbing, probably the rarest luxury during this period was the telephone. It seemed ludicrous to spend scarce money on such a contraption when all the people you knew were within walking distance anyway. Anyone contemplating aloud about getting hooked up would likely be asked by a suspicious neighbour, "why, who do you know with a phone?".

Sure, people in the Valley had a phone, but we didn't know many of them anyway, and we liked it that way. And who needed an indoor bathroom when an outhouse or chamber pail would do just fine, even if it did mean getting a little frost on your backside during the winter months.

These were simple country folk who on the surface at least seemed to live uncomplicated lives. The villagers made certain choices once in life and stuck to them dogmatically until death. Once you voted for a certain political party, you would be putting your "X" next to that party's candidate in each election for as long as you lived. Same with your choice of church, the brand of tobacco you smoked, and the type of beer you drank, that is, when you weren't drinking locally produced moonshine. And when registerable cars finally were affordable for more Fundy Bayers, the same lifelong blind loyalty applied. The adults of Fundy Bay liked Merle Haggard, Gentleman Jim Reeves, Johnny Cash, and Elvis, and didn't have much patience for those long haired Brits from Liverpool shaking their heads and singing in high voices.

The churchgoers in Fundy Bay knew that the preacher's story about walking on the wide path but entering through the narrow gate meant they would meet very few of their neighbours in heaven. They'd speak in hushed tones behind closed doors about the sins being committed in other homes, concluding with the usual "dear, dear" condemnation, but would do very little personally to address the community's ills. The analogy of the narrow gate was more applicable to the likelihood of the residents attaining a higher education, higher in this case meaning anything over grade nine or ten. But no matter, too much education wasn't good for a child. It just confused him and kept him from joining his father out fishing or farming. And if fishing or farming was good enough for his father, it damn well should be good enough for him.

In many respects, being isolated had its advantages. You could lead impoverished lives without ever knowing it. What meaning did a national poverty line drawn at $10,000 annually for a family of four have when you lived in a community where the average annual family income was less than $2,000 and the typical family membership numbered close to double digits? The only meaningful points of comparison for Fundy Bayers were their own neighbours, and they were no better off. This was a blissful time when the only measures of success that mattered were the number and brand of appliances you owned. This wasn't a case of misery loves company, since few were miserable and fewer still could afford company.

It wasn't until the late 1970s when residents started to purchase automobiles and televisions, learned to read in greater numbers, and travelled the newly paved roads leading to the Valley towns that they began to feel embarrassed about the conditions in which they had lived for so long. It was a classic case of the fall from grace in the Garden of Eden, except in this instance, the bite out of the apple came when little Johnny Goomar made his first trip fifteen miles away to Riverton, and suddenly realized how naked he really was.

The main road in Fundy Bay, referred to simply by the locals as the Fundy Bay road, was in the shape of a "U". The arms of the "U" were formed by the road leading in and out of Fundy Bay and the bottom of the "U" was the northern most section of the road running parallel to the rough, gravel shore road which snaked along the shoreline and past the huts owned by the area fishermen. The eastern side of the Fundy Bay road where it bottomed out and turned west to run parallel to the shore was known as "the corner". Immediately beside the corner was a fifteen foot wooden bridge known locally as "the bridge" which enabled travellers to traverse a body of water known simply as "the brook". The bridge was a popular hangout spot for anyone trying to obtain or maintain a certain reputation for toughness.

When the Fundy Bay road was officially christened "the Shore Road" by municipal authorities in the Valley eager to match tax bills with specific house addresses, it was viewed as simply another case of government ineptitude and the term was never used by local residents. We all knew that the true Shore Road was the gravel road running along the harbour. The government christened "Shore Road" continued to be know by us as the Fundy Bay Road. Whatever the name, the main road in Fundy Bay was part of the larger "Fundy Trail" which was promoted by the government to tourists as a "must see" and which connected many of the shoreline communities. In the case of Fundy Bay, that's about all it was, a trail. It was unpaved until the early 1970s and certainly wasn't much of a road.

Any drive through the community along the three mile long Fundy Bay road would enable visitors to see that the economy of the area was actually centred on two primary industries: the inshore fishery, primarily lobster fishing, and farming. The only two arteries off the Fundy Bay road in the entire village, excluding the real shore road, were the Porter road, where my father grew up on a five hundred acre farm, and the Crawford road, which ran along a cliff overlooking the Bay of Fundy.

Very few of the farmers or fishermen were terribly successful plying their trade, but it enabled them to at least work honestly for their living doing what had been passed on to them by their fathers, and to their fathers by their grandfathers, and so on.

It usually amazed outsiders to learn that few, if any, of the fishermen knew how to swim. However, as one of the old salts would invariably reply, "well, son, the trick is not to fall overboard." Many of the fishermen basically attempted to earn just enough stamps during fishing season to qualify for a minimum level of unemployment insurance for the off-season. This preoccupation with collecting stamps began in 1957 when the federal government introduced amendments to the Unemployment Insurance Act to allow self employed fishermen the right to claim benefits. The quantity of catch sold to an authorized buyer determined the number of stamps and the amount of U.I. benefits the fishermen would collect.

For many, inshore lobster fishing proved to a challenge in Fundy Bay. It seemed to the fishermen that the elusive crustaceans migrated further and further away from the local trapping grounds each year, and those that didn't seemed to be getting smaller and smaller.

For their part, the farmers generally choose to raise dairy cattle and vegetables, a questionable choice given the relatively small size of their herds and lands, and their inability to invest in the equipment necessary to mechanize their operations. In the minds of most, these farmers and fishermen were nothing more than hobbyists, a fact uncontested annually by the tax department. Therefore, to the casual observer, it seemed that these people were getting very little financial reward from all their attempts to harvest the sea and the land. However, to those who lived in Fundy Bay, one simple truth was understood, and this made it all crystal clear: those who loved the sea, fished; those who loved the land, farmed. These farmers and fishermen knew that the best prize life offered was the chance to work hard at work worth doing, something which had been understood and voiced by one no less esteemed than US President Theodore Roosevelt.

Being able to eke out even a substandard living was reward enough for these people, since they were able to enjoy the freedom of working for themselves, in the great outdoors, with the wind in their hair and the sun overhead. These men took pride in their work and in what might seem to be rather meagre accomplishments. They could see daily the results of their efforts: what they planted in the ground, grew. What was dropped into the sea was retrieved holding at least some catch.

A wonderful camaraderie existed amongst these primary producers. They regarded each other as peers, daily putting their strength and stamina to the test, and savouring those moments when they would gather to exchange and exaggerate stories and experiences.
These men would do anything for each other and would pass on what salaried workers voraciously protected as their due, some relaxation time, to be able to help their neighbour get his hay in before the rain came, or to help repair his traps before sunrise.

Amidst their labour, they would still find time to chat and needle each other mercilessly at every turn. One minute they would be discussing the weather forecast, the next they would be making predictions about whether or not hairless Joe Palooka was going to win his next fight in the daily comic strips. While huffing and puffing hauling their traps out of the water and into the boat, they might be engaged in some meaningless chatter about the latest adventures of their other comic strip favourite, Mandrake the Magician.

Even a blind person could soon identify the occupation of the head of the household by simply entering the front porch of the person's house. If you detected a pungent salty, briny smell, you were in the home of a fisherman. If the odours assailing your nostrils were a combination of hay and manure, you were in the home of a farmer.

It was a hard existence. Most of these people would be up before dawn, and would not retire for the evening until near midnight. There was no separation of work time from personal time. Your work was all around you. There was no escaping it. It was in the same ground on which you raised your family and built your home, and in the bay water whose waves constantly danced and sang, lulling you to sleep each night through an open window.

These people were honest and uncomplicated in their emotions and ambitions. There was nothing ambiguous or pretentious about them. When they laughed, they laughed the way a laugh was meant to be. When they were angry, they did not bottle it up inside until it tied a knot in their gut. Rather, they expressed their anger, dealt with it, and then moved on. Despite the hardships, you would never see a happier or more dedicated bunch of individuals setting out to work each day. This was a situation which couldn't be comprehended or appreciated by those deskbound nine-to-five civil planner urbanites who were preoccupied with poverty lines and redefining the fragile social fabric of communities such as these with their handouts. By providing handouts, they enticed entire generations to trade in their heritage for easy government money and created a vicious cycle of dependency that would not be broken in many decades.

Of course, not everyone in Fundy Bay found their calling in farming or fishing, although you would be hard pressed to find a family within the community which did not have some member of their kin so engaged. The main source of employment for the remaining residents, for those who actually sought employment, was located several miles away in the Valley. There were several small factories situated in various communities up and down the Valley, in communities such as Riverton, Centretown, Dodgeton, Queenstown, and Grahamville. These factories were always in the market for unskilled labourers who would be willing to drive up to sixty miles a day and work long hours at minimal wage for the furtherance of some faceless employer's growing regional empire. Fundy Bayers who decided to take such employment did not regard it as a career but rather as a means to an end. Besides, such employment was heavily seasonal and tenuous given the closure rate of Valley businesses, so the goal was to obtain sufficient stamps during the summer and fall months to enable them to hibernate in Fundy Bay all winter and spring, only emerging once every other week to drive to town to cash and quickly spend their unemployment insurance cheque.

At various times local preachers would quote Proverbs to point out that while a man plans his course, the Lord determines his steps. This truth would bitterly hit home to the village folk during certain winters when the factories decided to remain open, requiring the locals to make the long trip to and from work each day, navigating the now treacherous North Mountain roads in all kinds of snowy and icy conditions. After an early morning snow storm, it was bitter irony to see these reluctant factory workers, men and women, straining for all they were worth, risking cardiac arrest, desperately trying to shovel out their cars and trucks, all so that they could be on time for a job they couldn't stand.

It is said that necessity is the mother of invention. This was no doubt the reason why so many Fundy Bayers were proficient Jacks of all trades, as self reliance was a prerequisite for persons unable to afford to hire out work. Therefore, if your car needed some maintenance, or you wanted some rewiring done in your house, or your plumbing needed repair, or you wanted an addition built onto the house, you certainly had no need to call in high priced Valley professionals with fancy pieces of paper on the wall but with questionable skills. All you had to do was sound the call, and the neighbours would be tripping over each other to lend their services for a nominal fee.

Certain families came to be associated with possessing skills in a particular trade. For example, the Crawfords were known for being excellent carpenters, the Morgans for having considerable masonry skills, and the Newcombs for being expert brewmasters, albeit illegally. Many of these individuals became very proficient at their trades, and actually decided to legitimize their skills by seeking some formal accreditation. Two camps were basically formed: those who could do the job and had the papers to prove it, and those who could do the job. Most of those in the former group decided to seek their fortunes elsewhere and commuted daily to job sites many miles from Fundy Bay, being held in high regard throughout the Valley as highly skilled and in demand masons, plumbers, electricians, mechanics, and carpenters. Those without the piece of paper proving their skill level usually supplemented their other sources of income by accepting odd jobs throughout the community. Those skilled tradesmen who could not stand up to the pressure of regular work in their profession usually opted for a hum drum existence of seasonal work in the factory along with the unskilled masses.

Despite its limited numbers, Fundy Bay had two permanent church buildings serving the United Baptists and the Sanctified Methodists. At various other times, there were as many as four denominations active within the community when those of other faiths held services within their homes or outside in tents. However, no one church enjoyed a membership of greater than sixty persons and excluding those who attended church once a year at roll call service to remain in good standing, only twenty to thirty persons would be in attendance in each of the two mainstream churches each week. I was a member of the United Baptist church. For years as a youngster I thought the sign in front announced proudly that we were the "Untied" Baptists, which seemed rather confusing given our usual closing hymn, "Bless be the Ties That Bind".

FUNDY BAY

To enter Fundy Bay, coming from the Valley over the North Mountain, you first had to travel through the community of Mount Ruby. This was not only a nice name for a village, but also turned out to be an irresistible command for many of the menfolk. Ruby Goomar, one of the few spinsters of Fundy Bay, was mother to twelve children by the time she was thirty-two, and as local gossip had it, no two children had the same father. Despite or maybe because of her reputation and crowded abode, various religious men of the community were rather devout in their attempts to convert Ruby, frequenting her house while supposedly carrying the well wishes of the congregation. There were those parishioners who complained about what could be misconstrued as unseemly conduct by their fellow church goers, feeling that these would be missionaries were giving special meaning to the term "lay person". Deacon Goomar would usually remind these mean-spirited gossips that some were born to sow, some to plough, and some to spread.

Even though the residents of Fundy Bay were by and large as poor as church mice, the community itself actually had a very rich history. This was in fact typical of many other communities lining the Bay of Fundy coast of Nova Scotia, New Brunswick, and Maine. Most of the residents basically lived hand to mouth: if you ever commented on the squalor in which they lived, their hand would soon connect with your mouth.

Many well known commercial ships such as the SS Valinda and the Elizabeth Cann regularly visited Fundy Bay, as well as all the ports along the coast to deliver goods from Saint John and Maine to the local enterprises. One black eye on the community's record was the tragic sinking on Valentine's Day 1941 of the Rosie M ship and the loss of all crew members. Captain Balcom of the Rosie M had long been a favourite of the local gentry because of his ability to spin yarns about his many travels around the world, and his willingness to partake of the local stock, both alcoholic and female. He was buried in the Fundy Bay cemetery, and although he had never been married and his tombstone simply showed his name followed by "Lost at Sea", his grave was always decorated with numerous bouquets of flowers for every occasion for years to come, a lasting testament to his popularity and stamina.

Our next door neighbour, Edna Moore, recalled a time in the life of the community when three hotels were in operation. Also, several stores operated in Fundy Bay, although most of them seemed to close their doors after only a few seasons. The exception was the Anthony Brothers store, which operated from the early 1940s to the late 1960s, closing only upon the sudden death of the remaining brother, Harris. The Anthony Brothers store was a real treasure trove for young and old alike, a general store in the truest sense of the word. In the store you could find a wide variety of foodstuffs, hardware, fishing and farming supplies, toiletries, clothing, notions, books, crafts, magazines, tobacco products, and toys, and anything else that the poor folk of Fundy Bay could possibly be enticed into buying. My brother and I loved the jars of Anthony Brothers fresh baked beans with molasses, a potent mixture which was ten percent nutrition and ninety percent ammunition.

My Grammy Hayes, a university educated, enterprising woman always willing to consider new ways to supplement the family income, used to knit mittens and socks for sale in the Anthony Brothers store. All this plenty was crammed into every available space within the 30 feet by 15 feet store. Water pails were hanging from the ceiling, rubber boots were lined up along the back wall, china ornaments were on display everywhere, and penny candy sat in large glass jars on top of and under the front counter, always just beyond the reach of anyone less than five years old. In the store people could buy Fundy Bay ashtrays, Fundy Bay candle holders, Fundy Bay plates, and a variety of other products with "Fundy Bay" printed on them.

As the business became more and more popular, the Anthony Brothers houses, which were located on either side of the store, seemed to keep expanding at a rate eclipsed only by the increasing girth of the store owners. Even the locals thought success had gone to the Anthony Brothers heads when for two consecutive years, they gave out Anthony Brothers store calendars, an ostentatious reminder of their wealth in a community where certain residents could barely afford a thumb tack to hang up the calendar. It also irked many clients that the Anthony Brothers, despite their obvious success and means, refused to extend credit to anyone who did not own their own car, thereby excluding all by a handful of Fundy Bay residents. The grumbling continued for some time until the September of 1965, when the policy was credited with saving a local life. A despondent teenager named Marty Goomar, heartbroken after his father, Theodore, refused to give his permission to allow him to marry his sixteen year old sweetheart, fatally shot himself in the woods behind the Fundy Bay cemetery. In the brief investigation which followed, a suicide note written by Marty was discovered, and in it he declared he was going to first kill his father, then himself. It was then learned that he had walked earlier in the day to the Anthony Brothers store to purchase two bullets, being fairly confident of his marksmanship. However, having only enough money for one bullet and not extended any credit by Harris to enable him to purchase the second, Marty was limited to only one shot, the one which successfully penetrated his head. Harris' no credit policy was then vindicated. However, Theodore Goomar never got over the grudge he developed when he realized that Harris Anthony had insulted the Goomar family name by insinuating they lacked the means and honour to repay even a one bullet debt.

This unfortunately was not the last tragedy which somehow involved the Anthony Brothers store. Archibald Crawford, one of the renowned village drunks and orators, was out in the back field checking on the latest batch of moonshine when his two sons, Billy and Randy started a horrible fight over which one of them had gotten their second cousin, Cindy Goomar pregnant. Seems that they both wanted the honour, both had impressive credentials, and neither would relinquish their claim. A violent fistfight then broke out between the two brothers. Archibald entered the kitchen just in time to see Billy twirling a new fishing line around in the air like a lasso before casting it towards Randy. The heavy lead sinker at the end of the fishing line hit Randy on the temple and killed him instantly. The police easily reeled in Billy despite the garbled testimony given by Archibald, who was reportedly shaken by the fact that all during the questioning the police were within a few feet of discovering his prize still. Again, it was learned that the murder weapon had been bought by Billy earlier in the week at the Anthony Brothers store. Harris was quick to point out that Billy had purchased the line and sinker with cash. Nonetheless, in an attempt to avoid any future liability, he thereafter posted a sign near the front entrance of the store reading "The Anthony Brothers are not responsible for any damage or death caused by the use or misuse of any items purchased in this store".

For some time this had an adverse affect on their sales of foodstuffs, but this was made up for by a notable increase in the store's popularity amongst the young teenage male crowd within the community which associated their newfound consumerism as a sign of toughness. For his part, Billy Crawford was released from prison after serving only two years, but was killed shortly thereafter in a terrible car crash by the bridge in Fundy Bay, being hit by a drunk driver of a half ton truck. This was no surprise to the local soothsayers who often pointed out that anyone committing a violet crime would themselves be the victim of a violent crime.

One of the main attractions in the Anthony Brothers store for the children of Fundy Bay was the large, blue square salt lick located in the back row. The salt lick, meant for bovine palates, was conveniently out of sight of the front counter, enabling the children to sneak a lick during each visit without getting caught.

The salt lick was a staple at the store for many years, until the winter of 1963 when the local health nurse determined that it was responsible for a local epidemic of chicken pox amongst the young children. Morris Anthony agreed to dispose of the salt lick for humanitarian reasons, and since it was only a fraction of its original size, it was highly unlikely that any farmer would be buying it for his herd. The Anthony's replaced the salt lick with a display of dulce, hoping to cash in on the obvious adolescent desire for salt. This proved to be unprofitable, however, when Gertrude Halfpenny, the local sophisticate known for always giving her two cents worth, sampled the dulce and declared it to be a food fit only for commoners and the unbaptized, for those who were so poor as to have no choice but to resort to eating things harvested from the sea bottom.

The original Anthony Brothers store burned down in 1964 when I was six years old, and one year before Morris Anthony died. Harris built a slightly smaller store nearby, significantly situated just beyond the original site property owned jointly by the brothers. But it was no secret; with the condition of Morris' heart deteriorating to the point where he could no longer cross a room without becoming seriously winded, the retail venture was for all intents and purposes a one person operation. With Morris' death in the spring of 1965, Harris seemed to lose much of his enthusiasm for the business, and the variety of goods available stagnated considerably.

The new store seemed to serve as an unhappy reminder to its neighbour, Morris's widow, Elma, of her loss of status in the community, and she never missed an opportunity to speak derisively about the way in which Harris ran the store, how Morris and she had been left with nothing after the fire, and how she had refused to take one red cent from Harris after Morris death. In fact, after Morris' death, Elma never stepped foot again in the new store and would hire someone to drive her six miles to Johnstown in the Valley to do all her shopping, even though the taxi fare represented a good portion of her weekly food allowance. Elma always insisted that the driver of the car park in the driveway of the new Anthony's store when picking her up in case her weekly act of snubbery would otherwise be missed by her brother-in-law. This only intensified the rift that had grown between the once amiable families, and required the locals to be more discreet when discussing or displaying their latest purchases whenever Elma was within range.

It gave many of the older residents a feeling of discomfort when making the trip into Anthony's store, since they could sense Elma watching them through her parlour window, and they knew they would hear about their misplaced loyalty from her Sunday in church or at the next meeting of the women's missionary society. This presented a fairly lucrative commercial opportunity to the young and indifferent of the community, who would offer to go to Anthony's to shop on behalf of those faint of heart. Elma obviously knew what was going on, but she had no proof of who was hiring these mercenaries. She did spend a lot of time outdoors in the heat of day, and coincidentally during peak store hours, working in her many flower gardens, to monitor the goings on at the hated Anthony's store and the destination of these cads for hire.

Nonetheless, the new Anthony's store continued to be popular, and remained the principal source of retail goods for Fundy Bay residents for another four years until Harris' death in the fall of 1969 of an acute asthma attack. This brought an end to an era in the life of Fundy Bay, and to Elma's interest in horticulture. Harris' widow, Eva, sold the remaining stock to a store in Riverton in the Valley, and had the store torn down, which meant that for the first time since 1942, Elma and Eva had an unobstructed view of each other's homes and happenings. Although the two widows would never be mistaken for best of friends, they nonetheless regularly exchanged pleasantries, and would even be seen together occasionally enjoying a cup of tea or lemonade or reading books while sitting on Eva's front veranda on balmy summer evenings.

When Eva died of a stroke in 1970, Elma sat reverently with the immediate family during the funeral service, and even had to be comforted by Eva's son, Malcolm, during the singing of "What A Friend We Have in Jesus". At the graveside, Elma lingered longer than anyone, accepting the awkward condolences offered, and recounting special moments she and Eva had shared as neighbouring teenage brides. People paying their respects at the cemetery that day couldn't help but comment among themselves that the sister-in-law floral arrangement was more spectacular than any of the others and must have cost a pretty penny.

Most of the residents of Fundy Bay did not hold down a steady, year round job, and they liked it that way. The ultimate challenge for many was to qualify somehow for social assistance, of any variety. In fact, at various times of the year, close to three quarters of the village's residents were in receipt of some form of monthly government aid. Dad, being one of the few community members with a car and an annual albeit minuscule salary, had the pleasure of driving many of the hopeful cases to the various agencies seeking funding. The way Dad told it, the preparation these persons would go through in anticipation of their moment before the panel of experts or authorities would make seasoned actors like Olivier proud. The drive to the interviews was always a source of amusement to Dad.

One of the favourite and most effective scams was for the individual to place soggy chewing tobacco under his arm all during the drive to the Valley, as this would apparently give him severe palpitations by examination time, and he could be declared disabled by virtue of having an abnormal heartbeat. This newfound heart condition was good for a monthly pension from the easily duped government and proved to be a tidy sum which nicely supplemented any cash which could be generated seasonally by cutting timber, hauling hay, or hunting wild rabbits, pursuits not normally suited for those with such cardiac concerns.

Perpetrating insurance scams was also a noteworthy calling, although these did sometimes backfire. Orest Frizzel discovered this the hard way when he tried to sue for personal damages with a claim that a leak in his car's gasoline caused it to explode with him in it. Orest was left with nothing more than a burned out shell of a car, singed hair and eyebrows, and a ninety day jail sentence when the insurance investigators discovered straw in the gas tank, and were able to prove that he had torched his own vehicle. They also showed conclusively that his bodily scars and damage were attributable to falling asleep while smoking in bed while in the company of Judy Coutts, his ex and his neighbour's then present wife, an alcoholic woman known around the area for her honesty while under oath or under the influence.

Brent Goomar tried to parlay his taste for antifreeze into a government pension. Knowing through experience that it gave him seriously blurred vision he drank a healthy dose on the way to his examination. After convincing the physician of his near-blind condition and need for government assistance, Brent ran from the office in a celebratory mood, only to get run over and killed by a truck which he never saw coming.

Noteworthy causes for which government pensions were readily available to Fundy Bay residents included being blind, deaf, being in possession of a bad back or limbs, or just for being poor with children numbering in the double digits. Eldon Cobb, Gord's grandfather, was one of the recipients of a blind pension, and he never failed to parlay his stipend into a tidy sum each Friday and Saturday nights at the floating poker games attended by many of the other disabled members of the community. It was often marvelled how Eldon, with his darkened glasses pushed to the top of his head, kept pace with all the other players, never straining to read the cards in play at the center of the six foot long oval table or to up the ante in spite of the dim lighting and the ever present thick clouds of cigarette smoke.

Being poor turned out to offer access to various sources of assistance once the social services agents in the Valley started to do field trips to all the fishing communities and villages along the North Mountain. Using some statistical data generated by the federal government, these agents were easily able to demonstrate that the average family within Fundy Bay was well below the country's poverty line. This term was unfamiliar to most persons in Fundy Bay, and it might prompt them to ask if they served soup there and if they did, where could they get in line. After having been given some undecipherable economic and financial mumbo jumbo, the bewildered couple would be startled to hear that they were entitled to receive a monthly welfare cheque for a graduated amount dependent on the number of children they had at home. In addition, the new improved family allowance would provide the couple with another monthly sum of money to reward them for the good choices they had made in deciding to have twelve children. Now didn't this just fly in the face of Gertrude Halfpenny's remarks that the rich get richer and the poor have children!

Having children and inviting social services agents into the home soon became a growing business around Fundy Bay. Husbands who had long ago given up having more children even started staying home on Friday and Saturday nights, and another baby boom was created. There was soon a run on nails and tape at the Anthony Brothers store as parents decided that to make room for their thirteenth child, it would be necessary to build a third room onto the old homestead. But, hell, the first welfare cheque would more than pay for the sheets of cardboard needed for interior partitions and the sawdust used for insulation.

By far the least questioned scenario for being granted a government pension was for reasons of having a learning disability, either themselves or for a dependent child. By demonstrating to the government social worker that you or one or more of your children had a cognitive deficit, you could achieve your goal of obtaining a regular government cheque. And the size of the cheque grew with each additional person within the household similarly assessed. Better still, if you could add in your spouse to the ranks of the learning disabled, that boosted the cheque amount even more. Heck, hadn't your in-laws after all always insisted that their child must have been crazy to marry you? The only fly in the ointment was that among the younger generation, a notion had developed that it was not all that cool to be the recipient of a disability pension especially since the child never saw any of the money. The parents would placate their embarrassed child by promising never to identify to other family members or to neighbours that a disability pension was coming into the house. However, neighbours tended to get suspicious when they noticed that the family fridge was now regularly well stocked with store-bought beer.

Despite the widespread reliance on government assistance, many residents of the community did try to eke out a living by more industrious means. Melvin Newcomb, a borderline alcoholic who lived across the street from Edna Moore, went door to door peddling fish that he was able to catch fairly near to shore in rather infrequent jaunts out in a leaky punt owned by his brother and our next door neighbour, Merle. Melvin and Merle had both been quite spiritual in their youth, and commanded a good knowledge of the Bible, so Melvin convinced the elders at the Sanctified Methodist church to allow him to be the substitute preacher one Sunday, an invitation that was never again extended. Apparently in midst of telling the story of Jesus feeding the five thousand, Melvin reached behind the pulpit for his trademark fish bucket, hauled out two large harbour pollack, and proceeded to emphatically rip them from stem to stern all the while continuing the saga. Four small girls in the front bench vomited and Gertrude Halfpenny fainted when blood from the fish spurted all over their Sunday best and then onto the bread loaves which Melvin had just broken not two minutes earlier. The piece de resistance was when Melvin, apparently flustered by the reaction of his audience and himself covered in oil and blood, accidently skewered his index finger on a sizeable fish bone, causing him to utter a series of oaths that would make the heartiest of stevedores proud. People who were there later commented that while they did not learn any new words that day, they did hear a few interesting combinations.

From that day onwards, Melvin would ply this higher calling only when walking about the community with fish bucket in hand. Several of the community's housebound seniors were more than pleased to listen to his recital of scripture, or would offer him a meal of fresh fish while he provided them with some biblical teaching and insight. My Uncle Willie, himself a very enterprising lumber mill owner and operator, dubbed Melvin "the Reverend Fish Man", a term which was never fully appreciated by Melvin.

FUNDY BAY

△ △ △

CHAPTER TWO
The Beck Family

My father, Ainsley Herndon Beck, was born in 1909, and spent the first thirty nine years of his life on the Beck family farm, a lovely, secluded five hundred acre spread one mile from Fundy Bay. The farm was situated along the Porter road, on the downslope of the North Mountain, and extended down to the Bay of Fundy coastline. It had been in the Beck family for generations and had grown to be the largest farm in the Fundy Bay area. There were only eight houses along the two mile long Porter road, not counting the old Fundy Bay school. Although Dad rarely talked about his childhood in latter years and few family photos survived to fill in the gaps, he did often reminisce about owing from a very young age a motley dog named "Tigger", "Tig" for short, that was his constant and loyal companion through the years as he went about his farm chores.

Dad was the firstborn child within his family, which also included three sisters, two brothers, and parents Josiah and Rachel. Josiah was an enterprising farmer with a gentle nature and a love of the outdoors. Josiah was born in 1879 into a family of seven boys. He was the youngest of the family, and the only brother to measure in at less than six feet, barely reaching five foot nine. Stories were passed around the Fundy Bay United Baptist Church for years of how three of the Beck brothers filled a church pew normally capable of holding five adults. Josiah was also the only one of his brothers to remain in Nova Scotia to farm the land. The rest went off to Boston and New York to seek their fortune and fame. Three of them put their size to good use and became policemen in the Boston area, which provided Josiah with plenty of material for his stove-side storytelling sessions with his wide eyed children on cold winter nights. To the children, their uncles were like superheroes, willingly and ably protecting the good folk of Boston from the forces of evil.

What Josiah lacked in stature he made up for in industry and dogged perseverance. Within five years he had enlarged the Beck family farm by an additional one hundred acres, clearing the extra acreage of rocks, trees, and bushes all with nothing more than a few implements and a trusty team of horses. Rachel Abbott Beck was a trim, hard working woman with jet black hair and a fair complexion. She loved to sew, cook, read, attend church, and play games with her children. Her quiet, sincere faith was an influence on many people through the years who marvelled at her steadfastness and positive outlook on life, even in the face of ongoing trials and hardships. Rachel would never complain about her circumstances, no matter how grim, and she influenced her children to be the same way. Few would ever know when the Becks were feeling ill, as they preferred to keep such personal information to themselves. Rachel was renowned around the community for her ability to keep a secret and to refrain from judgement when others aired their dirty laundry in public. Rachel and Josiah both taught Sunday School classes in the Fundy Bay United Baptist church, and would sing hymns with their children on the walk to and from church each Sunday morning. They made a lovely couple, perfectly complementing each other in appearance, temperament, and ambition.

Josiah relied heavily on young Ainsley to help him with the burgeoning farm. Ainsley would be required to help steer the team of horses while Josiah manned the plough. Ainsley would help turn over the hay after Josiah had cut it with the scythe. Ainsley would milk the cows while Josiah shoed and brushed the horses. Ainsley would clean out the stalls while Josiah repaired the harnesses. Ainsley would be expected to watch over the family while Josiah took the horse and carriage to Fundy Bay or to the Valley to buy supplies.

Ainsley's fondest memories of his childhood were of the times when his father would tap him on the shoulder Sunday afternoons after church and say, "come on, son, we're going fishin' down at the Vaughn brook". Ainsley would go grab his fishing line, call for Tig, and walk alongside his father during the mile long walk to the brook. He'd listen to his father's stories and answer all his questions about how school was going, what he thought about the sermon that morning, and did he still have a crush on Oriel Bedard. Those hours spent with his father beside the clear, running brook, receiving very few bites but lots of encouragement and sage advice were better than Christmas morning to young Ainsley, and he savoured every minute. He didn't even mind his father's ongoing suggestions that he quit smoking given it was bad for his health and a waste of scarce money. Ainsley would usually shrug it off and say, "yeah, I'm goin' to, Dad." He had been smoking since 1918, when at the age of eight he was given a cigar by his Uncle Walcott in the midst of celebrations after news arrived that the World War had ended in victory.

During the winter of 1922, a cruel and devastating blow hit the Beck family: Josiah contracted pneumonia, and never recovered, despite the best efforts and constant bedside vigilance maintained by Rachel and the five youngest children. The huge drifts of snow all along the Porter and North Mountain roads prevented anyone from making the six mile trek to the Valley to summon medical help. No one in the community owned a telephone. On his deathbed, when all hope was gone, Josiah called over his eldest son who had just come in from the barn, placed his hand on his shoulder, and whispered, "you're the head of the household now, Ainsley. Take good care of your mother and the others." Ainsley, with his lip noticeably quivering and his eyes now moist, put his hand on his father's, and replied in a trembly voice, "Dad, I..". He never had a chance to complete his sentence. Josiah Beck, barely forty three years old, died at that moment, with his hand clasped firmly on Ainsley's shoulder, leaving behind his beloved family on a night which saw the start of what would be referred to around Fundy Bay that winter as "the big thaw".

While the other five children, aged two to eleven, wept profusely, Ainsley helped his mother arrange Josiah's hands on his chest, and pull the sheet over his body, occasionally saying "its going to be okay" to one of his younger siblings, or draping his arm around their shoulders. No one ever got to hear what Ainsley had wanted to tell his father that evening, and no one asked. Later that same evening, Ainsley was in the barn as always, milking the cows, feeding the sheep and pigs, cleaning out the stalls, brushing the horses, doing his chores to the best of his ability, the way his father had taught him. Somehow, though, the shovel felt much heavier that night, and it seemed to take forever to fill up the dented buckets with milk.

The Beck family mourned Josiah's death for the longest while, but through it all, Ainsley kept his composure, maintaining a stoic outwardly appearance, rarely changing his tight-lipped expression. Somehow, his calm demeanour helped the family get through this tragedy, as they drew strength from Ainsley. Even Rachel, herself a model of stoicism, was amazed at young Ainsley's composure and inner strength, and how he had been transformed almost overnight into a man. When Tig died later that winter, Ainsley barely seemed to care as he calmly carried the limp body of his old faithful companion up to the apple orchard and buried him there between the two largest trees that they used to occasionally laze around under during the heat of the day.

Ainsley had been a very promising and enthusiastic student, not only at the Fundy Bay school but also at the Fundy Bay Sunday School. He had been awarded several certificates to acknowledge his aptitude for scripture memory and his perfect attendance record. Ainsley had earned awards at school for his penmanship, arithmetic, and for winning spelling bees. On the daily mile long walk to and from school, Ainsley would test his siblings on their math and spelling skills, and they would do the same to him in return, only to find that they could never stump him. Due to his dependability and co-operative spirit, Ainsley had held the job at the Fundy Bay School since he was ten years old of carrying in wood for the fire. At the ripe old age of thirteen, however, Ainsley dropped out of school to assume responsibility for running the Beck family farm. There was never any questioning his decision. His father had given him one last task to do, and he was going to do it.

The only time Ainsley expressed any emotion about his father's death occurred the day after Josiah's passing. No other children were around at the time as they were either in the final stages of getting ready for bed or had already retired. As he was on his way out to the shed to fetch some more wood for the fire, he paused, turned to his mother, and asked, "Why did God let Dad die? I prayed that God would make Dad better, and it didn't do any good!"

Rachel could sense the bitterness and disenchantment in Ainsley's voice, and she tried to soothe him, talking about how God works in mysterious ways and how they had to accept that God knows best. Somehow, however, when Ainsley turned away and headed back to the shed for another armful, Rachel could sense that his heart had hardened towards God, and that things might never be the same again.

Ainsley got lots of help on the farm from his siblings, especially his brother Kendall and his sisters Melanie and Norita. They were nine, eleven, and eight years old respectively when their father died. The two youngest children, Faustine and Garratt were only six and two when Josiah died, so they were expected to be children and therefore were excused from the farming chores. Ainsley and Melanie especially lived somewhat vicariously through Faustine and Garratt, working hard and long to ensure that these two youngest ones would have every opportunity that seemed no longer available to the eldest. Rachel continued to be the doting mother all this time, expecting her five youngest children to do well in school, to mind their manners, to maintain a perfect attendance in Sunday School, and to say their prayers before retiring for the night. Two weeks following his father's death Ainsley had declared that he was too busy to go to Sunday School anymore, and no matter how hard his mother pleaded or offered help to ease his workload, he wouldn't budge from his resolve.

It wasn't easy to make ends meet during the best of times in those days, but without an adult male at home to run the farm, it made things especially tough. The family members living in the United States helped Rachel immensely by sending money regularly. They were devastated by the loss of their youngest brother and felt that it wouldn't have happened if he had only taken them up on their countless offers to leave the farm and bring his family down to Boston. After Josiah's death, the remaining brothers continued to coax Rachel to pack it in and move the family to Boston to be with relatives who could help. The possible move was briefly considered, but eventually was abandoned when Ainsley stubbornly insisted that he was capable of continuing on with the farm and ensuring that the family was provided for.

Rachel was able to contribute to the family finances by applying her skills as a seamstress. So renowned was her talent that people of Fundy Bay, Atlee, Mount Ruby, and even West Appleton would gladly walk or ride by horse all the way to the Beck farm to get their work done. Ainsley continued the commercial ventures engaged in by his father, selling pigs, cattle, grain, hay, milk, apples, pears, and eggs to the people of the surrounding area, all the while ensuring that he maintained healthy breeding stock and adequate sized herds. Ainsley began to cut and sell wood from the many woodlots owned by the family, and even had to hire friends to help him keep up with the demand from the wood burning residents of Fundy Bay.

Rachel continued to get hours of pleasure from working in the many flower beds around the farm as well as her indoor plants, giving special attention and care to the hyacinths around back of the house as Josiah had planted them for her the summer before he died. All during the summer and fall months she would keep Josiah's grave decorated with bouquets of flowers from her garden, never failing during her graveside visits to tell Josiah how hard Ainsley was working around the farm and not to worry about his refusal to attend church since she knew he'd come around, how young Garratt looked just like his father, how well the children were doing in school, and how much she still missed him.

It is said that time has a way of healing all wounds and hurts. The Becks carried on with their lives as Josiah would have wanted. The children continued to do well in their schooling, enjoyed playing with their friends, and loved walking past the livestock through the many fields of the farm down to the Vaughn brook for a refreshing swim on warm summer days. Rachel rebuffed any and all unwanted attention from amorous bachelors who were presumptuous enough to imagine that they could somehow rescue her from her loneliness.

Ainsley grew in strength and stature; he didn't drink and he wouldn't swear, but he did continue to smoke cigarettes he rolled himself. For the next eighteen years following his father's death, Ainsley devoted himself to his family and the farm. Seasons came and seasons went, and through it all, the Beck family trudged along, taking pride in being able to prove wrong the prognostications of their neighbours, friends, and relatives.

When he was twenty-three Ainsley acquired his first automobile, actually more of a jalopy which he obtained in a straight up trade for his more dependable bicycle. The once-proud car was a black Tin Lizzie, a 1923 Model T Ford which had definitely seen better days. Ainsley didn't know how to drive, and didn't own a license to do so, but the night of his acquisition he gathered up four of his friends and drove off to a barn dance in Atlee. The two mile drive took almost a hour as he kept driving into the ditch while he tried to figure out the gears and the steering. His friends gladly boosted him out of the shallow ditches, as the thrill of actually riding in an automobile was worth a little sweat. Ainsley made quite an impression that evening with the crowd as he parked his car just to the right of the various teams of horses that had transported all the others to the barn dance, and gave the equine gathering quite a start when the car backfired loudly the moment he turned the engine off. The dance halted temporarily since so many people filtered out of the barn into the front yard to look at this contraption, and to ask questions about how it worked. After promising to give rides sometime to almost everyone who came to gawk, Ainsley and his friends proceeded like conquering heroes into the barn dance and danced into the late evening hours. Despite the obvious faults and many malfunctions of his jalopy, Ainsley started a love affair that day with the automobile which would last a lifetime. He never had to take a driver's test, and simply sent away to the provincial government to get a license.

Despite his best efforts, Ainsley was not able to keep his jalopy running for more than a few months. Nonetheless, during that time, while he was sitting in the driver's seat, zooming past the homes of his waving neighbours, he would feel so free, released from his bondage, capable of doing anything he wanted, of achieving anything he set his mind to. He obviously impressed many during that time that he was a mover and a shaker, this young man from the largest farm in Fundy Bay, as he had many women vying for his attention. For the next five years, though, Ainsley went without an automobile, relying instead on his trusty team of horses for all season transportation. In clement weather, Ainsley would hitch up the horses to one of his two carriages, and would take his date on a two hour ride to Riverton to see a movie. During the winter months, he would bring the sleigh out of the barn, and get the team of horses to take he and his new date to Mount Ruby to a community dance, or perhaps a pie social, or maybe even a crokinole party. When the weather was especially cold, Ainsley would have to heat rocks up in the oven, wrap them in towels, and place them under layers of blankets in the sleigh to keep he and his date warm during their journey. Even if it did get a bit chilly, it provided a perfect excuse for Ainsley and his date to sit closely together under the blankets, sharing body heat while the carriage glided quietly along the road and the moonlight glistened off the fresh, soft snow.

As they matured into young adulthood, the Beck children started leaving the nest one by one, albeit with a bit of sadness and hesitation. Melanie was the first to leave, getting a license to teach school when she was nineteen. During her second year of teaching in Mount Ruby, Melanie started dating a young, enterprising man named Willie Crawford. Willie was a man of many talents and engaged in one successful business venture after another. He was for a time the community blacksmith. Then he started selling horses and making carriages and sleighs. Willie then expanded into making furniture for various stores out in the Valley. Then he started a very successful sawmill in Mount Ruby, and for a time employed either directly or indirectly almost half of the non-fishing and non-farming adult males within a three mile radius.

Many of the men who worked within the sawmill itself sported souvenirs of their hard earned pay, such as one or two shortened or lost fingers courtesy of the huge, whining saw blades. Others drove the mill trucks, picking up logs or delivering lumber to buyers throughout the North Mountain and Valley. Many others toiled in the woods, cutting downs trees to quench the sawmill's thirst for more and more timber. After her second year of teaching concluded, Melanie married Willie, retired from teaching, and settled with Willie in Mount Ruby. Being only two miles away from her family was important to Melanie as she made frequent trips back to the farm for social calls while Willie was busy working on his latest project.

As the second oldest son, Kendall tried to assist Ainsley as best he could with the farm chores. However, as he got older, he was increasingly stricken with asthma attacks, which meant that his contribution to the farm work lessened. He ended up missing a lot of school time, which concerned his mother and older siblings. At age seventeen, when he had finished grade eleven, he decided to accept the invitation of his Uncle Israel and moved to Boston to take a job on his Uncle Israel's profitable ice route. As soon as he obtained his license, Kendall was promoted to driver of one of the trucks and had a helper who unloaded the ice for all those customers needing their ice boxes refilled. Kendall's health improved in Boston, as he had ready access to more modern medical aid and less-polluted air. Nonetheless, he was very homesick for many months, and even spent his entire first two paycheques on gifts to be sent to his family back on the farm.

Norita proved to be a masterful understudy to her mother, learning all she could about sewing. From as early as anyone could remember she was a very serious girl, a perfectionist who could not tolerate it when she made even a slight mistake in her stitching. By age eleven, she was able to make some simple clothes for her younger siblings, and by age fifteen, was every bit as skilled as her mother. She shared seamstress duties with her mother from that time onwards, adding to their ability to improve the family's financial condition.

While working with her mother, she would often ask about her father, trying to get some new insight into his character and prying for a story that she might not have heard before. She treasured in her heart each time her mother would comment that her father would certainly have been proud of her for the way she had turned out and the skill she demonstrated. Her most prized possession was a faded, crinkled, black and white photograph of her father giving her a push on the swing set in the back yard, wide grins lighting up both of their faces. She had only been five years old at the time, and no one knew then that this would be the only photograph ever taken of she and her father together, or that her smile which radiated such joy would be so rarely seen in future years. At age eighteen, Norita accepted a job offer from a dress making shop in Boston whose owner had been suitably impressed by samples of her work provided by her Uncle Walcott and Aunt Evangeline. She boarded with her Uncle Walcott and Aunt Evangeline for three years before marrying a New England banker twenty years her senior.

Faustine was the acknowledged beauty of the Beck family, being blessed with pale skin and naturally curly auburn coloured hair. She had her mother's even disposition, and her father's hearty laugh. Where Norita was serious, Faustine was playful. As the youngest daughter in the family, she received a lot of special attention and privileges. She was a good student all through school, due perhaps in part to having so many willing tutors within her own household. Faustine was always pulling practical jokes on her older siblings, and with her quick smile and twinkling eyes, was usually able to get away with it unpunished. Faustine would sometimes change around some embroidery that Norita had been working on the night before, deliberately making a few errors. She would find it difficult to keep a straight face watching Norita's puzzled look as she examined the piece of work over and over, trying to imagine how she had so badly slipped up. At other times, Faustine would slip some ragweed under Kendall's pillow, and tried to contain her laughter as she heard him sneeze repeatedly before he finally clued into what had taken place. Faustine would even pull tricks on solemn, poker faced Ainsley. One of her favourite practical jokes was the time she partially sawed through one of the legs on Ainsley's milking stool. She and Garratt hid behind the hay bales in the barn so they could witness Ainsley tumbling off the stool, falling backwards into some newly plopped cow manure, a classic ending even she hadn't contemplated.

Faustine was very popular throughout the community, even being asked to vie for the title of queen of the Johnstown fair when she was sixteen years old. Although she didn't win the contest, she received many offers for dates from the teenage boys and young men in attendance. After graduating from grade school, Faustine decided that she wanted to be a teacher, so went sixty miles away to Teacher's College in Truro for two years to get her teaching certificate.

Faustine was as popular a teacher as she had been a citizen of the community, showering her students with love and good cheer. She taught for six years in a variety of one room school houses located mostly on the North Mountain. During her second last year of teaching, her grade nine class of two students included a bright, slightly overweight young girl who, unbeknownst to either of them, would several years later become Mrs. Ainsley Beck. A year later, teaching for the first time in a school located off the North Mountain, fifty miles away in Digby County, Faustine took a shine to a young bachelor farmer named Eachan Elliott. Apparently the feeling was mutual, since they were married eighteen months later. Deciding on a whim to shed their Nova Scotia bonds, they bought a car with their accumulated savings and drove off to the United States, unsure of where they were headed, but looking for something fresh. After a wonderful extended journey through many villages, towns, and cities, they got as far as Pittsburgh before they decided it was time to replenish their dwindling funds. Eachan soon found employment there in a steel plant, and Faustine got a desk job working for the local school board. Once they bought their first home, it was obvious that their search for a place to settle down was over.

Garratt actually had no recollection of his Dad, so looked upon Ainsley as the fatherly figure in the family. In fact, many of the other children did so as well, in varying degrees. Garratt was a handsome boy with a head covered in thick, wavy copper coloured hair. He was always full of energy, repeatedly coaxing his less enthusiastic brothers and sisters to play cops and robbers or hide and seek. In many ways he was the precious jewel of the family. All the other family members were extra protective of Garratt, making sure that he always had his homework done, rescuing him from playground altercations, and fetching him some soup or sitting alongside him playing board games whenever he was bedridden with a cold. Whenever any of the brothers and sisters made the trek to the store in Fundy Bay to buy some household supplies, they would invariably bring back some penny candy for Garratt. The entire family, even Ainsley, would be beaming with pride when Garratt would stand up on the church stage, rocking back and forth on his heels, reciting his verse without flaw during the annual Christmas concert. Garratt sometimes got tired of being hugged and kissed by his older sisters, and having his hair messed up and his shoulder lightly punched by his brothers. As Garratt grew older, he became less and less interested in school, preferring instead to help out Ainsley on the farm, or go out on dates with a variety of admiring teenage girls from the community.

When the Second World War commenced, Garratt felt deep within his soul a calling like nothing he had ever experienced: he wanted to enlist in the army. The family was shocked. They could not stand the thought of their precious brother being sent overseas to fight the Nazis. They pleaded with Garratt to change his mind; he was much too dear to them to lose his life fighting a distant war. In spite of all the coaxing and pleading, Garratt signed up secretly one day while buying some supplies in Centretown.

The secret didn't last long. His papers arrived in the mail a few days later and Ainsley was the first to spot them. Despite his own belief in privacy, Ainsley ripped open the letter to discover the horrible truth that Garratt had defied their wishes and enlisted. The entire family was grief stricken. That day while everyone badgered and implored Garratt to reconsider, Ainsley took his car and drove to Centretown to visit the recruiting office. Ainsley walked purposefully inside and declared to the officer in charge that he wanted to enlist in the army on the condition that Garratt Beck's enlistment be rescinded. After gaining a full understanding of the situation, the officer denied Ainsley's request, despite Ainsley's attempts at persuasion. Seems that there was a rule in place which forbade the army from enlisting the oldest adult male from any farm household.

Ainsley was devastated, and on the long ride back to the Porter road tried to concoct some scheme which would allow Garratt to stay at home. But it was no use; Garratt had made up his mind and off to war he would go. It was with sad hearts that the family bade Garratt farewell that September morning, when he headed off to Halifax to start his service in the army. Ainsley insisted on driving Garratt to Halifax in his recently acquired 1935 Chrysler Airflow. Not many words were spoken during the three and a half hour drive. Ainsley was in no hurry to get to Halifax, so ignored Garratt's good natured coaxing to "hit the gas" to see if the Airflow could go over eighty miles an hour as the manual said. When the car got a flat tire, Ainsley refused to let Garratt get out and help, telling him to save his energy.

It was difficult for both of them to say their goodbyes at the army depot. It more closely resembled a father bidding farewell to a favourite son than two brothers bidding each other adieu. Despite his sense of pride in Garratt's courage and determination, Ainsley was filled with a sadness and dread that he hadn't felt in over seventeen years. Garratt was surprised to see tears well up in Ainsley's eyes, and patted him twice on the shoulder in a gesture that needed no verbal accompaniment. They both knew deep down, although it was unspoken, that Josiah would be proud of his youngest son, so valiantly heading off to war. After an awkward moment when neither knew what to do to conclude this prolonged parting, Garratt held out his hand and simply said, "thanks for the ride, Ainsley. I'll write you all when I get overseas". Ainsley nodded then walked back to the car, with ever increasing regret that he had not acted on his gut instinct and given his teenage brother a hug. All during the drive back to the farm Ainsley was haunted by the many things that he had left unsaid. It sunk in for the very first time that it was now just he and his mother left on the farm, and he couldn't help but question the choices he had made in life.

When Ainsley arrived home, he announced to his mother that he was going to go into business driving taxi. He had given it lots of thought on the drive home and realized that he could still keep the farm going and drive taxi too. He felt now that he was thirty years old, he should start thinking about having a career, and farming would always be there.

For the next ten years, Ainsley worked even longer hours than he had before, going through a succession of cars in that time: a 1937 Ford Model 74, a maroon 1942 Whippet, a green 1943 Nash Rambler, a blue 1944 Chevrolet, a maroon 1947 Studebaker Commander, and a grey 1949 Chrysler Desoto. The car he loved the most was the Studebaker. It was pointed in the front and in the back, so that by a casual glance you couldn't tell which way it was headed. It was built very low to the ground, however, which proved to be somewhat impractical on the pot hole filled gravel roads around Fundy Bay.

There was only a handful of cars in all the neighbouring communities on the North Mountain, so Ainsley enjoyed a virtual monopoly with his taxiing business, as proven by his ever increasing bank balance. There was never any shortage of women eager to go out with this good looking gentleman farmer with the fast cars and wallet full of cash. Ainsley was very generous to the women he dated, taking them to places and things they had never had access to before. He rarely dated any one woman for any length of time, preferring to play the field at a time when most men his age were thinking of marriage. The succession of women in his life almost seemed to be a by-product of his hectic work schedule, as he would soon grow tired of being asked "when can I expect to see you again?". His busy schedule clearly dictated that women had to be available to see him when it was convenient for him, even if this meant never getting really close to any one person. Besides, he had to spend some time with his mother when he wasn't working, since she was now home all alone, spending many nights on her own in the large farmhouse with no neighbours' houses in sight, while he would be stranded in a snowstorm a hundred miles away.

Ainsley would often go to church with his mother, as this seemed to cover over a multitude of neglect on his part. His mother would proudly step out of Ainsley's new car on these Sunday mornings, being escorted into church on Ainsley's arm. She would have preferred it if he could stay awake through the sermon, but at least he was there. Something might sink in, even while he was dozing.

During the winter of 1948, Ainsley did not have to worry about his mother being lonely as Garratt's pretty wife Phoebe and their four year old son Taylor stayed at the farmhouse while Garratt was posted in Germany. Those were happy times for Rachel as she delighted in all the shenanigans young Taylor would get up to, as he reminded her so much of Garratt when he had been that age. Ainsley also enjoyed having young Taylor around, helping him build a snowman in the front yard, pulling him on his sled up the Porter road, taking him for sleigh rides to the Anthony Brothers store to get some candy, telling him stories about his father and grandfather, and even taking him ice fishing in the Vaughn brook. Something stirred inside Ainsley that winter, and this thirty-nine year old bachelor eventually came to realize that he wanted to be a father more than anything else.

Ainsley continued to frequent community dances on weekend nights. He was a popular figure at these events, often bringing a girlfriend, and one or two other couples. He became quite well known in the area not only for his square dancing ability, but also for his skill at calling the dances. The apex of his calling career came one night when Don Messer and his band were playing at dance in Fenton, six miles from Fundy Bay. Don Messer's regular caller had taken ill during the afternoon, so Ainsley was volunteered by the booking agent who recalled hearing him call a dance a few weeks ago in Mount Ruby. Without any hesitation, Ainsley went to the stage, shook hands with Don Messer, then proceeded to call the dance of a lifetime. Afterwards, everyone including Don Messer himself congratulated Ainsley on the fine job he had done. His date was suitably impressed and gave him his reward later that night on their extended drive home.

△ △ △

CHAPTER THREE
The Hayes Family

When he was thirty nine, Ainsley Beck met a young teacher named Lenore Hayes, a woman fifteen years his junior, at a Mount Ruby community dance, and almost immediately had designs on marrying her despite the fact that he was dating four women at the time, two of them also teachers. Lenore was the sole teacher in the one room schoolhouse in Mount Ruby and was conveniently boarding in the community there at the home of Ainsley's sister and brother-in-law, Melanie and Willie Crawford. That gave Ainsley plenty of opportunity to visit Lenore, without appearing overly pushy. Ainsley's sister, Faustine was delighted to see Ainsley dating that delightful girl she once taught.

Lenore had lived most of her life in Atlee, just two miles south of the Beck farm, located near the crest of the North Mountain. Atlee was a community consisting of only sixteen houses with a population of about seventy people spread over a couple of square miles. Lenore was the eldest child in a family comprised of six children and headed by Oliver and Penelope Hayes. Penelope's father, Boden Wolfe, had been a very successful farmer, land baron and financier, and was first cousin to Captain Joshua Slocum, who earned fame as the first person ever to sail around the world alone.

The Wolfe family farm comprised over six hundred acres and was believed to be the largest farm on the entire North Mountain. At one time, ten different men were employed on the farm, tending the herd of beef cattle, cutting wood, and sheering the sheep. Boden Wolfe was often referred to by fellow businessmen as "the most honest man you could ever meet". He was a deeply religious man, who would spend at least sixty minutes each evening after the children were in bed reading and reciting scripture. It troubled Boden to foreclose on those who were unable to keep up their loan payments, and he always did what he could to give people a little more time to come up with the money. It was his faith in God which allowed him to accept the death of his dear wife Gracie in 1893. She had gotten ill giving birth to their fifth child and never recovered. On her deathbed he pledged that he would do all he could to raise their five daughters, ranging in ages from seven to newborn, in a manner which would make Gracie proud.

In 1899, Boden decided to build a new five bedroom home in Atlee for his family, in part to enable them to entertain all the relatives which continued to visit from Ontario and the United States. At the time it was the most luxurious home around, made with the finest materials and sporting many special touches. Boden named the house "Spirit of Grace", which served as much an expression of his faith as a reminder of a dear one departed. Boden's business ventures continued to prosper, which enabled him to hire nannies and housekeepers to provide care to the family and the house all during the children's formative years.

Another tragedy struck the family one year after moving into the new house. Boden's youngest daughter, seven year old Gracienne, discovered a shotgun shell dropped by a tramp who had been by the house earlier that morning looking for a job or something to eat. She unfortunately mistook the shell for a piece of chalk, and as she tapped it on her new slate given to her by cousin Joshua, the shell exploded and almost completely severed her right hand from her arm. Gracienne was rushed to the doctor, but there was nothing they could do to save the hand. She had gone in shock from the loss of so much blood and was required to stay in the Centretown hospital for two weeks while she recovered. Boden was devastated by this sad incident, feeling that somehow he had let Gracie down. He commuted each day to the hospital, barely getting any sleep, but trying to keep up appearances for the sake of his other children. Boden was mortified that his little baby, darling Gracienne, was going to have to go through life with an ugly hook for a right hand. He lectured his other daughters about the importance of giving Gracienne lots of love and support always, and never to make her feel self conscious about her new hand.

The Wolfe family continued along, pouring out a special dose of love on Gracienne. When Gracienne was seventeen, the family doctor recommended that she be referred to a specialist in prosthetics located in Boston who was doing marvellous work providing children with replacement limbs. Boden wasted no time making the trip to Boston with Gracienne, and she was eventually fitted with a fairly realistic looking prosthesis. While it didn't quite match her skin tone and was very stiff to the touch, the new hand enabled Gracienne to go out amongst strangers without worrying about the cruel and thoughtless comments and questions which normally invariably followed.

Linette, the heavy set eldest daughter, seemed to thrive on physical labour, loving nothing better than doing chores around the farm. Dressed up in her loose fitting, soiled work clothes, and with an old hat pulled down over her head, she would often be mistaken for a man by passersby. She did blend in perfectly with the other hired help working on the farm, enjoying their company, camaraderie, and well seasoned language much more than would be possible with some slicked up Joe hell bent on romance and marriage.

Sibella, the second eldest daughter, was the first to marry, being wed in 1914 to Power Davis, an insurance salesman from Toronto. She was always the adventurous one of the family and didn't seem to have the least bit of dread heading off to a strange city to start a new life. The marriage proved to be a happy one, resulting in five children, all blessed with their father's inner drive to succeed in commerce. Although Sibella and Power returned to Atlee to visit each summer, they never had any inclination to settle there. During her visits and in her frequent letters, Sibella would regale her father and her sisters with stories about the shopping and entertainment available in Toronto, the beauty of the city lights, and the thrill of navigating through city traffic.

Penelope and Amelia had more academic pursuits in mind, and put their love lives on hold until schooling was finished. It was very rare for children from the North Mountain to finish grade school let alone tackle university. Undaunted by this, and with the support of their proud father, Penelope and Amelia both headed off to university sixty miles away in Wolfville, Nova Scotia. Penelope graduated from Acadia University in 1913 with a degree in music. For the next seven years, Penelope taught school around the North Mountain in small communities like Mount Havelock, Port Ethan, Mount Ruby, and Atlee, and provided music lessons whenever possible in her spare time in communities along the mountain as well as some in the Valley. Amelia wasn't content with just one degree, so after graduating from Acadia with a science degree majoring in biology and chemistry, she headed off to Dalhousie University in Halifax to get a masters degree in biology, then obtained her masters degree in chemistry from the University of Toronto. She often said that doing her graduate studies in Toronto was one of the most fun times of her life, as she boarded at Sibella's roomy house in downtown Toronto and got to experience the fun of big city life with her sister as a guide. After her graduation in 1918, Amelia accepted a job as professor of chemistry at the University of Toronto, a post she would revel in and excel at for the next thirty-nine years.

The 1920s saw three more of the Wolfe girls get married. Penelope married a dashing young farmer named Oliver Hayes in 1920, and they moved into the modest Hayes homestead in Mount Havelock, one and a half miles from Atlee. Linette finally decided at the age of forty to tie the knot in 1926 with seventy-five year old farmer Mercer Parsons, a man with snow on his rooftop but plenty of fire in the furnace. Mercer proved to possess an abundance of vitality, as he and Linette enjoyed twenty years of married bliss on the Parsons' farm located on the side of the North Mountain overlooking Riverton. Over the years they provided board in their home to scores of down and out men who helped out on the sprawling farm, picking apples, caring for the herds, and doing all sorts of manual labour. Mercer may have well have become a centenarian if not for complications which arose after his nasty fall in the autumn of 1946 from a ladder while picking apples in his upper orchard.

In the spring of 1928, Amelia married Victor Lahey, a ferret faced, shifty eyed, smooth talking Torontonian that no one else in the family had much use for. He was a dreamer, a would be entrepreneur who would go on at length about his grand get rich schemes, but who never seemed to get his ideas off the ground. The marriage produced two children followed by a hasty divorce when Victor proved unwilling to leave his womanizing and drinking ways behind.

A mere month after Amelia's marriage, Boden Wolfe died at age seventy-two, leaving behind an estate valued conservatively at $120,000, a huge sum for those times and parts. His only regret seemed to be that Gracienne had not married or even had a serious boyfriend, a situation he blamed on himself. His estate was shared equally among the five daughters, and the farm was left to Penelope since she and Oliver and their three children had outgrown their modest home in Mount Havelock. Also, Oliver had been an invaluable help in keeping the Wolfe farm operation running during the last few years of Boden's life as his health declined. The inheritance proved to be a huge boost to the girls in establishing their own careers and lives and in getting through the Great Depression.

Although Boden did not live to see it, Gracienne did eventually marry, in 1938 at age forty-five to a seventy-three year old retired shopkeeper named Grantham Moore. Apparently what Grantham lacked in life expectancy he made up for in friskiness and endurance. Perhaps inspired by his hard working brother in law, Mercer, Grantham lived to be ninety-six, and he and Gracienne continued to act like newlyweds throughout their twenty-three year marriage. They made their home in a beautiful Victorian house in Riverton, directly overlooking the river. They had a modest sized orchard of pear trees on their property, but usually the harvest was only sufficient to allow Gracienne to put up some preserves for the winter. Gracienne and Grantham really didn't do much of anything besides enjoy each other's company to the fullest, sitting most evenings in their huge living room with its twelve foot high ceilings, holding hands on the couch while listening to the radio. Gracienne was holding Grantham's hand when he died at home during the winter of 1960 of a massive heart attack after having to shovel quite a bit earlier that night when driving back from Atlee.

Penelope and Oliver Hayes had many wonderful times together and with their children throughout a marriage which lasted forty two years. Although Penelope gave up school teaching once she was married, she applied herself in many other ways to "help with the family finances" as she called it, although it seemed to most people that she was the principal breadwinner of the family. She taught music lessons for many years out of the home. She also was post mistress of the Mount Havelock post office for thirty years. She knit all sorts of clothing, doilies, and assorted items for sale in Anthony Brothers store in Fundy Bay. During each election she served at the polling station as presiding officer representing the Liberal party. In the midst of this Penelope found time to raise six children, sew all their clothes including their undergarments, serve as organist at the Mount Havelock and Atlee community churches, help out on the farm, and entertain an endless stream of visitors and relatives so royally that return visits were assured.

People used to regard Oliver as a slow moving and slow taking man who never seemed to be in a hurry no matter what the activity. He took on driving the rural mail shortly after being married, and with his trusty team of horses would cover a three mile route extending from the Darnell Mountain road to East Appleton. This was not a full time responsibility however, since mail was only delivered three times a week. Therefore, Oliver continued to run the Wolfe family farm, or "putter around doing some farm chores" as Penelope jokingly referred to it, as Oliver was never terribly enthusiastic about or successful at it. He tolerated with remarkable patience throughout the years the continual summer visits from Penelope's out of province relatives, despite the fact that most of them were obviously much more well to do than he could ever hope to be and didn't mind flaunting it.

Penelope and Oliver waited two years before starting to have children, but once they started, they found that it quickly became habit forming. Lenore was born in 1922, followed by Bryce in 1926, then Enid in 1927, Franklin in 1929, Galen in 1930, and finally, Marian in 1932. Lenore was a heavy child from birth. By age ten she weighed well over a hundred pounds, and by age twelve reached her full adult height of five feet, two inches. Penelope taught Lenore at home until grade four, since the one room school house in Atlee was one mile away and Lenore would have had to do this daily walk all on her own, there being no other school children her age in all of Atlee. When Bryce was old enough to start school, it meant that Lenore could finally go to the schoolhouse for the first time, as she now had someone to walk with.

Lenore was blessed with a keen ear for music, taking piano lessons from her mother at age six and mastering the instrument in no time. Those proved to be the only lessons she would ever need. By age ten, Lenore was playing the piano and organ at community sing songs due to popular request by the residents who loved to see this young prodigy flawlessly play songs that gave much older pianists trouble. When she was fourteen, Lenore taught herself how to play the guitar simply by observing others during events in the community hall and singalongs in her house. Once moved into the "Spirit of Grace" house in Atlee following Boden's death, these in-home singalongs became more common, as the Hayes home came to be the drop-in centre of the community for young and old alike. Through it all, the Hayes family were willing and gracious hosts, and there was always a pot of coffee, a cold drink of lemonade, and some homemade sweets waiting for the next person who crossed the threshold.

Being the eldest of the family, Lenore was expected to help look after her younger siblings, which she usually did quite willingly. However, when Penelope announced to her five children that she was pregnant once again, nine year old Lenore threw up her arms and shouted, "I'm sick and tired of looking after kids!"

Age twelve brought two special treats to a full grown Lenore. During the summer, she received an unexpected treat when her father announced that he would take her to the dance in Port Ethan. Her mother would not have allowed it, but she was away with young Marian on a once in a lifetime trip to Toronto to visit Sibella and Amelia. Lenore was fascinated by the live band and captivated by the dancing. As she sat there in her Sunday best watching the older folks dancing, she wished with all her might that she could have a chance to get up just once with someone other than her rather awkward father to give it a try. But she knew that it was too much to hope for. Just after her father turned to her to say that they would have to leave soon, a handsome young lad named Dewey Nixon strolled across the room and asked Lenore to dance. This was a thrill of a lifetime for young Lenore, and with her beaming father watching, she proceeded to do all the steps just right, a payoff for an evening spent keenly observing the others dancing. The memory of this night had to last a long while, since it would be six years later before Lenore would be allowed to go to another dance.

Later that summer, when Aunt Sibella and Uncle Power were visiting from Toronto, Uncle Power decided to take Penelope and Lenore to Halifax for a day trip. Lenore had no idea what they would do in Halifax once the three to four hour drive along the gravel roads was over. To her utmost surprise and delight, Uncle Power first treated them to a dinner in a fancy downtown restaurant, then took all of them to the Capital theatre to see the movie, "Peg of My Heart" starring Clark Gable. Lenore sat mesmerized throughout the film, as she had never seen anything like it before. And Clark Gable was so handsome. When she got home and told the other children of the community about her experience, she was treated like a celebrity, as none of the others had ever been outside the county, let alone do something so grand.

Lenore continued to excel at school, although she had no one to push her, always being the only one in her grade at the one room school in Atlee. The children referred to the school as "Frog Leg Academy" due to the number of frog ponds surrounding the building and the constant "ribet, ribet" and chirping sounds which filtered in the schoolhouse windows throughout the day. The school building was plain but highly functional. It had been built at the time of Confederation in 1867 shortly after provincial legislation had passed guaranteeing free education for all children. Like so many other small rural communities which had no church, the schoolhouse in Atlee was used on Sundays for church services, and averaged thirty to thirty five worshippers a week, a highly respectable number in a community of only seventy persons.

Lenore was the first person ever to obtain her grade eleven from the Atlee school. It was a proud moment not only for the Hayes family but the entire community. It hadn't been easy, as this gifted student from the small one-room rural school had to write standard exams administered to all grade eleven students throughout Nova Scotia, including those attending the big city and town schools. Despite her success, grade eleven was as far as Lenore could go in school, since Frog Leg Academy and the other one room schools in the area did not offer grade twelve. This would mean that Lenore would have to go to school six miles away in the community of Glory located in the Valley, and board with a family there for the year.

Penelope and Oliver felt terrible that they could not allow their daughter to continue her schooling, but they just couldn't afford to pay her board and they were too proud to ask their Toronto relatives for assistance. So Lenore stayed at home for two years, helping her mother around the house. She also started being a regular at the weekend house dances in Mount Ruby, as well as at the dance halls in Port Ethan and Hurbertsville. The Hill family held regular weekend dances throughout the year in their home perfectly situated at the intersection of the Darnell Mountain road and the Mount Ruby road. The Hills were very poor, so decided to host these dances in their home with its hardwood floors and spacious living room, so they could raise enough money each week to buy a bag of flour or sugar from Anthony Brothers store. Lenore thoroughly enjoyed these times, being much in demand by the single men of the area looking to hoedown then settle down with a good churchgoing woman who knew how to cook and sew. She couldn't help but take notice during these dances of that clean-cut Beck fellow, always arriving with a different girlfriend, and making such a splashy entrance with his fancy car. He often ended up being the caller at these dances. Lenore liked dancing when he was calling, as he always seemed to know how to get the crowd moving and mixing it up just right. But he was so much older than her that she never entertained any serious thoughts of ever dating him, even if he ever did take notice of her.

Lenore decided when she was twenty-one that it was time to get out of the house and pursue a career. After what seemed like an eternity of helping to care for her younger siblings, she decided that nursing would be a natural calling. So, in 1941 she headed off to Halifax for a two year nursing course at the Victoria General hospital. Unfortunately, the time spent at home had done nothing to prepare her for the loneliness she would feel in the solitude of her residence room in Halifax. So, after only spending two months with the training, Lenore packed it in and headed home, ashamed that she had started something that she was unable to finish, but nonetheless glad to be home.

Lenore's ego had been bruised by this experience, as she had never been anything but a success at any of her previous academic ventures. Despite the warm, embracing feeling she got whenever she woke up and realized she was back in her own bed in Atlee, Lenore was sensible enough to know that life on the farm was not a realistic alternative for her at this stage in her life. It was in the midst of World War II, and Lenore noted how teachers were in such short supply, especially those willing to work in the rural areas. Therefore, on the basis of her grade eleven diploma, she wrote away for and was granted a teaching license. For the next two years, Lenore taught at one room schoolhouses in East Hurbertsville and Willards Cove. Boarding at rooming houses during these two years, she found that she was still fairly homesick, but being relatively close to home helped ease the feeling. Also, having a steady boyfriend for the very first time in life didn't hurt either.

Two years of steady teaching were enough to convince Lenore that being an educator was her passion. She also realized that her position was rather tenuous, having never been formally trained for the profession. Therefore, the very next fall Lenore packed her bags and headed off to Teacher's College in Truro, Nova Scotia to start the two year program there. Lenore still felt terribly homesick while in Truro, but the choice of vocation seemed better suited to her personality and gifts than had nursing. She had broken up with her boyfriend before heading off, since this seemed the sensible thing to do. Besides, he had thrown her for a bit of a loop by proposing marriage when she had announced her plans to head off to Teacher's College.

Lenore found that if she lost herself in her studies it would prevent her from sitting around pining away for the folks back in Atlee. This escapism into the books usually meant that she would have all the year's assignments completed by after the first three months, leaving lots of time for going to movies, socializing, or helping the other girls with their homework. Lenore's romantic life was rather quiet during these two years, since most of the eligible men were off fighting in the war. Lenore was an obliging, compliant student who would go out of her way to avoid trouble. However, even she could not accept the validity of certain rules which all college students were expected to follow religiously. For one, being forbidden to ever set foot in a Chinese restaurant seemed to Lenore to be nothing but outright prejudice, and she could not see how the war effort had anything to do with it. Besides, they made the best banana splits in all of Truro, at a time when bananas were a rare commodity. Lenore and her friends would occasionally sneak downtown and dart into the restaurant, sliding quickly into the unobtrusive seating available, hoping all the while that they weren't spotted by any of the college staff. Lenore wasn't used to this adrenaline rush, and didn't really enjoy it, but one taste of the banana split would usually convince her that it was worth it. In true Baptist fashion, Lenore would afterwards feel guilty for about a week for having broken a college rule and would promise herself that it would never happen again.

Lenore graduated from Teacher's College in 1944, making her parents and family very proud. She then proceeded to prove the adage that variety is the spice of life by teaching at four different one room schools over the next seven years, in communities like Glendon, Atlee, Glory, and Mount Ruby. After completing her second year of teaching at Atlee, Lenore decided to upgrade her license so spent the summer at Dalhousie University in Halifax. This time in Halifax, being more mature and less tied to her mother's apron strings, Lenore was able to complete her training, and it allowed her to receive an increase in her annual salary to $650 the following year. Once teaching in Mount Ruby, Lenore officially met Ainsley Beck, and her life would never be the same.

Bryce Hayes was an industrious, hard working boy from a very young age. He seemed to be more content out in the woods chopping down trees than he did playing with the neighbours or his younger brothers. Bryce inherited his mother's inner drive and couldn't stand to sit around with nothing particular to do. Penelope and Oliver used to chuckle to themselves to hear Bryce quoting his grandfather Hayes to his friends and brothers to explain why he couldn't come and play, saying "idleness is the root of all evil", and "an idle person is the devil's playfellow". His friends would usually just snicker and shake their heads, but Bryce knew he was right. Besides, he loved more than anything having a chance to earn some spending money, helping the neighbours put in their hay, or peel their wood, or cut their grass with the scythe. And Bryce took after his grandfather Hayes and his mother when it came to possessing a deep Christian faith. He refused to take part in the smoking and drinking adopted by so many of the community's youth, bored with nothing to do and nowhere to go. Bryce preferred to spend his time on money making pursuits rather than on such self indulgences. Bryce was an incredible help to his parents, always willing to chip in and lend a hand, never complaining about the uneven distribution of work amongst the siblings. He also was blessed with a wonderful sense of humour and a penchant for gently but effectively teasing his family and friends.

It was obvious to all that Bryce was destined for success, with such as hard working upbringing and industrious spirit. He was a good student, although he yearned to be outside in the fields or woods, earning money rather than learning some subjects that he would never use anyway. But out of respect for his mother, Bryce continued in school until he graduated from grade ten. He then decided that it was time to get involved in the war in Europe, as Hitler's forces seemed to be getting more powerful with each passing day. So in 1941, at age sixteen, Bryce enlisted in the army and was posted to Europe. This was a bittersweet moment for his family, so proud of how handsome their dear Bryce looked in his uniform, yet so worried about what waited him in Europe. The family spent much time together in prayer for the next four years as Bryce continued to be involved on or near the front lines in the war effort. If a month would go by without any letter from Bryce, the family couldn't help but fear the worst. When they received word in 1945 that the war was over and Bryce would soon be returning home, they were ecstatic.

A few months later, Bryce arrived home, being welcomed back to Atlee with a huge reception and dance in the schoolhouse. His war medals were admired by young and old alike, as he patiently answered all their questions and made sure he went around the room to chat with everyone who showed up. The tittering young women who seemed to hang on his every word were noticeably crestfallen when Bryce started talking about "my belle Noelle" and passing around a small black and white photo of a young woman with a perfect smile and slender figure.

During the latter part of the war, Bryce had met and fallen hopelessly in love with a beautiful young French girl named Noelle Deschamps, who spoke very little English. Noelle's parents had both been killed during the war, along with three of her four brothers. She and her remaining brother, Andre, had been sent to England by some of their relatives afraid that otherwise they too would be soon killed. Bryce met Andre when she was cleaning up tables in a small coffee shop in Bristol, and found that although he could not speak her language and her English was not very good, they nonetheless had an immediate rapport. He did regret, however, not listening to his mother's urgings to continue with his French lessons at school.

Bryce continued to see Noelle whenever he could. Their dates would consist of taking walks in the park, going to church, watching the ducks swimming in the pond, listening to music on the radio, going to dances, and making simple conversation. Bryce could always make Noelle laugh, with nothing more than a flick of his eyebrows, or by doing a silly pirouette. When he was away, Bryce would write Noelle uncomplicated letters, assuring her that he was okay, and telling her how much he longed to see her again. Before returning home at the war's conclusion, Bryce decided to propose marriage to Noelle, and to his surprise she said "oui, bien sur".

Neither of them had enough money to pay her trip back to Canada, and Noelle did want to return to Nice to say "au revoir" to all her friends and relatives before heading off to North America. So, Bryce promised to send her the money to come over in six months time which would allow both of them time to settle their affairs.

The Hayes family was thrilled to hear about Noelle, and eagerly awaited her arrival. She was unable to make the trip until eight months following her last date with Bryce, but they had stayed in fairly regular contact by mail. In the meantime, Bryce and his family made all the arrangements for the wedding, to take place two days after Noelle first set foot on Nova Scotian soil. Ten different relatives from Toronto made the trip, and when Noelle's plane landed at the Halifax airport one sunny fall day in October, she was startled to see not only her beloved Bryce, but thirty five members of his family. Their initial embrace and kiss that afternoon were somewhat awkward with the audience watching and analyzing her every move and gesture. In her heart, Noelle already felt homesick for her beloved France, and wondered if she had made the right decision. However, she noticed that same twinkle in Bryce's eyes that she hadn't seen in many months, and something about the way he lovingly and reassuringly clasped her hand while introducing her to every one of his relatives that day made her think that their love would be enough to carry her through.

The next two days were a whirlwind of activity, starting with a drive for what seemed like hours on a long dirt road, further and further away from civilization, finally pulling into an attractive house sitting proudly and solitarily on the farm that Bryce had described to her so many times. Noelle was touched by the sincere efforts of Penelope and Lenore to communicate with her in French, although lacking confidence in their ability to verbalize their message they usually had to revert to writing the words. Noelle stayed at "Spirit of Grace" house for the next two days waiting for her wedding day, overwhelmed by the hospitality and attention lavished on her by Bryce's family and the sheer number of guests Penelope was able to provide room and board to in the midst of finalizing preparations for the wedding. All of the Toronto relatives settled in for a stay, enjoying the good food and lodging provided by the somewhat harried and distracted hostess. Noelle was also amazed at how well the hand sewn wedding dress fit since Bryce's mother had had nothing more to go on than the small black and white photograph Bryce carried around in his billfold.

The day of their wedding was characterized by clear autumn skies and a warm breeze blowing across the fields. The wedding was held in the Mount Havelock Baptist church, and the bells ringing out over the community that day told of a special union to take place, between handsome young Bryce Hayes and his beautiful French bride. The morning of the wedding, Noelle was struck by how the girls in the family were fussing and fretting about their clothes, their makeup, their hair, and their shoes, to the point where it seemed that they had forgotten that it was her wedding, not theirs. Nonetheless, everything went smoothly that day, although it wouldn't have mattered to Noelle. Once the ceremony started, she was overcome by the depth of her love for this country soldier, so tall and dashing in his uniform. She had no family at the wedding, represented only by a single handwritten letter containing felicitations from her aunt in Nice.

After the ceremony, the wedding party went to the Mount Havelock community hall for a rousing reception, the highlight of which may have been a reading by Bryce of a bilingual poem he authored for the occasion, titled "Ma Belle Noelle". The poem flipped from English to French and back to English again, all in mangled syntax, but no questioning the love and emotion that had gone into writing it. Noelle was overjoyed at the effort and was the only one laughing when Bryce was waxing poetic about her hair, commenting that "il a la coleur des carrots", intending to compare its colour to carrots, but unintentionally linking it to rabbit droppings.

After a brief honeymoon in Maine, Bryce and Noelle returned to Nova Scotia and settled in Centretown in the Valley. Bryce had decided to leave the army and took a job with Milford's furniture store, acting as part time salesman and full time delivery man. It didn't pay a lot, but really didn't matter as Bryce and Noelle didn't have expensive tastes and were not materialistic anyway. They regularly changed their furniture, taking advantage of his employee discount, and the newly discarded pieces usually were sold at bargain prices to family members.

Enid Hayes always felt like she was in the shadow of her older siblings. She always did well in school, but never quite as well as Lenore. Enid got to be fairly proficient at playing the piano but would refuse to sub for Lenore or her mother when they were unable to play the church organ due to illness. Also, being fairly overweight, Enid always seemed to inherit Lenore's clothes, rarely having any new items that were all her own. She helped out a lot around the house and farm but could not compete with Bryce's contribution. Enid even felt outdone by her younger siblings, as they were always that much younger and cuter in their actions.

Through the years, Enid continued in her quest to find something that was uniquely hers, some accomplishment that had alluded the others. Upon graduation from school, she went away to Teachers College and obtained her teaching license without a hitch. After two years of teaching in the one room Mount Havelock school Enid started to date a strapping young man named Curtis Porter. He was the first steady boyfriend she had had, as most boys visiting the farm had been coming either to see Lenore or to see young Marian. Curtis had an ambition to build houses and had already designed and constructed several solid outbuildings for his parents on their Mount Havelock farm. He was getting fed up with the lack of construction going on in those parts and would talk about going to the city to gain some experience working for a large builder. Enid encouraged him all she could, sensing his restlessness and frustration. After another year spent working on his father's farm, supplemented by the occasional job helping a neighbour with a minor building project, Curtis decided it was now or never.

A few months earlier he had met a swift talking builder from Halifax one day when he was out in Johnstown buying some farm supplies at the Co-op. The builder had left him his business card and told of endless opportunities in the city for anyone willing to do an honest day's work for a good day's wage. Curtis, who had found formal schooling to be a bore and waste of time, got Enid to write a letter to Jonathan Kervin, asking if the offer of employment still stood. Three weeks later a letter arrived in the mail offering Curtis a full-time job in Halifax as carpenter's assistant, working for Kervin Construction. In a wink of an eye Curtis made up his mind to pack up everything he owned and move to Halifax. But the thought of leaving Enid was too much to bear. She had been his first girlfriend, and he loved her deeply, although he had never really been able to express his feelings in words. He was sure that Enid cared deeply about him, but he had to take a chance. After telling Enid about his decision to head to Halifax to pursue his dream, he laid it all on the line, telling her how much he cared for her, how he couldn't even think about being in the city without her, and how he wanted her to be his little heifer. She was somewhat overwhelmed by this sudden verbalization of his affection, and managed to simply reply, "well, okay". Therefore, two weeks later, during the spring of 1950, Enid and Curtis got married, and amidst many tears and sad farewells, headed off to live in Halifax, the first of her brothers and sisters to move outside the county to live.

Enid and Curtis, both simple country folk by heritage, soon found that they loved the city life, and Curtis discovered that building houses was his dream come true. He took special care in designing and building their own home, nestled into the woods on the edge of a quiet, clear lake in Halifax County. It wasn't a large home, but the construction was of the highest quality. Enid would often sit out in the evenings on the front veranda, gently rocking in the chair Curtis built her when they got back from their honeymoon, watching and talking to him as he stood out on their small wharf, casting for trout.

In many ways, Franklin was the misfit of the Hayes family. He was tall and lean rather than short and stocky. Whereas all the others had a fair complexion and sandy or rouge coloured hair, Franklin had dark brown, almost black hair and a dark complexion. Neighbours used to tease Penelope when discussing Franklin, saying "if we didn't know you were such a fine Christian woman, Penelope, we would guess that Oliver didn't father that one". Since a young age Franklin rebelled at going to church, always thinking of excuses why he should stay home. He didn't much like helping out with farm chores, but he didn't have much choice but to pitch in and do his share. Franklin seemed to be happiest when he went off fishing or to a dance with some of his friends, although his mother used to worry somewhat about the company he kept. However, as Franklin used to say, "look, Ma, I gotta be friends with someone".

Bryce used to get terribly frustrated trying to enlist Franklin to help him cut wood or in other money making schemes, as Franklin would repeatedly rebuff his offers, preferring instead to head off with his friends with no particular destination in mind. When Penelope discovered cigarettes in the front pocket of Franklin's overalls one day, she cried. Here he was only fourteen and already she felt she had no control over him. His stubbornness was legendary within the family. He was the only family member not to warmly greet the Toronto relatives when they made their annual summer pilgrimage to the old Wolfe family farm. Often he was downright rude, refusing to come in from the woodshed to say hello to his newly arrived uncles and aunts.

Franklin was dating girls steady by the time he was fifteen. He never seemed to have any problem finding different girls to go with. Penelope and Oliver never liked the way these young girls would giggle and grin as a way of acknowledging their presence rather than the customary, "hello, Mr. and Mrs Hayes, how are you?". Franklin never asked his parents what they thought of his dates and didn't take kindly to any criticism of them offered by anyone in the family.

When he was barely seventeen, Franklin announced that he was leaving school, having just completed grade ten. His parents had suspected that this was coming, but quizzed him as to whether or not he had any plans for employment. It was then that he confessed that his latest girlfriend, Wilda Hogg, was pregnant and that he was going to go live with her and her family in their three room shack down on the Porter road. Penelope and Oliver were devastated, although not overly surprised. Unfortunately, Bryce, just recently back from the war, overheard the news, and proceeded to tear a strip off his none too receptive younger brother. After the tirade, Franklin simply said, "well, I guess I have nothing to say to any of you, so see you around", and headed out the door with nothing more than the clothes on his back. His parents ran after him, coaxing him to come back and talk about it, after all there might be something they could work out. Anyway, he should at least make plans to marry the girl. What really disturbed them was the cold look in his eyes, the nonchalant way in which he shrugged off their invitation. He didn't even seem to care enough about them to get angry. After a slight pause, during which time he at least agreed to come back tomorrow to get some things they would pack up for him, Franklin headed off on his old hand-me-down bicycle.

Things never really smoothed out between Franklin and the rest of his family, despite their best efforts to accept his decisions without passing judgement. He seemed fairly content to be living away from home, even in the squalor of the Hogg household, but then again, it was never easy to tell what Franklin was thinking. He was a boy of few words when his family was around.

About a month later, after not having seen Franklin for about three weeks, Lenore was outside when she spotted Wilda approaching with the youngest of her four brothers. Lenore could see that Wilda was uncomfortably pregnant, probably close to eight months along. Never one to waste words, Wilda stopped about ten feet from Lenore and shouted, "tell Frank I want to see 'em".

Lenore was taken aback at this, replying, "what do you mean? He isn't here. We haven't seen him in weeks."

"Don't lie to me, Lenore. I know he's here. He left two nights ago sayin' he was goin' back home", Wilda said.

"I don't know what to say, Wilda. I'm not lying. Come inside and see for yourself".

The two of them marched inside, leaving the blank faced Hogg youngster outside to contemplate his role in all of this. After a rather circular discussion in which the Hayes family members got more and more worried and scared and Wilda got more and more angry, it was agreed that Franklin's whereabouts were unknown. Everyone promised to let the other side know if they heard anything from him. Bryce promised to take a trip to Fundy Bay and Mount Havelock to see if anyone had seen Franklin. Galen agreed to go look up some of Franklin's friends to see what they knew. The sisters were fit to be tied, fussing about the kitchen, wringing their hands, crying for poor confused Franklin. When Lenore declared that Franklin was probably dead, they moaned all the louder, wondering what had gone wrong in his life.

The next two days were agony for the family. They were unsuccessful in their attempts to get any word about Franklin, except from old Fingal O'Brien, who thought he had seen Franklin heading off the Darnell mountain with Ainsley Beck a few days ago. Bryce road down to the Beck farm to speak with Ainsley, but his mother declared that he probably wouldn't be home for another few days. Three days after their encounter with Wilda, a letter arrived from Franklin, postmarked Halifax. In his brief letter, he declared that he had decided to join the army since nothing good was happening around Atlee. He said he didn't mention it before since he was sure that the family would try to talk him out of it. He concluded by saying not to worry, he was a man now, signing off the letter with "regards, Franklin. PS. How's Wilda?". The family only felt slightly comforted now that they knew their son was alive. Under different circumstances they might have been happy that their son was going to experience the discipline of army life. But they couldn't get Wilda out of their thoughts. How could Franklin be so insensitive to her, to leave her at this time, carrying their child?

This drama was almost too much for the family to bear. It was decided that Bryce would go that day down to the Hogg home and tell Wilda the news. Bryce hitched up the horses and made the trip, mulling over in his head the entire trip how he would express the news. He hoped he wouldn't run into old Moody Hogg, as he was always drunk and cantankerous, rarely bothered to shave, and was always wearing the same sweat stained undershirt with his belly hanging out over his unbuckled pants. When Bryce got there, he saw Wilda sitting on the front step, perhaps hoping to catch sight of a returning Franklin. His attempt at some opening pleasantries were interrupted with her question, "So, have you found Frank?" Bryce proceeded to tell her the news, couching it in as gentle terms as he could, trying to lie convincingly when he said he was sure Franklin loved her and would be coming back when he could. To his amazement, Wilda just laughed, saying "I guess he couldn't take it when I told 'em the baby wasn't his".

At that moment, her half drunk father, old Moody Hogg, staggered out onto the front steps, yelling "Wilda, get your pregnant ass in here, and get me something to eat."

As she turned to head toward the doorway, she shot an imploring look at Bryce, patted her stomach, motioned to her father then whispered "he's been real lonely ever since Mamma died last year."

With that she headed back inside, and as she walked past Moody, he hauled off and kicked her in the behind, yelling "and don't be talkin' to no strangers".

Bryce stood motionless, not sure what he should do, when Moody yelled, "get on home, army boy", before slamming the door.

As he contemplated going in and talking to Moody, the door opened again. Moody was standing there waving a shotgun, yelling "and tell that no good, lyin' brother of yours to stay away from my Wilda if he knows what's good for 'em."

Bryce thought better of trying a knight-in-shining armour rescue attempt, and turned and walked toward the cart.

He was very distraught all the way home, his heart suddenly overflowing with compassion for young Wilda, as he could barely comprehend the abuse she must suffer at the hands of this ogre of a father, and wondered if she and the baby would ever escape. Two weeks later, in a letter to Franklin, Bryce told of how Wilda's baby had been stillborn, and how she had snuck away to live with her Aunt Haidee in Fenton, seven miles from Atlee, and how she had asked about Franklin the last time he had seen her. Bryce didn't tell Franklin the rumour going around that the baby had aborted after Moody had struck Wilda hard in the stomach with a piece of stovewood in the midst of one of his drunken rages. None of the family, including Franklin, ever saw Wilda again, although they occasionally heard stories of her whereabouts and latest doomed relationship.

To the amazement and eventual delight of his family, Franklin continued to serve in the army. He rarely wrote the family, but during his unannounced visits home, it struck everyone how at peace and mature he suddenly had become, and how handsome he looked when he smiled and when he tossed his head back to laugh at even the corniest of jokes. He would usually arrive bearing gifts for his parents and sisters. It seemed that overnight he had forgotten all the ill feelings he once harboured towards the family.

Eight years after joining the army, at the age of twenty five, Franklin got married in a quiet civil ceremony in Richmond, Ontario to a plain, never married farm girl named Celestine Lapointe. True to his modus operandi, Franklin failed to notify his family of the ceremony until after the marriage was a fait accompli. He did send them a post card from Vermont where he and Celestine were honeymooning, advising his family of the end of his bachelorhood and telling them how Celestine was going to make him very happy. Although slightly hurt, the family couldn't help but feel that Franklin's worst days were behind him.

Galen was often teased by his older brothers and their friends as being the sissy of the family. When he was young, he liked to play dolls with his sisters. He was also a momma's boy, never venturing very far from his mother's apron strings. When he got older, he would usually balk at helping out Bryce in the woods or doing the farm chores. He would instead make some excuse and go ride his bicycle with his well to do friend, Milburn, or play with Milburn's latest toys. Any aspersions cast about his masculinity did not seem to dissuade any of the young girls of the neighbourhood, as no small number of them seemed to want to hang around, perhaps attracted by his sparkly blue eyes, or his wavy brown hair, or his kind and gentle manner.   Galen was an excellent student, consistently getting higher marks than his older brothers and sisters, even Lenore, had achieved in similar grades. All during his last year of school, Penelope and Oliver pressed Galen to decide on a career he would like to pursue. His two choices always left them feeling quite unsettled: banjo player or mortician.   The family would try to convince him of the virtues of more acceptable and well paying vocations, such as accounting, law, or even medicine since he certainly had the marks to go into these fields. Galen remained noncommittal during his final year of high school.

A month after graduation, Galen announced to his parents one evening that he had decided to follow his heart and become a mortician, even though he knew their thoughts on the matter. He explained how he had researched it very carefully and how it was a very lucrative field. He thought he would ease their tensions somewhat by pointing out that as a mortician, people are just dying to give you their business, but the attempt at humour was lost on his bewildered parents. They continued to try to talk him out of his morbid choice, but to no avail. He had made up his mind. They could only shake their heads, and say, "well, son, we hope you know what you're doing".

Galen's prediction proved correct. It turned out to be a very lucrative field. During each summer visit, Uncle Power, always appreciate of professions which guaranteed an above average income, would quiz Galen "How's the undertaking working out? I suppose people are just dying to give you their business", and each summer Galen would obligingly laugh along as Uncle Power guffawed. Galen worked for a time as an assistant undertaker at Parr's funeral home in Centretown while studying to get his license. Sometime later, old Latimer Parr made Galen an equal partner, as he had been very impressed by Galen's skill, his steady hands, his enthusiasm for the job, and his gentle and sincere manner in dealing with grieving families. Latimer, a lifelong bachelor, often remarked that Galen reminded him of the son he never had.

When Latimer turned sixty, he decided that he had seen and sewn enough, so he offered Galen the chance to buy out his fifty percent share of the operation. Galen didn't hesitate for a moment. It was his dream come true. He couldn't wait to rush home and tell his mother and father. They were much more suitably impressed by this time, having noted over the past few years how well Galen dressed, the nice car he always drove, and how happy he always was. They also took pride in hearing from people how Galen had been such a source of comfort to them during their time of mourning as he was so sensitive and compassionate in his dealings with them. The family also could not overlook the well known fact that after being an undertaker for thirty-five years, Latimer Parr had become one of the richest men in Centretown. Before retiring he had adorned his cemetery plot with the largest, most expensive tombstone in the Valley, with the complete text of the twenty-third Psalm engraved on its reverse side. Neighbours joked that Latimer, who had all his adult life had stood six feet tall above ground, was now preparing to be at rest six feet under ground.

One woman in particular who had been impressed by Galen's tender spirit was Dorothy Dewar. She had visited the funeral home several times to view her deceased grandfather, and each time she was touched by the words of comfort offered to her and her family by the young, dapper funeral director. He handled all the financial aspects of the funeral arrangements with class and tact, never pressuring them to choose something they couldn't afford, or demanding early payment. She had noticed that he didn't wear a wedding ring and was certain that he had paid special attention to her during each of her visits. A month after her last visit, she decided to phone the funeral home and speak to him, again thanking him for his kindness, and then asked him to her parents' house for dinner. Galen was thrilled to hear from Dorothy, and quickly accepted the invitation. Galen had only very casually dated during his teenage and young adult years. There was never anyone with whom he wanted to get too serious with. But now that he was twenty-eight years old, he felt that he should start getting out more to mingle with people who still had natural colour in their cheeks.

Dorothy's parents were somewhat dubious about their twenty-three year old daughter dating an undertaker. And they were certainly less than thrilled when Galen arrived for dinner, driving the hearse and parking it right smack in front of their house for all to see. Galen's apologetic attitude helped somewhat, as he explained that his car was being fixed, but nonetheless five minutes wouldn't go by without either Osborn or Horatia Dewar pulling back the curtains a bit to see if anyone was outside staring toward the car or the house. It didn't help when the nosy next door neighbour, Hedwig Klemens, dropped by, asking for some sugar althewhile craning her neck to see around the doorframe and asking suspiciously how Osborn was feeling.

Following the dinner, Dorothy excused herself from the table, and asked Galen to join her for a stroll around the flower gardens out back. They spent over two hours outside, admiring the flowers in bloom, then sitting on the bench talking about what they liked and didn't like. When Dorothy mentioned that it was getting cool, Galen took off his suit jacket and draped it around her shoulder, commenting that she was going to get her death of cold, then accepted her hand. Dorothy couldn't help but notice how the jacket had a recognizable chemical smell about it, but she couldn't quite place the scent. She felt a wave of guilt go over her as she wondered to herself if the flower in his lapel had come from one of the floral arrangements in the funeral home. As he got more bold, Galen stroked her hand gently, commenting on how warm and soft it felt to the touch, and complimenting her on her small wrists. After sensing a slight pressure, Dorothy could have sworn that Galen was pausing to take her pulse, but quickly shook this off as a silly overreaction to dating an undertaker for the first time. She didn't really relate to his sense of humour, despite his constant introduction to each supposed funny story that "this one's gonna kill ya!" However, there was something pleasant about his demeanour, in the way he spoke about his profession with pride, and how he looked her straight in the eye when she spoke. He seemed so sincere, she thought, really just a boy in a man's body. He had seen so much of death, yet seemed quite naive about life. Galen made her feel like a teenager again, somehow, just in the way he looked at her with respect and listened to her with attentiveness. She had dated many men but he was different, and it wasn't just the car he drove.

Galen and Dorothy started dating soon after that. Dorothy didn't let the mean spirited jokes from her friends and neighbours bother her. It did upset her when her mother would quickly throw out the flowers Galen brought during each of his visits to the house. Horatia was always suspicious that they had come from the funeral parlour and that it would be bad luck to keep them as a centrepiece. She refused to laugh along when her father would try to get Galen's goad, commenting on his aftershave, saying, "now what exactly is that cologne you're wearing, Galen? Formaldehyde or methanol?"

Galen grew to love Dorothy dearly, and to depend on her for a daily smile. Dorothy also came to love Galen almost as much as she respected and admired him for his steadfast character, his patience, and his gentle spirit. In 1960, after two years of constant dating, they were married. Their wedding day was lovely, and both families were pleased to see the union. Many friends and relatives decided to poke good natured fun at Galen one last time during the occasion. Galen and Dorothy both had to laugh along with the other guests when during the meal at the reception, the four black suited ushers from the wedding marched solemnly into the room carrying a coffin, placing it at the head table right in front of the newly married bride and groom. After the waves of laughter subsided somewhat, a knocking sound was heard coming from the coffin. The head usher, looking suitably puzzled, reached down and opened the lid, and out popped Galen's best friend and best man, Johnny Parr, who, after accepting a round of applause, proceeded to make a speech to the happy couple, then read announcements and well wishes from persons who couldn't attend in person. Afterwards, Galen and Dorothy braved the confetti shower one more time, loaded into Galen's car and headed off on their honeymoon amid the din of tin cans being dragged along the road, oblivious of Johnny's final joke. In place of the usual declaration adorning the wedding getaway vehicle was a huge sign painted in black, red, and white, announcing "Just Buried: R.I.P.", for all trailing motorists along Galen and Dorothy's route to see.

Galen and Dorothy's marriage proved to be as solid as an oak casket, producing lots of wonderful times and love sufficient to weather a fair share of heartache and pain. Although they never had children of their own, they became a favourite uncle and aunt to all progeny of their siblings. Galen's business success just continued to grow by leaps and bounds, and five years after his wedding, he opened a second funeral home in Queenstown, the town in which they settled. Six years later, Galen opened a third outlet, this time in Riverton. With his drive, determination, and solid character, as well as Dorothy's talents in the accessory end of the business, they basically cornered the after death market throughout much of the Valley, making oodles of money not only on the funeral services, but on retailing caskets, floral arrangements, and eventually even tombstones. His success was always admired, but never envied by his proud brothers and sisters. Galen and Dorothy were always generous with their relatives, never lording their success over the others.

Marian Hayes experienced all the usual highs and the lows that come with being the youngest of a large family. Most of her clothes were hand-me-downs. However, she enjoyed having older siblings to take care of her at the playground, and to help her with her homework. Marian was very popular around the community, partly because of her angelic like features and her outgoing personality. But as her mother used to say, "Marian looks like an angel but acts like a devil". Marian did seem to have a knack for getting into trouble, but was equally gifted at feigning innocence and weaseling her way out of any punishment, often convincing her parents to inflict a spanking on one of her brothers or sisters. This didn't exactly endear her to her siblings, but usually with one wink of an eye and a flash of her perfect grin, any residual feelings of animosity would melt away. Marian was not a particularly gifted student, but did manage to maintain average grades throughout school. By the time she reached thirteen, she was dating regularly, in spite of her parents's disapproval and admonishment. She often had to meet her boyfriends on the sly, pretending to be going to visit a girlfriend down the road. Off she would head on her bicycle in the direction of the accomplice. It required Marian to establish a fairly elaborate web of confidants and sympathizers who would be willing to lie convincingly for her, able to withstand very penetrating and persistent questioning from Marian's parents.

Despite this apparent bent towards deception and trickery, Marian was a very kind person, always willing to help out anyone in need. She was a very hard worker, even giving her brother Bryce a run for his money in the energetic department. Whenever she set her mind to do something, she would go to it passionately, single minded in her resolve to complete the task as soon as possible. Friends and relatives, although quite ignorant of Muslim traditions, often remarked that Marian was like a whirling dervish in the way she set about doing a task. She was always in big demand to help out at the church, the school, the community hall, or in any capacity which required someone with stamina and enthusiasm. And due to her unsurpassed popularity amongst children her age, if Marian was enlisted to do a task within the community, it usually meant getting several other volunteers without needing to coax. But despite her goodwill and hard work, Marian would usually find a way to get her nose out of joint, feeling slighted somehow if she didn't get her due relative to others. And always being one to speak her mind first, and mind her manners second, Marian would usually end up undoing all the good she had done with a few words spoken in haste and anger. As Reverend Upton used to remark, "Marian is like a cow who gives you a bucket of beautiful, fresh milk then kicks it over". Somehow, that all too often summed up Marian's reaction to the multitude of injustices she perceived, so often feeling poorly done to and overlooking all the kindnesses and favours that had been showered upon her by those being accused of wrongdoing.

Marian's choice of boyfriends used to trouble her family. For some reason, she was never attracted to the good students or the boys in Sunday School with perfect attendance. Instead, her heart usually went to those louts who would light up a cigarette whenever they were out of sight of their parents, who would utter oaths under their breath when more civilized persons were questioning them about their life ambition, who would sneak out to the backfields with their friends to split a bottle of beer someone managed to steal from their parents, those destined to drop out of school at any early age if they hadn't already, and those who wouldn't think twice about trying to take advantage of a young girl's naivete. Penelope and Oliver were not oblivious to what was going on. The trouble was, they were unable to do much about it. It was necessary for their children to walk almost everywhere they went, so they had to allow them to head off down the road, hoping that they were actually bound for a safe and proper destination.

When electricity came to Atlee in 1948, the Hayes family got connected right away. In addition to all the luxuries this now allowed them to consider, they hoped that being one of the few families in the area with such a precious commodity would motivate sixteen year old Marian to invite her friends to her house during the evenings to play games, to see how bright everything looked at night without oil lamps, and to sit around with the family and listen to the radio, visit, and chat, like all the other guests at their home enjoyed doing. This seemed to work for a time, as the novelty of electricity and its many uses proved to be an unbeatable drawing card all during the day, and especially after sunset. Visitors enjoyed getting a cold drink from the new fangled refrigerator that Lenore had bought for her parents by saving up her teacher's salary. The family quickly noted how bedtime moved later and later, as no one wanted to turn out the lights and retire for the evening.

Marian continued to press the limits of her parents' patience and understanding all during her mid teenage years. They noticed that her grades started to suffer as her social life grew even more active. They had hoped that when Lenore took over as teacher of the Atlee school that Marian would fare better, but if anything, she became even more disinterested. Lenore did admit to being harder on her younger sister than others, never wanting to be accused of playing favourites, but apparently oblivious to the concept of reverse discrimination. By age seventeen, Marian decided that she had had enough of formal schooling, so declared that she wanted to study to be a hairdresser. This wasn't exactly the higher calling her parents had wished for their youngest daughter. All of the other children were established in their careers by now, and Penelope and Oliver simply wanted Marian to make a solid choice for a life vocation. They couldn't understand how anyone could make a living at hairdressing, when everyone in Atlee got their hair cut at home by a family member, and wouldn't dream of paying for a cut or curls. Marian had been impressed by the number and look of hair salons that she had seen during a visit to Halifax with her Uncle Power and Aunt Sibella two years ago, and therefore couldn't be dissuaded. That fall, Marian enrolled in a six week hairdressing course at the vocational school fifty miles away in Langville.

As usual, Marian had a boyfriend at the time, a tall, lanky twenty year old named Harlan Reeves, who worked at the huge sawmill down near the head of the Vaughn brook, located on the Beck family property. Conditions were pretty primitive for people working down there on the mill operation. The men came from as far away as the French shore of Nova Scotia looking for work. Those who were lucky enough to get hired lived in crude shacks erected in the woods for the workers. Things got pretty cold in those shacks during the winter. The men would work for weeks on end, then after saving up some money, would hire Ainsley Beck to taxi them home to see their families again briefly before returning for another tour of duty. Harlan was a tough, hard working young man who could hold his own with the roughest and crudest men on the work crew. He hailed from Riverton originally, but by now was pretty much on his own, roving from job site to job site, looking for paying work wherever he could find it. He was unlike most of the others, however, in that he owned a truck, albeit a fairly unreliable beat up old Ford. This did give him some ability to escape the confines of this heavily wooded encampment. Marian's parents didn't think much of Harlan, as he used rough language openly in front of them, seemed to have no respect or use for his elders, and was as ill tempered and unpredictable as a caged wildcat. They especially were concerned when Marian would visit Harlan at the mill site, as they knew what he men were like who worked there They wondered why any daughter of theirs would want to be caught near a place like that.

Marian continued along with her course and surprised even her dubious parents by graduating second in her class of twenty. Having decided that she wanted to make a go of this, Marian set about her hairdressing career with a vengeance. She was the first member of her graduating class to get an offer of employment and started to work out of a small salon in Centretown. It didn't take long before she was the darling of the salon crowd, being inundated with requests for her cut and curl services from the ladies of the town. Apparently her straight talk and angelic looks were a welcome change to the patrons of Della's Beauty Boutique. She would often work late, keeping an eye out for Harlan's truck, knowing that he didn't like to be kept waiting even for a minute or two. She boarded in a small, but neat apartment in a home along Main Street in Centretown, and loved to have her friends and relatives drop by for a visit. Unfortunately, fewer and fewer of them wanted to drop by when Harlan became a frequent guest at the apartment.

After a year of hairdressing, Marian decided that Harlan's head of hair was the only one she wanted to run her fingers through, so at age eighteen she accepted his invitation of marriage. Harlan had just gotten a steady job working with the government paid highway crew, and therefore felt quite confident in his ability to provide a good living for a family, despite the fact that it was seasonal work. Anyway, he intended to continue cutting wood whenever the road project was on hiatus.

Marian felt especially proud that she had finally bested Lenore, as she was the first of the two to get married. The family felt quite hurt that the only family member invited to participate in the wedding party was Franklin, apparently the only Hayes that Harlan could tolerate. After the wedding reception was over Penelope told Marian quietly in their mother daughter talk that if Harlan ever lost his temper and threatened her with violence that she was to come home right away until things calmed down. Apparently Marian didn't appreciate this piece of advice one little bit, and stormed out of the room yelling "you've never given Harlan a chance! He loves me and I love him. You just can't stand to see me happy!" With that she and Harlan headed off on their honeymoon, full of optimism for a lifetime of wedded bliss and fewer blisters.

△ △ △

CHAPTER FOUR
The House: Hillcrest

In 1949, when he was thirty nine years old, Ainsley Beck decided that it was time for another career change, as taxi driving was losing its allure despite its financial rewards. Besides, it was keeping him from being able to see more of Lenore Hayes. So, when the rural mail route between Glory and Fundy Bay came up for tender, Ainsley bid on it and won the contract. Now that he had a government job, Ainsley felt that he could guarantee a decent living to any prospective wife. He knew, however, that he was poorly situated on the Porter road since many times during the winter the road there would be plugged and unpassable for days on end. It usually took several teams of horses dragging some heavy logs to break up the snow enough to allow a car to pass through. Therefore, although it saddened his mother's heart greatly, he decided that it was time to move off the farm and into the centre of Fundy Bay, where the roads were generally opened shortly after a storm due to the larger population there.

Ainsley took an instant shine to a one and a half storey house called "Hillcrest", built around 1840 and owned by Mandell Embree, well to do publisher of the Riverton Times weekly newspaper. Hillcrest was situated on an acre lot directly overlooking the Fundy Bay harbour and wharf. In the back yard on a government easement separating the Hillcrest property from the shoreline sat the Fundy Bay lighthouse, a picturesque white structure proudly flashing its beacon to all seafarers, directing them to the approaching harbour which was impossible to locate in the thick fog routinely blanketing Fundy Bay. The lighthouse keeper was Ainsley's neighbour and first cousin, Rollie Collins. Rollie kept the lighthouse supplies in a small shed located on the far northeast corner of the easement.

Ainsley was certain that this nice centrally located home on the shore of the Bay of Fundy would be the piece de resistance in his quest for Lenore's hand. After a bit of traditional rural dickering (his mother referred to it as "humming and hawing"), Mandell Embree agreed to sell Hillcrest to Dad for $1100 cash. Being the only taxi driver and one of the few car owners in Fundy Bay and the surrounding area, Ainsley was never short on cash. Therefore, he simply reached into this wallet and counted the agreed upon amount into the hands of the somewhat started seller. And with that, and following some legal paperwork which followed, Ainsley was the proud owner of a century home. Dad very soon moved his mother and himself from the Beck family homestead into Hillcrest since at age sixty-five Rachel had no desire to live on her own in the family's farmhouse and was not able to do so even if she had been willing.

Over the next two years, Ainsley dated Lenore steadily, culminating in a proposal of marriage during the last waltz of a square dance in the Mount Ruby community hall one Saturday night. Lenore said yes, and within a few months they were married at the Mount Havelock Baptist church, Ainsley finally saying goodbye to bachelorhood at the age of forty-two. All of the older villagers who knew what hardships Ainsley had faced during his life were happy and relieved to see him finally settle down with a woman of character. Even Lenore's mother had said to her on her wedding day, "I hope you'll love Ainsley an awful lot because he's had it pretty hard in life". After a short honeymoon in Prince Edward Island, Ainsley and Lenore returned to Fundy Bay and Lenore moved in with Ainsley and his mother, choosing to sleep in the spare bedroom so as not to disturb mother Beck. Ainsley felt somewhat guilty about asking his new bride to settle for the smallest bedroom, so went out and bought her a brand new set of bedroom furniture to compensate.

Lenore decided to marry Ainsley even though he had shown questionable tact and devotion at times during their courtship. For example, Ainsley continued to date Celesta Ashe while he was supposedly going steady with Lenore, and he went so far as to bring Celesta along to his wedding shower in Fundy Bay. Whenever Lenore took Ainsley to task for continuing to date Celesta, he would reply, "look, woman, I stopped going with Rosabel, Nellie, and Malfrida. What more do you want?" The simple answer never dawned on Ainsley during those pre-marriage days. Lenore knew that as a bachelor Ainsley had displayed a voracious appetite for female company and was somewhat stuck in his ways, so decided not to push too much when it came to matters of fidelity, at least not until they were married.

She did feel a bit disappointed at Ainsley's insistence that she give up her teaching career. She had recently notified the superintendent of schools of her intention to accept the vacant job at the two room school in Inglis, out in the Valley. But Ainsley was adamant: no wife of his was going to have to work. That was his role. Somehow, the fact that Lenore had just been offered a salary of $1100 and was capable of making more money than Ainsley did not seem to matter. So, Lenore finally relented, and agreed to stay home to take care of Hillcrest, Ainsley, and her new mother in law.

Mom never really liked Hillcrest. Perhaps having to share the house with her mother in law for the first seven years of marriage got her off to a bad start, and it probably changed Grammy Beck's opinion of the place too. Mom had many fond memories of Fundy Bay from her youth but had never really thought of taking up residence there before marrying Dad. As a child she had enjoyed riding in her Uncle Power's latest car on trips to Fundy Bay during the summer to go shopping at the Anthony Brothers store or to buy homemade ice cream at the parlour run by Caius and Austine Mason out of their home located fifty feet from the bridge. She would spend hours during those three week summer visits by her Uncle Power watching him and scores of local men and teenagers fish off the Fundy Bay wharf for smelt.

Mom clearly remembered the ice house beside the Fundy Bay wharf which the fishermen would use to store their fish. During the winter the fishermen would cut huge blocks of ice from the frozen Pebble Lake, bring it to the ice house, and pack the blocks of ice in sawdust. This would enable the ice to keep for months right through the summer months when refrigeration was needed most.

As soon as she moved to Fundy Bay as a new bride, Mom remembered something else about the community that she hadn't enjoyed at all during her summer visits as a youth: the awful smell that permeated the community from two sources. Firstly, in the cold weather months the impoverished locals burned easy to come by shore wood in their stoves as their sole source of heat. The salt laden wood caused stoves to rush out prematurely, but most of the residents could not afford to buy wood when it was readily available throughout the year just above the high tide mark on the beach. As the stoves rusted, they would be patched together in some fashion, often with questionable regard to safety, to enable the homeowners to get just one more year out of Ol' Faithful. The second source of the stench which filled the air during certain times of the year was the smoke billowing from the fish shacks while the fishermen smoked their fish. Mom soon discovered after moving to Fundy Bay that things had not changed all that much since she was a young visitor to the community, except that the ice cream parlour had long since closed.

Mom often said that whoever designed Hillcrest must have been drunk at the time. That really didn't help identify the guilty party since just about any of the neighbours could lay claim to being drunk the majority of the time. No question about it, the layout was very unusual and not terribly functional. Mom's pet peeve was the layout of the kitchen: there were no fewer than five doors leading off the kitchen, including one doorway opening up to a back set of stairs leading directly to one of the bedrooms. The other four doors joined the kitchen to the front porch, the dining room, the living room, and the pantry. Upstairs, rather than having a central hallway with bedrooms feeding off it, two of the bedrooms flowed directly into each other, and only a small two foot by five foot utility room we called the washroom separated the middle bedroom from the third bedroom, the one connected by stairs to the kitchen. Therefore, to get to the middle bedroom, you had to pass through one of the other two bedrooms. This design faux pas proved to be extremely annoying over the years, as my brother Johnny and I were relegated to the middle bedroom while Dad and Mom occupied the adjoining southern bedroom overlooking the Goomar property on the hill. The middle bedroom was rather tiny, and therefore by fitting two twin beds inside the room it meant that the door separating the two bedrooms could not be closed since it was blocked by my bed.

Hillcrest was basically tucked into the southwest corner of the property, meaning that the remaining acreage circled the house to the north and east. The perimeter of the property was soon lined with a variety of trees, as Dad continued to plant various saplings and bushes year after year, being especially fond of horse chestnut trees. Over the years this became a source of annoyance to Mom who complained that the foliage reduced her visibility and therefore her ability to keep track of all persons and vehicles passing by along the road. A two story outbuilding we referred to as "the shop" was attached to the house, and served as a woodshed, garage, and storage area for Dad. The woodshed portion of the shed was a ten foot by six foot section adjoining the house, and served as the passageway between the house and the rest of the shop. Dad kept the woodbox located in the woodshed piled high with wood for use in the kitchen stove. By the end of a typical fall or winter day, the box would have been emptied, meaning that Dad would have to restock the box each morning before heading off to the barn. As Johnny and I got older, stocking the woodbox became one of our duties, one we didn't especially enjoy in the dead of winter as we would have to venture out into the frigid woodshed to retrieve and maybe even chop the necessary stovewood.

Mom didn't like the elevation of the property much more that the house layout. The neighbours across the road, Donnie and Brenda Goomar, lived in a two story house situated high on an incline overlooking our house. Therefore, they had a direct view into our kitchen, dining room, and front bedroom, a fact which never seemed to be far from Mom's mind. The lack of privacy in the front bedroom was initially not a concern of Mom's since that was Grammy Beck's bedroom. When Johnny was born in 1960, his crib was placed in the west bedroom where Dad and Mom slept. However, when Grammy Beck died in 1958, just five days after my birth, Dad and Mom decided to move into the front bedroom and put Johnny and I in the middle bedroom.

The day his mother died was probably the saddest day in Dad's life. He had lived with and cherished her for forty nine years. For almost twelve years, they had lived together alone on the Beck family farm, with the rest of the family off pursuing their own lives. She had sustained and supported him, and he had stuck by her faithfully ever since his father had died so long ago. They knew and understood each other in a way that rarely happens among parents and their children. Although he had walked away from the church years ago, Dad took great comfort in knowing that his mother kept him in her prayers daily, knowing that God recognized her sincere faith. He had never resented the choices which he had made in life and which were thrust upon him, mostly because of the love he felt for his mother, feeling that more than anyone she had been robbed of something special for which there could be no compensation. She had lived a full life to the grand age of seventy four, the last thirty five years as a widow, her devotion to her husband failing to diminish throughout the years as she kept alive in her heart the love they had shared during their too brief time together.

Grammy Beck took great delight in her six grandchildren, the last of which was born as she lay ill at home with a malady which would lead to her death five days later. As she lay in bed and cradled this young infant in her feeble arms, stoking his wispy hair with her trembling fingers, she made a request that his name be changed from Edward to Paul, in honour of Paul Beck, who had been Josiah's favourite brother and who had continued to send money and letters from Boston to help support her and the children years after Josiah's death. With her fading vision she saw no imperfection in her newborn grandson, rather a perfect, warm, responsive child who had slipped through one door to begin the marvelous journey called life just as her own sojourn was coming to an end with another door about to close. Dad was with his mother when she died. He fought back the tears as he firmly held and gently stroked her hand. He would never forget the peaceful look and quiet smile that came over her face when she closed her eyes and breathed her last, as if she could finally see the welcoming faces of the two she had loved and honored for so long, her Lord Jesus and her husband Josiah. Dad mourned the death of his mother for a long time, but in his own way, quietly, without discussion and without tears. But there was something about the way he would linger over my crib, or would take time out from his farm chores to rock me in his arms, which made Mom feel that Dad had come to understand better the ongoing saga and chain of life and faith, and how the ending of one chapter is simply the beginning of another.

The lighthouse in the back of the property sat opposite our bedroom window, so Johnny and I never had to worry about having a night light in our room. The lighthouse made us all feel secure at night, and during the day, although it blocked our view of the harbour, its proud appearance and faithful service to the Bay traffic made us feel glad for its presence. As young children, Johnny and I always were intrigued by the structure, wondering what it must look like inside. We would see Rollie Collins disappear through the side door and wished that we could just have a peek inside, even if only for a moment. One fall day as Dad was working in the back garden and Johnny and I were languishing around with nothing to do, Rollie ambled up from the supply shed on his way to the lighthouse to do some repairs, check out the view from the top, or torture some emaciated prisoners, whatever it was he did inside there. Rollie and Dad started shooting the breeze, and before we knew it, Dad started toward the lighthouse with Rollie. We looked at each other disbelievingly, our eyes as wide as saucers. We decided not to wait for an invitation, so shot after Dad just as Rollie got the side door unlocked.

This was incredible! We were finally going to get to see the inside! Dad asked Rollie if it was alright if we came inside. Rollie paused for a moment, looked us over as if to see if we could be trusted to keep a secret, then said, "well, I guess it would be alright this one time". Rollie then led the way inside carrying a flashlight, with Dad behind him, and Johnny following closely behind Dad. As we stepped inside at ground level, to my surprise, we were immediately faced with a flight of stairs which went downwards, and not upwards. And the stairs were definitely not built for persons with short legs, as each step represented another one foot drop into the bowels of the lighthouse. As the youngest visitor, I was finding it very difficult to keep up, despite my eagerness and burning curiosity. I was only half way down the stairs when I saw Johnny disappear from sight, in hot pursuit of Rollie and Dad who had vanished into a narrow, darkened corridor, with only the echoing sound of their voices providing evidence of their trail.

My heart was pounding by this time. I looked downwards and realized that I had to pick up the pace. I descended the stairway as fast as I could, throwing all caution to the wind. But when I reached the bottom stair, it was a different story. In fact, it seemed like it was a storey drop. I knew there was no way I could make the leap on my own: the dim light from the partially open doorway above did little to illuminate what lay below me. I was only six years old and I was sure that the drop would be more than I could handle. I then realized that I could no longer hear any voices, and suddenly I was very scared. I was trapped in this gigantic structure, with no one there to help me. I called "Dad! Dad! Johnny! Come get me!" as loud as I could, but to no avail. No one showed to give me a helping hand. As my eyes adjusted to the dark I could make out a passageway in the direction that I was certain Dad and Johnny had disappeared. I felt tempted to take a leap of faith, hoping that I would hit solid ground, but something told me that perhaps I would land in deep water, perhaps a moat added to dissuade would be thieves of lighthouse bulbs. And the longer I waited and yelled, the more frustrated and scared I became, knowing somehow that I was going to miss out on my long awaited chance to tour this ominous building with its frightening creeks and groans. I couldn't believe that I wasn't being missed by the others in our party. Surely they had noticed that I wasn't with them. Wouldn't they know that I would not have retreated to the safe confines of home, that I wanted more that anything to accompany them on their adventure?

Finally, I could stand it no longer, so I started to cry. Then I started to sob in earnest, feeling lonely and terrified, abandoned yet again, and suddenly so many long ago forgotten memories of my earlier childhood came flooding back into my consciousness. All I wanted was my Daddy to come and scoop me up in his arms. And just when I had all but given up hope, along came Johnny and Dad, looking rather puzzled as to why I was standing on the bottom step, howling, the tears tumbling down my cheeks. After a moment to compose myself, I suddenly brightened up, realizing that now I could have my tour. Then, just as quickly as my spirits had risen, they were dashed as Rollie returned, saying, "OK, let's go gang". I was speechless. No words could express my disappointment, which later turned to anger. Dad tried to placate me by promising that we would go on another tour sometime soon, and Rollie concurred, promising, "Oh, yes, there'll be another time, cheer up, young lad!".

Six months later we all stood in sadness with a flock of our neighbours as a crew of government workers descended on our beloved lighthouse and tore it down within a matter of hours and filled in the foundation with gravel and earth, to make way for a more reliable, metallic structure which didn't resemble any lighthouse that we had ever seen. Granted, it wasn't prone to wood rod, but it was an eyesore. Surely even the government officials could see that. It did have a light on the top of it, but how what about the "house" part? It was an open structure, with no walls, resembling a tripod more than anything. Sure, all of a sudden our view of the harbour was much clearer, but that was small consolation when the postcard picture was being spoiled by this grotesque monstrosity.

After tearing down the lighthouse, the workers descended on the supply shed and demolished it in less than an hour, appearing rather proud afterwards of their efficiency. As the foreman pointed out, this new fangled metallic lighthouse promised very low maintenance. They wouldn't even need to bother any of the locals to tend it. Rollie was noticeable by his absence during the cruel ceremony. Some said he was watching from his living room window, unable to compose himself to come for a closer look. No doubt he could hear the creeks and groans emitted by his trusty old friend as it twisted and swayed with each pull of the long rope secured around its circumference, finally losing its battle and succumbing to these merciless invaders, toppling to the ground with a loud crash. Rollie's once proud position as lighthouse keeper had been stripped away, his responsibilities now consisting of being the one designated to phone the toll free government number to report any sudden lighthouse outages. But who were they kidding? In the years which followed, there was only one incident of a burned out bulb in the new beacon, that coming after the granddaddy of all thunderstorms. And on that occasion Rollie wasn't even home, so Dad had to phone in the service call, a fact which undoubtedly led to Rollie's services no longer being required.

The good service record for the new lightstand was accomplished by following a regular maintenance schedule. A helicopter would descend upon Fundy Bay periodically in apocalyptic fashion, carrying a sinister looking worker wearing dark sunglasses who would scramble out, scale the ladder on one of the legs of the structure, and replace the still working existing bulb. Then, before the rotary blade had even had time to come to a halt, the worker would climb into the helicopter and head back across the Bay of Fundy to Saint John, New Brunswick from whence he came. Fundy Bayers failed to appreciate this advancement in efficiency as they continued to mourn the loss of that grand, white, wooden lighthouse which had served the community so ably for so long. And perhaps because I had never had time to get back inside the original lighthouse for my promised tour, I felt a deep loss at its passing.

Like almost every other house in Fundy Bay, Hillcrest was without indoor plumbing, or "running water" as it was called by Fundy Bayers. The only water running in Hillcrest was when we opted to urinate in the upstairs thunder mug rather than venture out into the shop. The shop at Hillcrest had a three seater outhouse in it, somewhat of a status symbol within Fundy Bay since it was more of an "inhouse" being connected to the house so you never had to venture outside into the elements. Since the toilet was located on the bottom level and in the far corner of the shed, it afforded Johnny and I a perfect opportunity to indulge our adolescent fantasies. We therefore went with our base instincts and drilled holes in the toilet's ceiling and side wall so we could hopefully catch cousin Erica or any other visiting female, hopefully attractive but not necessarily so, in a compromising position. I don't recall ever getting a glimpse of anything special, but that probably wasn't as important as the adrenaline rush we experienced just thinking we might.

No doubt that people growing up in Fundy Bay had a very earthy sense of humour about what more refined persons would consider to be vulgar and unmentionable, and things to be kept private. But the truth was, the conditions in the typical Fundy Bay home did not allow for privacy in matters related to the bedroom or the toilet. The Valley people fortunate enough to have indoor plumbing were spoiled into thinking that human waste was a passing thing, something to be taken from sight with one flick of the handle to become the concern of others further down in the economic chain. For Fundy Bayers, waste management was something they all had to take personally since their every movement left behind some waste that had to be dealt with. It made for a never-ending cycle of fill and empty, dig and fill. Lime wasn't wasted on lawns to treat acidic soil. It was used to ensure that persons sitting in the outhouse would be able to breathe comfortably during their next visit.

At Hillcrest, we were well equipped with a number of pails and pots in addition to our three holer outhouse. Tucked away in a small three foot by two foot alcove in the front porch, to the side of the handpump and sink and behind the door leading to the cellar, were two pots sitting on the top of the clothes hamper, one for momma bear and one for the two baby bears. The small alcove became our place of solitude, somewhere where we could turn our face and other parts to the wall and perform our most private of functions with everyone else in the family respecting our need for a moment alone. When anyone in the house saw the door between the kitchen and the front porch pulled partially shut, they would understand what was in progress and would continue along to another room in the house. Such cooperation was necessary for privacy, since the door separating the kitchen and the front porch could not shut all the way due to warping and a poor fit. Rather than replace or resize the door, we simply accepted the remaining five inch gap in the doorway as too small a space to be concerned about. To visitors prone to queasiness, the visual and olfactory detection of the two pots in various stages of fullness sitting on top of the hamper often left them pale and searching for words as well as their coat and hat. To true Fundy Bayers, it was not even an issue. Hell, they'd excuse themselves and add to the content whenever the urge hit them, without even breaking a sweat. And our display was at least done with some degree of modesty and decorum. The Newcombs next door kept their slop pail on the floor right outside their kitchen door. Visitors there would often amble into the front porch to discover Merle Newcombe standing overtop of the pail, testing his aim and their nerve. And the Newcombes would only empty the pail once a day, so depending on the time of your visit, you could expect a memorable sensory experience and perhaps even a close encounter of the turd kind. Small wonder that Ethel Newcomb had very few takers for her freshly baked goods amongst those crossing the threshold.

The front porch at Hillcrest was also the place where all of us save Dad would take our baths, again with the door shut as far as it would go. These baths were ritualistic affairs, things which would be done weekly or daily, depending on the age of the person. In the case of the children, weekly was deemed to be adequate. Therefore, on Saturday or Sunday night Johnny and I would take our turns in the front porch having a bath, using nothing more than a kitchen chair, a basin of warm water, some soap, a washcloth, and two towels. Mom referred to this as a "sponge bath" although no one ever used a sponge. Dad preferred to take his sponge baths on Sunday afternoon while sitting on the dining room couch.

Having the front porch sub as a bathroom worked quite well, except when the occupant forgot to either pull shut the kitchen door or lock the front door which led directly from the outdoors to the porch. In these times, when you were in the midst of doing your best Niagara Falls imitation and suddenly realized that you had forgotten to secure the two doors, you simply had to stay alert to any sudden attempted entry into the room. If it was from within the house, it was no real problem as you could announce your presence and that would be the end of it, although the innocent intruder might have advanced to within two or three feet of you before you were able to halt their progress. The real problem was company entering the house from the outdoors. The Fundy Bay custom was to enter first, knock second. This allowed for very little time for the startled occupant to react and avoid complete embarrassment. The only hope was that you could reach the alcove, if you were not already there, and hide there unnoticed without making a sound while the visitor passed through to one of the other rooms, perhaps at the invitation of a family member who would become aware of the predicament you were in. This also required the vulnerable occupant to be able to shut off the tap on a moment's notice, to choke the chicken until it was safe to release. Certainly, being able to hold your breath was not your primary concern.

It was inevitable, however, that each of us would be caught off-guard at one time or another. One time I was blissfully having my Saturday night bath in the front porch, sitting on a chair and listening to Mom's transistor radio, when all of a sudden my Uncle Bryce and Aunt Noelle barged in without knocking, to find their embarrassed looking nephew wearing nothing but a strategically placed washcloth. On more than one occasion I was trapped in the porch's alcove, forced to put my bladder control to the test, while Mom tried in vain to quickly dismiss a chatty visitor intent on hovering near the front door and refusing all offers of a seat in the other room.

In Hillcrest, when you needed to do more than just lower your level of liquids, you had one of three options: go to the toilet in the shop, use the pail in the woodshed, or use the pail in the spare bedroom upstairs which served as a storage room for much of the year. The availability of either of the latter two options depended greatly upon the time of year. In the warmer weather, Mom generally insisted that use of the upstairs pail be discontinued. This didn't affect Dad since year round he relied on nothing more than the outhouse in the shed, a place where he could go and enjoy a good, long smoke in peace while he performed other functions. Johnny, Mom, and I were generally more likely to opt for the pail, as we feared having spiders traverse our bared bottoms if we ever chose to use the outhouse. Johnny and I had to overcome this fear when friends were around and a group "shit chat" was in order, since you didn't want to appear wimpy in front of your peers. Besides, you put considerable reliance on the law of averages that the chance of having spiders attack your exposed parts were greatly reduced when all three toilet holes were occupied and it was standing room only. Inevitably someone in the group would be overcome by arachnophobia and would revert to the hover and release approach whereby all contact with the toilet seat was avoided.

In the winter, Mom would eventually agree to move the pail into the upper spare bedroom as a concession to the sub-freezing temperatures, but not before pushing our endurance to the limit. In the freezing cold of the unheated shop, sit down use of the pail was an experience which separated the men from the boys, and often the skin from one's posterior. Johnny and I considered this a true test of our mettle, and when we survived the challenge, we considered ourselves to be the true hardy boys. The initially warm deposits in the metal pail would soon generate condensation which would cause the lid of the pail to freeze to the rim in between customers. Therefore, even though the pail would be very heavy once half or more full, a person could pick up the handle to the lid and have the entire pail rise up off the ground, never coming unfrozen from the lid. Once the determined soul managed to pry the lid free they would be enveloped and almost overpowered by a stench like stale ammonia. After gaining composure, it took considerable willpower to lower one's behind onto the icy rim of the pail. But once that was accomplished, and the ice had been melted away by the body heat, you could experience other interesting aspects of physics, such as standing up and having the pail remain stuck to your bottom. When you finally got the pail removed from your derriere, you were left with ring around the rosy. All this time you were wearing a heavy parka to enable you to withstand the cold. With all of these unpleasantries, it was small wonder that Fundy Bayers followed a low fibre diet, especially in the winter months.

Since Mom had the official title of "emptier of the pail", she would always check with the returning family members to ask if the pail was getting full. Johnny and I in our mischievous ways, would play tricks on her and always tell her that no, it wasn't nearly full yet. By the time Mom would go out to fetch the pail, it would be filled to overflowing and weigh close to twenty pounds. Mom would simply say, "you boys!" and would do her best to haul the pail out to the toilet for emptying.

As there was no indoor toilet in the house, each of us had a pot under our beds for nighttime relief. We differed slightly from our next door neighbours, the Goomars, in that whereas our pee was stored under the bed, theirs was in the bed, they being community famous for their bedwetting skills. In either case, we came to closely associate the smell of urine with sleep and would start yawning and getting drowsy with the slightest hint of that unmistakable scent in the air. It was certainly reassuring to know that the pot was there to take care of emergency calls during bedtime hours. And when nature called or a trumpet sounded, everyone listened. This was the inspiration for Johnny and I once adolescence hit to develop bladders of elastic, capable of going for hours without once considering the need for an outpouring. It was also the reason why Mom and Dad would spend twenty minutes to half an hour each night, Mom in the front porch, Dad in the shop, privately experiencing and expressing the highs and lows of flatulence before retiring for the night in the echo chamber they called their bedroom. Mom did not have her functions in check to the extent we males did so after finishing her prayers, she would go from kneeling to squatting as unobtrusively as possible. However, in the still of the night there was no mistaking what was in progress, so Mom often had to endure the indignity of suddenly having a flashlight trained on her by her cackling sons right when she was at her most vulnerable, keeping in mind there was no door between the two bedrooms. This lack of privacy in matters related to the bathroom and bedroom also resulted in some rather repressed and muted late night and early morning couplings in the master bedroom. These sessions served to plant the seeds of voyeurism within the maturing, adolescent boys uncomfortably silent in the next room hoping that the ordeal would soon end and wishing that their Dad would just leave their Mom alone.

Like most homes in Fundy Bay, there was no source of heat upstairs in Hillcrest except for whatever warmth you could generate under the sheets. The entire house was heated by two wood sources: a wood stove in the kitchen and a wood burning furnace in the basement which vented through one three foot square central register in the living room. This made for some interesting Monroesque moments through the years, especially whenever a long legged, heat seeking female was stationed on top of the register enjoying the hot air billowing upwards. The middle bedroom occupied by Johnny and I was situated directly above the living room, and had a small register in the corner, which thanks to the law of physics allowed heat to pass from the living room register right upstairs. The only other way to get heat in the upper chambers was to leave the doors open going upstairs and keep stoking the fires to help compensate downstairs for the loss of heat rising upstairs. Therefore, in order to get things moderately comfortable upstairs in the bedrooms, you had to endure stifling heat downstairs if you happened to be spending time in either the kitchen or the living room. However, the dining room, with no source of heat except what circulated around the house on its way to higher ground, was usually tepid and to Johnny and I, the most bearable. It was difficult to know how to dress in our house in the winter, as you felt like wearing a parka when you were upstairs in the west end bedroom, a sweater when you were in either of the other two bedrooms, a thick flannel shirt when you were in the dining room, a thin short sleeved shirt when you were in the kitchen, and nothing but a grin and sweatbands when you were in the living room.

Relying on wood heat had its drawbacks, such as the inability of being able to regulate the heat or leave the furnace unattended while you did other chores. Dad would stoke the furnace before coming to bed, with the hope that the midnight inferno would provide enough heat to allow us all to keep from freezing until he went down again at five o'clock in the morning to get the home fires burning once again. This meant that, having retired several hours earlier, Johnny and I would be transported in our dreamworlds from skating on Pebble Lake and playing hockey at Halley's Pond to playing baseball at the Quarry and cavorting on tropical islands with scantily clad neighbour girls during this brief nightly period of overheating. Then faster than you can say "pyjama soaker", we would each be transported back in our mind's eye to visions of sitting in spilled ice cream, sledding down the cemetery hill, and running for miles barefooted in dark, unfamiliar, snow covered woods wearing only a thin tee shirt and shorts while being closely pursued by a hungry grizzly.

You actually learn to sleep very contentedly with a mountain of blankets on top, with the feeling of the mid morning chill on your face. Once we had each scrambled to bed and burrowed deep into the blankets, Johnny and I would exchange a few pleasantries, say our prayers, then go off to sleep. The smell of day old urine would sometimes assail your nostrils while you first lay in bed if Mom had forgotten to empty the pots that day, but once the room temperature fell to arctic conditions the only noticeable hum was the sound being made by Mom downstairs as she worked away happily in the kitchen. Johnny and I would be very reluctant to stir from our cozy dens, but when saying goodnight, we arranged a special handshake that would be administered in the dark. We would each be squirrelled away under our blankets and would stretch one of our arms out in the dark, groping around for a brotherly hand to shake. This usually proceeded without incident. However, one night as I was flailing my hand around in the dark trying to connect with Johnny's outstretched hand, I recoiled when I suddenly dunked my hand in something wet and cold. The sound of Johnny's wicked laughter made me realize that I wouldn't like what I was about to discover, and when I turned on the light on the nightstand, I saw Johnny grinning from ear to ear holding up his pot three quarters full of day old urine. Throwing caution and several mild oaths to the wind, I bolted out of bed, ran downstairs to complain profusely to Mom, and washed my hand at least ten times before returning to share a room with my proud, unrepentant, still chuckling brother.

Johnny was a person who enjoyed testing his willpower, and our bedroom with its Sahara like conditions in the summer and its arctic temperature in the winter afforded a perfect proving ground. It was never quite clear what he was proving, although insanity comes to mind. During the coldest of the winter nights, when the frost had long ago passed the pumpkin and was now covering every window in the house, Johnny would accept a self proposed challenge and would throw back all his ten quilts, strip down to his waist, and would allow himself only a thin sheet for a cover for the night. I usually didn't get much sleep those nights, and it wasn't from feelings of guilt since I had egged him on. Rather, it was from a curious chattering and knocking sound which kept waking me up, and it always seemed to be emanating from Johnny's side of the room. In the morning, Johnny would be complaining of a sore jaw and aching knees as he bolted through the kitchen on his way to fill to overflowing the pot in the front porch. Mom would chastise Johnny once she had realized what he had done and would try to get Dad to chime in with his disapproval. Dad sometimes tried to reprimand Johnny at these times, but he obviously found it difficult to keep a quiet grin from creeping across his face as he imagined his son actually surviving several hours of self imposed shivering and shaking.

As much as I admired Johnny's tenacity and inner fortitude during these arctic trials, I was much more impressed by the endurance he demonstrated during his midsummer night's Saharafest. On still, hot summer nights, the heat almost got unbearable for we Fundy Bayers used to the refreshing Bay breezes to keep us cool. Upstairs in the bedrooms was like an oven, trapping all the risen heat in the house with no apparent means of releasing it to the outdoors. Our windows would be open as high as they would go, but on these sultry nights, no breeze was to be found. On a night such as this, Johnny would declare to me after we had been sent off to bed that it was time for a test of his willpower. I would chuckle, knowing what lay ahead, and would offer up a few words of encouragement. On these nights, when I would lie on top of my bed, wearing only thin pyjama bottoms and with no bedding on top of me, Johnny would locate his flannel pyjamas from the back of his drawer, put on the top and the bottom, and proceed to wrap himself tightly in about eight heavy blankets before saying "goodnight". I could only shake my head in admiration and await to hear the tale the next morning.

By mid morning, upon suddenly awaking, if I concentrated fairly hard I could usually detect a distantly recognizable and off-putting aroma, something like a poorly maintained locker room, dead rat, or stale cheese. In the morning, when Johnny emerged from his cocoon, he would look almost as bad as he smelled. It wasn't necessary to butter him up about his accomplishment since it looked and smelled like he had turned into butter during the night and had since gone rancid. He usually commented that he felt like he had lost ten or more pounds. His clothes were absolutely saturated with sweat, and his hair looked like an oil slick, stuck to his head like some cheap toupee. When he would venture rather sheepishly downstairs for breakfast and to get dressed, he didn't have to announce his arrival. Every person and fly in the house could spot his movements with no trouble at all. Mom, the sole washer and bedmaker in the family, would just stand there dumbfounded, saying, "Oh, no, you didn't do another one of your endurance tests again did you? Johnny, why in the name of creation do you do these things? Now I'm going to have to wash your pyjamas and all your bedding! And your mattress is probably soaked through!" Johnny would look too pale and weak to pursue a discussion and would simply slide off to the porch to deposit his sodden bedclothes in the hamper, and then proceed to wash himself with cold water to try to get rid of that sluggish feeling, hoping that we had some industrial strength shampoo on hand to take care of that greasy mop sitting on top of his head.

In the winter, it would take several hours to be able to reheat the upstairs each day, so no one would dress upstairs in the cold. Instead, we all set out our clothes for the next day downstairs before retiring for the night and would waste little time in scurrying down the stairs each morning to put them on when it was time to rise. As a child, there was always something comforting and homey about being transported each winter morning from your dark arctic chambers to the bright, balmy kitchen filled with the smell of bacon and eggs being prepared for your breakfast. On Christmas mornings while Johnny and I were youngsters, we could barely contain our excitement waiting for Dad to venture down to the cellar to start the furnace fire, then to the kitchen to start the stove fire, to get the living room warm enough to allow us to rush down and view the bounty dropped off the night before by good ol' reliable Saint Nick. The truth is, the temperature wouldn't have mattered to us one bit at that magical moment, since the euphoria of having proof once again that Santa Claus cared enough about us to drop by with such thoughtful gifts was sufficient to warm not only our hearts but all of our extremities for quite some time.

In the summer, with windows open, we would be lulled off to sleep by the sound of the waves crashing against the wharf, and would awaken to the sound of seagulls calling, or of a fishing boat put-putting out to sea to check the lobster traps. During summer vacation and during weekends, Johnny and I would often be woken by another sound, the sound of sticks clashing and a ground hockey game in progress, as our competitive so-called friends had hastily put together a game before we could join in, all in the hopes of catching up to us in our hotly contested scoring race. We knew all too well the rules since we had helped draft them: once teams had been set, you had to keep them for two consecutive games, and no one could join in until the two game series was over. On these days, Johnny and I would bolt out of bed at the sound of the opening faceoff, pull on some clothes, decline Mom's offer of breakfast, grab our hockey sticks and indignantly stomp off to Newcomb's yard to glare at the players sheepishly carrying on with their contest, and await the next game so we could make up for lost time and points. Johnny and I usually tried to get on the same team for the next two game series, so we could together exact our revenge on these snakes in the grass.

Running off the kitchen on the way to the door leading to the shop was the pantry. This was a lovely room, about ten feet by seven feet, complete with shelf lined walls, a long counter as principal work area, a large wall storage closet, two large built in cabinets, a display case for dishes, and a deep built in flour bin often frequented by ants in the summertime. Johnny and I had our small wooden table and chair set in the kitchen, and this made for hours of fun while Mom worked away baking pies and cookies for us to enjoy. Mom would also hide our favourite treats in the pantry, putting them on higher and higher shelves as we got older. My particular passion was miniature mallow cookies, free of the sticky jam which ruined most makes of the larger mallow cookies. Johnny and I would spend hours each week trying to hunt down the latest hiding spot Mom had selected for these cookies, waiting until she was upstairs doing chores before commencing our exploration. And sooner or later, our search would be rewarded. Once the package was discovered, we would rip the cellophane wrap, and fit as many mallow cookies as we could in the extended span between our thumb and middle finger, usually five or six cookies at a time. Mom would be cross when she would later discover that the hiding place had been detected, promising to stop buying the cookies since a week's worth of cookies always disappeared within a day of their purchase. No question about it, we were manic for mallows.

On one particular sortie, I was convinced that Mom had placed the mallow cookies on the very top shelf, a lofty perch even for someone with adult sized arms. Johnny and I discussed our strategy, both being certain that the cookies were to be found at the top shelf, just inches from the ceiling. So, being the lightest and more adventuresome brother, I volunteered to make the climb. First I climbed up on the work counter, soon discovering that even outstretched I could not come close to the top shelf. However, I did catch a glimpse of the familiar packaging, so I became all the more determined to proceed. I asked Johnny to pass up one the chairs from our play table set, and he did so, taking the time to warn me to "be careful". I set the small wooden chair on the counter top, then climbed on top, struggling to find the center of gravity on the wobbly chair. I reached out my arm and found that I was only a centimeter or two from the prize. So, I went up on my tiptoes, stretching for all I was worth. Just as my fingertips brushed against the package, suddenly the small playchair slipped and I came crashing down to the floor, turning towards Johnny as I fell. Before I landed, my face, right above my left eye, slammed against the portable chalk board standing against the wall, with its metal border. I was momentarily stunned, but when I stood up, all I could see was a pool of red blood lying on the floor, growing in size by the minute, with a searing pain by my left eye. When I put my hand up to my eye, it became covered with blood. Johnny was wide eyed staring at me, with his mouth wide open. All he could say was, "are you okay, Paul?". But I wasn't okay.

Suddenly, I felt nauseous, and panicky at the sight of so much blood. I started to cry, and I ran out of the pantry, through the kitchen, through the dining room, into the back hall, and up the stairway, managing to yell "Mommy! Mommy! Mommy!" through my wailing. I couldn't even open my left eye now as it was filled with a warm liquid, but with my right eye I could see that I was leaving behind a trail of blood. Mom came over to the head of the stairs, carrying her dust mop, wondering what all the commotion was about. When she saw me and could see the damage that had been done, she started sobbing uncontrollably, pulling me close to her bosom, holding onto the back of my head, and repeating over and over, "Oh, dear God in Heaven! Oh, dear God in Heaven" in a trembly voice that I had never heard Mom use, not even that winter when I had tonsillitis and she looked at the thermometer to see that it read 105 degrees, realizing that it was impossible to see a doctor since all the roads were plugged with snow. I knew that this was serious, but with my face pressed tight against Mom, I somehow felt that everything would be alright. When Johnny appeared at the foot of the stairs, looking wide-eyed up at Mom, Mom just yelled, "Johnny! Go get a dishtowel from the cupboard and soak it with cold water! And hurry!"

When Johnny came back with the overly wet towel, Mom simply squeezed the excess water out onto the floor, impervious to the mess she was making, folded the towel two times, then pressed it against my eye. She then spoke firmly to Johnny, still in a trembly voice through her tears, "go to the barn and get your father, quickly!". Mom continued to hug me and press the cloth against my eye. It felt cool, and the pressure felt good. When Dad came running upstairs still wearing his manure covered boots, I knew things were serious. I never saw Dad move so fast inside the house before, and he had never dared venture past the front porch wearing his rubber boots. "Ainsley! Come hold onto this towel, while I go phone Doctor Fergus! Make sure you keep pressure on it." With that Mom scampered downstairs and phoned the good doctor located six miles away in Johnstown. Mom was so emotional by this time that she was practically screaming into the telephone, so loudly that I could hear her say "Paul has got a huge cut above his left eye, and that his eye is hanging out! What should I do?!" Well, now I was really scared! My eye was hanging out? With this I started to cry. Dad tried to comfort me, all the while tears welling up in his eyes, and trying to keep Johnny calm as he was asking, "what is it, Dad? Is Paul going to be okay?". When Mom returned, she seemed a bit more composed, telling Dad, "the doctor says to put pressure on it like we've been doing, and use cold water on the towel. He says we should come out as soon as we can, but I told him the roads were full. So he's going to phone the plow and try to get them over here as soon as possible."

By the time the plow showed up, Mom had made about ten phone calls to the municipal office, imploring, chastising, threatening. Dad had spent his time shovelling out the plugged driveway, with the help of a cast of neighbours who had come to know the plight from their wives who had listened in on the distress calls on the party line. In between rants, Mom took some time to swab up the mess I have left throughout the house, but for once, it didn't seem like her heart was in it. By the time I was admitted to Doctor Fergus' office, five hours after the initial injury, the bleeding had long ago stopped, and the gash had actually closed somewhat. Doctor Fergus spent considerable time examining the wound, and complimented Mom on her quick thinking which had no doubt saved the eye. He did numerous tests on my eyesight, appearing pleased that I was able to identify each letter he pointed to, regardless of its size. He even decided that stitches were not required, due to the satisfactory healing process which had started. But even my stoic Dad could only shake his head in consideration of what might have been when Doctor Fergus held up two fingers with the smallest space between their tips, saying, "if the blow had been this much further towards the eye, your son would have lost his eyesight". With that adventure on the downswing, Mom vowed to keep the mallows in a more accessible location from now on, conceding to the addiction that Johnny and I obviously had.

Johnny and I often opted to eat at our small wooden table in the pantry rather than join the adults in the kitchen. The kitchen table was too tall and impersonal for Johnny and I, although we did find that it made a great play fort for us from time to time, with lots of headroom and offering at least some privacy from the adults who walked around outside, only their legs being visible from our hideaway. Problem was, the kitchen was the main room for socializing in Fundy Bay homes, so the kitchen table was often surrounded by women friends and relatives who were busy chatting away with Mom. Not being easily discouraged, I would often push my way under the kitchen table anyway to resume my games of pretend, imagining that I was the sole occupant of this ground level fortress. Despite the protestations from my mother, I would remain underfoot for some time, as the visitors assured her that I wasn't causing any harm. Whenever my imagination would be exhausted and I would be contemplating my escape, I couldn't help but notice when glancing around the variety of garters and nylons being worn by all of the women around the table. And their legs came in all lengths and sizes. I would try to guess whose legs and undergarments belonged to whom, finding it hard to make the match by distinguishing their voices being muffled by the table overhead. This childhood penchant for looking up women's skirts was soon thwarted when I became tall enough that my head started to hit the underside of the kitchen table when I was seated on the floor underneath. It wasn't so much a case of my head getting tender as it was having exhausted Mom's patience.

The shop attached to Hillcrest served as a woodshed for Dad, a garage, and a dump for all our non-perishable garbage that could be thrown "up over head" and forgotten about for a decade or two. Fundy Bay didn't have any roadside garbage collection, so disposing of one's refuse was a problem faced by all. This hardship was mitigated somewhat by the fact that few people in Fundy Bay had anything worth owning, so would generally make their few possessions last rather than cast them aside seasonally like the more affluent Valley types. Nonetheless, even Fundy Bayers would eventually wear out their hand me down jacket, their third hand shoes, their patched up mittens, and even their patience in holding onto that paint can with a just a few teaspoons of primer red left inside. When the moment of disposal finally arrived, the Fundy Bayer had various options: dig a hole in the ground and bury it, throw it into the Bay of Fundy and let the world's highest tides take their course, burn it, throw it over the nearest bluff, abandon it in the neighbouring woods, leave it in a bag outside the house with a "do not touch" sign on it so someone would steal it, get it trucked ten miles to the nearest dump so they could burn it, or pack it into the nearest outbuilding and promise yourself that you will clean it out someday real soon. Dad usually opted for the latter, the outbuilding being up over head in the shop. The entire floor was one big dumping ground.

Johnny and I used to like to explore up over head because we always found so many interesting things. It was anyone's guess what type of spores we might have been breathing whenever we would stir up the mess, raising clouds of dust that would leave us coughing at length. But that was merely a hazard that came with an explorer's job. The things that Johnny and I would uncover during these archaeological expeditions were wondrous and terrifying all at the same time. I remember finding a fairly dusty black candy that didn't taste terribly good but stood out as one of the few edible items uncovered. Mom wasn't so impressed when she heard about it, especially when she looked at the bottle it had come in and realized it was one of Grammy Beck's heart pills from a prescription which had expired twelve years ago. And cough medicine certainly ages nicely, acquiring a real potent kick after five or six years of dormancy.

I was quite intrigued by the dead cat which I found wound up in a large hand cranked egg beater, as it seemed to me a testament to modern technology and feline curiosity and persistence that any beast could actually force the beater blades to continue turning when they were up against such fleshy resistance. Obviously not a case of an irrepressible force running into an immovable object. Those blades had definitely moved, but in hindsight or by the sight of the cat's hind end, it might have been better if it hadn't.

This wasn't the only macabre discovery, far from it. One day while exploring the southwest corner up over head, I uncovered a very interesting looking big metal trunk suitable for storing clothes, bedding, and the like. The lid was very heavy but when I finally managed to open it, I discovered a rather emaciated looking cat inside. The poor critter had obviously been on the wrong side of gravity. But ol' Puss hadn't died in vain: she had taught us a valuable lesson, to be wary of such inviting looking hiding places. After that, we never again hid inside the old refrigerator or Dad's old metal milk cooler.

One day I was rooting through some old dried up straw, when I commented to Johnny, "gee, this would have made a nice nest for a mouse or something". Well, faster than I could spell Rodentia, I reached down and picked up a skeleton of a small mouse, holding it up for Johnny to see. With a comment as dry as the mouse Johnny remarked "Well, I guess that poor guy didn't get the hint that it was time to leave home". Johnny and I discussed the poor fella's fate a bit, feeling sad that he must have lived a solitary life with no one to take care of him. After another five minutes of rooting, I uncovered victim number two, and announced to Johnny, "Guess he wasn't lonely afterall". Perhaps the two of them had made a suicide pact after getting the cold shoulder from the family of mice living happily and snugly inside the walls of our house. You could bet that their shoulders weren't the only cold thing if they tried wintering up over head with no source of heat. It was kind of tragically romantic when you thought about it. Which is probably why we didn't for long.

Mixed in with all the interesting treasures we would uncover up over head was a lot of junk that had been deliberately placed there by Dad for reasons already noted. One day I uncovered an old flour sack stuffed full of nothing but old toilet paper tubes. Now there was no way our family had gone through two hundred and fifty four toilet paper rolls during a normal garbage bagging cycle, not even during that time we got food poisoning from the Thanksgiving turkey. That bird certainly had the final laugh, well, at least it would have had it not been beheaded before getting to see our sorry, repentant faces as we repeatedly scurried to our three holer outhouse. So the only plausible explanation I could think of was that Dad must have been speculating in toilet tube futures. After all, you never know when they might become valuable. Which is probably the same reason Dad had three boxes containing old well worn shoes. I couldn't see what use they could possibly have, except to someone studying early gauche Canadiana ruralitis. But I had to admit that the genuine imitation leather uppers did stand the test of time. If only the soles had worn as well. The shoes did seem to be a good companion piece to the two bags full of holey mittens, although at least in that case you could admire the fine workmanship that had gone into creating these hand warmers.

The temperature up over head got to be over one hundred degrees Fahrenheit on hot summer days, which only seemed to make the dustiness all the more unbearable. But it did offer certain greenhouse potential. So Johnny and I decided to follow in Dad's farmer footsteps, avoiding the cow plops, so planted some seeds in some empty paint cans we found, placed the cans right beside the western window up over head, and sat back and waited for our crop to grow. We probably should have consulted Dad on this one, but we were quite sure that the seeds would need moisture. So each day we would dutifully lug upstairs something to water the garden in a can. Problem was, the something we were lugging was our full bladders. We were pleased to see the little seedlings spring forth and apparently thrive on this briny diet, but soon became disenchanted when they wilted and died. We didn't even have a chance to ask Dad what had gone wrong, as one afternoon he had detected a rather pungent odour from up over head, which by midday reached oven like conditions, and discovered a paint can that visiting cats must have been using as a toilet.

Our feline friends were usually blamed for our adolescent indiscretions of the urinary kind. It got so cold in the winter that we couldn't bring ourselves to venture out into the three seater outhouse. So Johnny and I would often step out into the sub-zero degree shop, wait until we heard Mom's humming disappear into the living room or beyond, then we would man the hoses and dampen Dad's previously dry kindling and stovewood. The cool of the winter would often hide our tracks for a few days, but eventually Mom would pick up the scent and curse the neighbour's cats and their feline ways.

Even our cherished play fort became no more than a glorified urinal. Dad had built the play fort himself for Johnny and I in the back field, tucked under the huge chestnut tree which marked the boundary line between our property and the Newcomb place. The fort was made of wood, and measured six feet long, three feet wide, and five feet tall. For a while we enjoyed using it to play the usual innocent childhood games, such as lynch your neighbour, massacre the invaders, and bomb chestnuts on unsuspecting passersby. But we soon found that it made the perfect stand up urinal for those who wanted some privacy and preferred not to be exposed in the great outdoors. It wasn't long before only the hardiest of souls or those with the worst head congestion would even venture inside. Which is probably why we stopped going in altogether save to answer nature's call and restricted our play to the fort's roof from where no one had boldly gone before. This time, the roving dogs of the neighbourhood, those of the four legged variety, were blamed for the fort's aroma. Dad and Mom would discuss how the competing male dogs must be engaged in an epic urinary struggle, with the fort being marked and taken by an aggressive canine, then reclaimed by the new top dog, only to see the prized territory fall into the paws and jetstream of another. Their imagery was not all that unrealistic, since to Johnny and I, the fort was our Water Loo. We did learn some valuable life lessons in that rustic old fort, such as the dangers of splashback, the attraction that hornets have to brine, don't shoot between the cracks in the wall when your neighbour happens to be walking by, and don't cry "foul" when your father decides to tear down your favourite outbuilding because it is for that very reason that it is being levelled.

Another feature about Hillcrest which used to fascinate Johnny and I was the fact that there were four wall closets in the upstairs, and these also served as entry way to the two foot space between the walls. Therefore, even a grown adult could stand up and walk between the walls through much of the upstairs, passing by the chimney, and continuing part way into the other rooms. This didn't really help us sleep any better at night, knowing that a crazed ghoul could be lurking right behind our bed, on the other side of the wall, waiting for us to fall asleep so he could claim his next helpless victim. The only between-the-wall intruders Mom worried about were of the four legged variety, either mice or wharf rats. Once the chill of the fall became constant and unpleasant, the large rats living in the Fundy Bay wharf would decide to migrate several hundred feet to the warmer hospices just up the bluff. They found our shed and house a welcoming haven, despite the multitude of traps and poison intended to discourage any long stayovers. The space between the walls was especially inviting, given that the chimney was in the middle, a much appreciated source of heat for the guests. It was a common at night when lying in bed to hear the sound of little feet running along the floor just inside the walls, usually followed by Mom moaning, "oh dear, there's another one of those doosed mice. Ainsley, you're going to have to set some more traps".

It seemed rather ironic that Mom made such a fuss about the sound of mice running through the walls when it was only after the sound stopped that the real problem began: locating and disposing of the odourous dead. Seemed much like the buzzing mosquito scenario: you worry when you hear the whine of a mosquito around your head, but it is when the whine stops when you are in trouble.

Trying to kill these rodents proved to be a rather hopeless struggle, one which mostly served to frustrate the hunter and only slightly challenge the hunted. Dad tended to rely more on warfarin then he did on mechanical traps. The trouble with warfarin was the recurring fulfilment of Ainsley's Law: rodents who are poisoned always crawl off to die in the most inaccessible locations, exacting their final revenge on their adversary. Mom would usually be the first to detect a successful kill by the unmistakable odour of a rotting corpse. Dad would then be summoned to locate the carcass and dispose of it so we could all enjoy fresh air again while we slept. It would be at these times that Dad would usually vow to use traps next time, realizing that his prey would at least be stationary when caught by those means. Poor Dad would often have to spend hours inside the walls upstairs, trying to rely on his sense of smell to lead him to the victim. Problem was, parts of the inner wall sanctum were too narrow and too low to allow a grown adult to pass through. It was at these times that either Johnny or myself were often pressed into service against our wills. The smell inside the walls seemed unbearable at these times, yet we knew that we had to act now or forever hold our breath. Eventually with the help of Dad's trusty lantern and our own keen sense of smell, we would locate the hapless creature looking rather wasted by this time. After a moment of sympathy for the deceased, we would proceed to carry the catch downstairs to the kitchen to show our relieved Mom. We would then dispose of the dead and continue on with our day, while looking forward to an odourless night's sleep knowing that could be sabotaged depending what was on the menu for supper that night.

Like all homes in Fundy Bay, Hillcrest had no proper basement, but instead had a damp cellar with a very low ceiling. Adults had to remain in a crouched over position when walking through the cellar, for fear of knocking themselves out on the support beams. Like other homes with a wood burning furnace, the cellar was used to store firewood. Therefore, in addition to the entry way to the cellar from the interior of the house, there was an external entrance on the west side of the house, through two large wooden cellar doors placed at a forty-five degree angle to the ground. This allowed Dad ready access to the cellar when bringing in his winter supply of wood during the fall. The cellar doors were also a source of worry for Mom as she imagined that any would be thief, murderer, or insurance salesman could also gain ready access to the house that way.

All summer long the cellar had a damp feeling about it, but during the winter, when the wood furnace was humming, it could almost be considered cozy except for the dim lighting attributable to having only one ceiling light for the entire cellar. As children, this made venturing to the rear corner of the cellar a frightening experience, since the furnace blocked off most of the light, and also served as an impediment to any necessary retreat from whatever lurked in the shadows. Nonetheless, Johnny and I would be called upon to make the trek fairly regularly since Mom kept her jars of homemade pickles stored in a small cabinet at the rear of the cellar in the darkest corner. Usually there was nothing to greet us but our own shadows, but our hearts would be pumping madly by the time we tiptoed slowly past the furnace. On a few occasions our fears would be realized and we would be greeted by a large, rather unfriendly wharf rat which had ventured south for the winter. This would elicit screams of "Help!" from us as we scrambled to scale the rickety, narrow wooden stairs leading to the front porch. Dad would then be summoned to rid the cellar of this intruder, a task he would undertake quietly but with determination, since he did not want any rodent gnawing away at his winter supply of potatoes which were stored near the furnace in five open wooden barrels.

Probably my worst fright was when as a small child I ventured to the cellar on my own to retrieve a jar of beets and stepped on a loose board which Dad had placed on the dirt floor to bridge a rather large puddle which had formed. Unfortunately, the other end of the board had somehow slid underneath a near empty barrel which had some dahlias bulbs inside. When I stepped on one end of the six foot board, it caused the barrel to rise up and the dry stocks of the dahlia bulbs rubbed together making a rather hissing sound, which I was sure was the sound of a snake about to strike. I ran screaming upstairs as fast as my trembling legs could carry me, into Mom's arms. Once she ascertained that I was not injured in any physical way and assured me that there couldn't be any snake downstairs, she dispatched Dad to the cellar to check out the scene of the crime. Despite Dad's subsequent explanation of what had happened, it was a long time before I agreed to be the errand boy for any more subterranean assignments.

The front door of Hillcrest led directly into the porch, which housed the sink and handpump, the washing machine and dryer, as well as the interior cellar door. The handpump was our sole source of water for cooking and cleaning and drew water from our own dug well located in front of the house tucked behind the Japanese quince bush. The problem was, Mom had discovered through personal taste tests that our well water was not fit to drink. Although the water was probably every bit as drinkable as that which was being blissfully consumed by all the neighbours, Mom ruled that it would be necessary to get all our drinking water from another source. However, it was apparently alright to ingest the well water indirectly when rinsing toothpaste out of one's mouth or by eating vegetables which had been cooked in the well water. After a bit of shopping around, it was determined that the water from Merle Newcomb's well located just to the west of our property line had a much more pleasing taste and would suit our purposes. Therefore, with Merle's permission, we had a reliable source of drinking water despite the fact that its purity or superiority had never been scientifically proven.

The minor problem remaining was in getting the drinking water to our house. We didn't have any pipes running to our house from Merle's well, and indeed, any suggestion of installing such would have undoubtedly bankrupted his patience and good neighbourliness. In fact, there were no pipes running to the well period, at least none that worked. The well did have two rusted off pipes sticking out the side of the well, but these hadn't worked in years, and undoubtedly, the other end of the now defunct pipes were lying at the well's bottom. Merle's family drew the water from their well by bucket lowered into the well. Therefore, all during my childhood, a daily ritual was going for water from Merle's well. Dad drew this assignment while Johnny and I were in our preteen years, since the steel bucket used by Dad for the purpose was much too heavy when full to be lifted by well intended youngsters. However, a rite of passage for young boys was being led to the well by Dad and being taught how to tie a proper knot, and then being allowed to lower the pail into the well, while Dad held onto our shoulders. Dad would have to reach around and grab the rope if and when the pail actually took on water, since it was a bit too risky to allow ones so young and inexperienced attempt to test their strength while doing such a delicate balancing act.

The water level in Merle's well was usually ten to fifteen feet below ground level. Therefore, once the wooden well cover was removed, any uninitiated person sent to fetch a pail of water was faced with a rather formidable challenge while staring down into the cool, narrow, rock lined well which would make a chilling and unyielding grave with one wrong step. One thing for sure, no one would be able to save you in time, since the water in the well was over six feet deep, and even if you could somehow flail your way to the surface in time to utter one last scream, your call would resound within the well cavity itself but would not project outside to any would be rescuers.

Once any initial wooziness settled, the fetch it person would tie a secure knot on the handle of the steel bucket, lower it down until it was hovering approximately one foot above the water level, then would jerk the rope back and forth until the pail was tripped upside down. At that exact moment, the person would let the rope slip a few feet so the overturned bucket would drop into the water and take on a pail full. It was then a matter of mustering up the strength to dead lift the pail ten feet to the wooden curb of the well, all the while maintaining your balance while straddling the two foot square opening to the well. This wasn't as easy as it seemed when the well cover was covered with rain, snow, or ice. Once when he was about eight years old and walking down to the barn to see Dad, Johnny decided in passing the well to take a peek at the water level just to have something to tell Dad about. It was starting to get dusk, and the fading light didn't allow Johnny to readily see the water level since there was too little light to cause a reflection from such a depth. In his eagerness to get a closer look, Johnny leaned over too far, lost his balance and plunged downwards into the hole. In that terrifying moment, he reached out his hands instinctively and managed to grasp onto the curb. The only thing visible from ground level were

Johnny's two hands clinging for dear life onto the partially rotten wood. As he dangled precariously over the black water, it felt to Johnny as if all the spirits of those who had gone down the well before him to their death were chuckling and calling out for him to join them. His cries for help echoed inside the chamber but failed to bring the much needed help. Just when his strength was ebbing to the point where he could no longer even hold held up to look towards the sky, he felt two strong arms grab onto his, and without a word, he was lifted straight up into Dad's welcoming embrace. Johnny just collapsed into Dad's arms, sobbing for having been caught doing something so stupid, and relieved that the spirits of the well had been cheated out of so young a companion. For quite some time after that, Dad accompanied Johnny to the well for the twice a day water chores, and Johnny wouldn't have had it any other way.

When we got older, we especially liked to tease Freddie Newcomb, who was the water retriever for their family, by giving him a sudden push with one hand when he was hovering over the open well, while grabbing onto his shirt at the same time with the other hand to avoid any unintended plunge. This didn't seem particularly mean spirited or dangerous at the time, and usually elicited the hoped for screams from a terrified Freddie.

Once the pail of cool water was retrieved from the well, it would be hauled one hundred feet into our house, where it would be placed on the narrow, linoleum covered wooden table Mom had in the porch especially for that purpose. Anyone wanting a drink would simply proceed to the porch and ladle out a glassful.

As far as hot water needs were concerned, every person owning a wood burning stove in Fundy Bay pretty well had to make sure it was one with a hot water tank on the side. This tank would hold several gallons of water, and being attached to the ever warm wood stove, would provide a ready source of warm, and sometimes hot water to anyone in quick need of such. As a testimony to how hard the water in our well was, the hot water tank which started out black or silver in colour, would soon be copper coloured due to the deposits from the water. Also, the inside bottom of the tank would be coated with several millimetres of rusty looking sediment formed over time. When it was wash time, the water from the tank would not suffice, so it would be necessary to keep huge tubs of water on the hot stove during the day, to keep adequate supplies of heated water at hand.

Hillcrest had a few nice design features which helped outweigh its negatives. For one, it had a modest veranda with eastern exposure with a nice view of the Bay of

Fundy. On hot summer nights, it was very pleasant to take a lawn or rocking chair out on the veranda and enjoy the cool breezes blowing up from the Bay while listening to Rollie Collins sing hymns next door from his veranda. Hillcrest also had a six foot by five foot enclosed sunporch on the southern side of the house facing the road. Unfortunately, access to the room was impossible from inside the house. Instead, you had to enter the sunporch from the veranda, a minor nuisance which probably was responsible for the lack of usage of the room once Grammy Beck died.

Grammy Beck had loved that little sundrenched room, a place which offered quiet repose and escape from the hustle and bustle and monotonous chit chatting in the main house. It gave her a tiny oasis where she could apply her green thumb, without having to listen to complaints about the bugs which were most certainly living in the soil and waiting to infest the house. In the midst of the tiny sunporch, Grammy Beck had placed a small but sturdy rocking chair where she would sit and soak in the beauty of the fruits of her labour, a magnificent, aromatic floral display of every colour and scent. Many of her dear friends from the community would drop in while they were walking by, just to talk briefly and compliment her on the splendour of her surroundings in that cramped room, and she would just as graciously invite a bumblebee or two inside to enjoy the flowers in their own special way.

Mom had no interest in investing the time necessary time to maintain the flora in its out of the way location, so when Grammy Beck died, most of the plants did likewise, except those which Aunt Melanie rescued and lovingly preserved in her Mount Ruby home. The flowers seemed to be drooping the day after Grammy's death as if in mourning, somehow knowing that their faithful guardian was about to assume her resting place deep in the cool earth, never to return to grace them with her presence. The sunporch never again was a room filled with life and beauty, but rather seemed haunting in its emptiness and loneliness, cut off from the rest of the house, its windows painted shut and its sprung door kept locked lest someone steal their way inside to make off with a ray of light or to revive a memory of a happier time. The sun still streamed into the room searching for the receptive audience which once filled the space, to supply life and pleasure. But its warmth and light were now wasted, with no life to be found there, having no affect except eventually causing the neglected, faded linoleum to curl and crack. The room was now special to no one, pleasing to no one. The only memory of its glorious past was an unmistakable smell of geraniums which still lingered in the stale air years after Grammy Beck's death. Soon the sunporch door would be opened only on rare occasions in order to use the room for such ignoble purposes as storing lawn chairs and boxes of discarded knickknacks. But for that brief instant, when the door swung open, a small amount of fresh air would sneak in, causing a momentary stir amongst the remains of insects and leaves littering the floor, raising hopes for the return of a nurturing hand, and a loving touch. Suddenly, with the slam of the door and the turning of the key, the promise of life would vanish, and death would again settle into its appointed place, to be undisturbed and unchallenged for yet another season.

△ △ △

CHAPTER FIVE
The Neighbours

A common practice around Fundy Bay was for the residents to name their homes, and to place the name plate proudly over the front door. The names reflected the geography of the area as well as the mood and humour of the people, including names like "Utopia Hall", "Fundy Spray", "Tides Inn", "Bayside Manor", "Sleepy Hollow", "Harbour House", "Fundy View", "Shore Nuff", and "Fish-Inn". Our house, located on a bluff overlooking the harbour's wharf and just up the hill from the bridge, was called "Hillcrest", although Mom insisted that the sign be taken down and stored in the shed since it clashed with her idea of what a modern entrance way should look like.

Growing up in "Hillcrest", I enjoyed getting to know our very interesting neighbours, as there was an almost non-existent turnover in home occupancy. Across the road from my house lived Donnie and Brenda Goomar in a house purchased for them by my Uncle Willie, who was also Brenda's uncle. Donnie was a certified electrician, but seemed to get more of a charge out of drinking beer than by plying his trade. Donnie was a heavy drinker for most of his life, which may have partly explained why he suffered from nocturnal enuresis. Actually, bed-wetting ran in Donnie's family, literally. He and each of his four brothers had suffered from the same condition since early childhood. The parents, Ed and Norma Goomar, were at a loss to explain why their children had been so stricken, but neighbours often theorized privately that it may have something to do with the fact that the Goomar house had no indoor or outdoor toilet, so the family would pry up a particular floorboard in the unheated porch and pay their respects to Mother Earth whenever nature called. Speculation was that this may have had some psychological affect on the children, since they and any visitors to the house passed over the family waste with each crossing of the kitchen threshold. Odours were not a problem since the Anthony Brothers store was always well stocked with powdered lime.   Norma confessed to Mom once that in the still of the night, if she stood outside the bedrooms in the hallway and listened, the sound which greeted your ears was like that of a tap running, intermingled with a chorus of snores, all emanating from her five sons. When as a young bride Brenda first spent an evening with Donnie, she was horrified to discover that her partner for life had soiled their brass marriage bed.   Her feelings of entrapment passed with time, however, as did the finish on the bedrails.   She learned to grin through any number of comedic suggestions and remedies from the neighbours, and somehow could even muster a chuckle when yet another grinning soul would recommend that she get a copy of the book "Rusty Bedsprings" by I.P. Nightly.   In fact, it wasn't long before the soggy couple were bringing another generation of bed-wetters into the Goomar family. It was no wonder that Donnie and Brenda received free wall calendars each Christmas from Johnson's Mattress and Box Spring outlet on highway #1 outside of Dodgeton.

Just east of Donnie and Brenda Goomar's place lived Rollie and Mary Collins, along with their five children, Ronnie, Veronica, Sarah, and the twins, Peter and Jake. Rollie's parents used to live in the Goomar house before it was purchased by my Uncle Willie. Rollie's mother was a sister to my Dad's mother, making Rollie and Dad first cousins.   Rollie was born in 1906 and it didn't take him long to become a model citizen of Fundy Bay. He was a fisherman all his life, and had the typical optimistic outlook on life which was necessary for that trade. He was a burly man, not good looking, but so jovial in his demeanour that everyone just had to smile whenever he was around. Rollie was never terribly successful as a fisherman.   If the truth be known, at least in the latter years he barely made enough to make ends meet. Nonetheless, he was regarded as the elder statesman of the fishing community, commanding a level of respect amongst his peers that would rival that of any company president. When he spoke, the other fishermen listened. He never abused his authority, however, and was always open to some good natured needling, even at his own expense.   Rollie was elder deacon of the United Baptist church, and was its most enthusiastic choir member. Rollie was the only one allowed to make the Sunday morning trek up three flights of church stairs to the belfry to pull the rope on the church bell, announcing that church would be commencing in fifteen minutes. This was a position of honour, a privilege reserved for someone who had served God and the church well and stood the test of time.

On warm, summer evenings, Rollie would sit out in his rocking chair on his veranda, singing Gospel songs at the top of his lungs, truly making a joyful noise unto the Lord and all of Fundy Bay. Rollie showed a definite bias for those songs with a nautical theme, such as "Will Your Anchor Hold in the Storms of Life?", "Fishers of Men", and "Jesus, Saviour, Pilot Me". On these evenings, our whole family would take some time to sit together out on the veranda, as would all the other neighbours at their own homes, to listen to Rollie singing away, each of us saying nothing, just taking in the meaning of the words and enjoying every discordant note. Every so often someone would yell out a request, and Rollie would usually oblige. Even the Goomars and Morgans down the street would sit out and enjoy the show, enjoying a cold beer while they listened. No one ever talked to Rollie about his concerts next day or anytime; somehow, that might have embarrassed him. Rollie knew that an audience was out there, he just wasn't able see any of their faces.

As children growing up at a time when families had to rely on face to face visits to exchange news, my brother and I especially looked forward to the Sunday night visits by Rollie and Mary. They would usually arrive around seven thirty and would stay until nine o'clock. Dad and Mom loved these visits as much as we did. Rollie was a masterful storyteller, knowing how to draw people into his yarns, how to hold their attention through the various plot twists, and then how to conclude in the funniest way possible. And best of all, Rollie had the most contagious laugh any of us had ever heard. It would start deep down within his stomach, a real belly laugh. Then it would build in volume and intensity, as the seconds passed, taking us all along for the ride, all the while causing Rollie's eyes to water profusely. It would culminate in a high pitched wail as Rollie would almost be crying from the sheer joy of the experience, breathless and exhausted. My brother and I, although we always sat in the next room so as not to be trapped into any forced conversation, would turn down the radio or pause whatever we were doing at the time whenever we heard Rollie starting to laugh. We, and everyone else in earshot range, would just spontaneously start to laugh a genuine, feelgood type of laugh along with Rollie, keeping pace with him and enjoying every second of the ride, hoping it would go on just a little bit longer. His was the type of laugh that can only come from a clear conscience and a love for life with all its ironies and twists of fate. The ultimate experience in merriment was when Rollie Collins and Edna Moore would be at the same social event, as they would invariably end up sitting close enough to one another to converse, and this would soon turn into an exchange of witticisms and puns, leading to gales of rollicking laughter that would have melted the frown off Queen Victoria.

To most of us, it seemed that Rollie and Mary were a mismatch. As joyful as Rollie was, Mary was equally as serious. While Rollie was carefree and happy go lucky, Mary was cautious and a worry wart. Rollie would see the best in everyone, whereas Mary was quick to criticize and pass judgement. Rollie loved being around people any chance he got, whereas Mary liked to stay within her own home and putter around. Mary was nonetheless a very efficient woman, and on those rare occasions when Mom actually left the house to go on a trip to town and needed a babysitter for her two boys, Mary would quite willingly volunteer. We didn't enjoy her as a babysitter as much as, say, Connie Baxter, grandmother to our good friend, Tommy Goomar, since Mary didn't ever want to play. She was a hard worker, though, and would make sure that Johnny and I stayed out of trouble as well her way, since she usually decided to take the opportunity to scrub the kitchen floor, prepare dinner, or wash some leftover dishes, all above and beyond the call of duty.

Mary would not tolerate alcohol or tobacco in her house, or any use of them on display in her front yard. She refused time and time again to take office in the church despite frequent requests made, and generally did not say much at any community social function. She was a stern looking woman with thick glasses and would usually only speak when spoken to. Nonetheless, she could be counted on to help anyone in distress, or to work diligently on a cause when others would shirk the responsibility. She hosted the annual picnic of the women's missionary society year after year, always going to an incredible amount of work and expense to outdo the effort she had put forth last year. Everyone knew that the Collins' couldn't afford to put on such a spread, but it would have been no good to protest. All the children of the women in the group looked forward to the picnic as much as the members, as it was the only meeting where we were allowed to attend. The food was always exquisite, and the tables were overflowing with home baked desserts. Each year we all walked away stuffed, wondering how we could have fit so much food in our aching stomach, all while congratulating Mary on a job well done.

The Collins' children, my fourth cousins, took mostly after their father, in looks and disposition. Ronnie Collins, a community favourite from an early age because he was a chip off the old Collins block, decided early on to follow in his father's footsteps, quitting school after grade nine to fish fulltime with his father. Ronnie could do no wrong in most people's eyes, since he was his father personified. However, his fondness for cigarettes kept him in his mother's bad books.

He worked very hard to learn the fishing trade, and by age twenty had decided to start fishing with his own boat. It didn't take too long for young Ronnie to establish himself as one helleva lobster fisherman. Being tall and strong, with an even temperament and lots of energy, Ronnie worked hard and long to make this venture a success. He was usually the first fisherman in Fundy Bay each day to head to sea, and the last to leave the wharf at night for home. He soon sold his first boat and bought a much larger one, which he named "Lila T". The "Lila T" was in fact the largest inshore boat fishing out of Fundy Bay or any community east of Digby. The significance of the name escaped everyone, until it was learned that in the midst of his daily fishing outings, Ronnie had each day been sailing to Hurbertsville hoping to catch a glimpse of a raven haired beauty who took afternoon strolls along the beach there.

They had met on the Hurbertsville wharf by chance, and then each day after that by design. Her name was Lila Trainor, an unspoiled beauty who instantly took a shine to this strapping young fisherman with the wavy black hair and the devilish look in his eye. It was later discovered that when she agreed to go steady with Ronnie, Ronnie then and there decided that he needed a larger vessel to allow him to haul more lobster traps, to show Lila that he would be able to provide for all of her material needs. He proudly sailed his new boat to Hurbertsville the day after his purchase, and took along a bottle of local Fundy Bay moonshine for Lila to christened the from bow with. Needless to say, she was very touched by the chosen name, and from that time on vowed that she would do everything to turn that "T" into a "C".

Veronica Collins was a beauty by anyone's standards, tall and thin, with an hourglass figure, long, silky dark brown hair, and dreamy blue eyes. She oozed sophistication from every pore. She had a quiet demeanour, much like her mother, but was quick to smile and laugh like her father. Her visits were also welcomed by my brother John and I, but unlike visits by her father, these were no laughing matter. We both had serious crushes on her, and it was no doubt obvious to Veronica and Mom. Our frequent trips through the living room where they would be seated would eventually evoke some gentle laughter on their part, as they would understand that Johnny and I were just making excuses to glance in Veronica' direction. Sometimes we would decide that the living room was the best place afterall to do our colouring, or to play our board game, quietly of course, while we took in the beauty of this lovely creature. Veronica never failed

to ask each of us a question about ourselves, which simply proved to us that she was also carrying a torch for one of us, but which one? She was always so coy about her affections. The fact that she was at least fifteen years older than us was simply an accident of nature, and did nothing to stifle our longings. Of course, we had no idea what we were longing for, since we weren't even old enough to go to school.
Nursing seemed to be made for Veronica. She had a gentle, caring spirit, yet could be very firm when she needed to be. She went through the training program in Halifax with ease and graduated second in her class. Upon graduation, she announced that she was taking a position at the children's hospital in Halifax and would be moving there permanently. Veronica was missed in Fundy Bay by everyone, especially by the community's pubescent males. In such a small village, it could take years for someone to rear another as beautiful as she, so for the adolescent boys, it was back to the Sears catalogue while fantasizing about having enough money to enable them to move to the city.

We really didn't get to know Sarah all that well. She took after her father in most respects, including inheriting his husky built. She was quick with a joke, which she would deliver in her normal, loud voice, and could always make Mom laugh out loud, no matter how tired or frustrated Mom might be. Sarah started dating some of the local Fundy Bay boys at a very early age, which horrified her protective, image conscious mother. Sarah continued to date a variety of boys, both from within and outside the community, and got married at the age of eighteen to a boy she met at a dance in Port Heath. He turned out to have some ambition, and they moved away to Halifax shortly afterwards. This was a shock to many that a local girl would go so far away, and most Fundy Bayers gave the young couple only a few months before they would come to their senses and buy a place in Fundy Bay. As it turned out, they had a baby just a few months later which apparently didn't surprise anyone, so it was assumed that this was the reason why they had moved away, to avoid the scorn they would have faced from their church going neighbours. After the baby's birth, people took it for granted that they would see very little of Sarah from then on.

The twins, Peter and Jake, were without doubt the life of the party, every party. They were constant companions throughout their younger years and would take turns playing the straight man and the comedian. Like everyone, they apparently loved to hear their father laugh, so they went about ensuring that his laughter was no scarce commodity. Their propensity for looking for the double entendre in everything said kept them in trouble with their teachers pretty well all through elementary and high school.

Their wit was so sharp and polished that they came to be a regular comedy act at all community concerts in Fundy Bay as well as the surrounding coastal villages. The act which was most responsible for keeping them in the local entertainment spotlight was their Deke and Duffy routine, about two hard working but not so swift Fundy Bayers, Deke being the farmer and Duffy being the lobster fisherman. Their accents were exaggerated, and their vocabulary was a shameless cross between Newfoundlandese and Cape Bretonese. Peter, as Deke the farmer, would dress in manure stained, baggy work overalls, a plaid shirt with rolled up sleeves, a dirty old farmer's cap pulled down to his eyes, and a filthy old pair of rubber boots. Jake, as Duffy the fisherman, dressed in a pair of black hipwaders, and old bulky cloth jacket buttoned up to the neck, and a stained sou'wester hat complete with fishing lures stuck in the side. Deke and Duffy would amble out onto to the stage, to the recognition and applause of an adoring audience who knew their every joke and cue. The crowd would sit on the edge of their seats as the routine progressed, waiting for their favourite part which the had retold a hundred times to their friends, elbowing their neighbour when the punch line was about to be delivered, and slapping their knee and laughing freely when it came across even better than the last time. Deke would rock back and forth on his heels while he spoke in the recognizable drawl of the Fundy Bay farmers, while Deke would be concentrating on carving pegs to be used to plug lobster claws. The two buddies and neighbours would tell increasingly exaggerated stories about the hardships they were facing in their respective lines of work. Their Deke and Duffy routine would be much too earthy and colloquial for mainstream television or radio, but played just right in the small community halls of rural Nova Scotia. The routine would go something like this, with Duffy intently carving away:

"Duffy, I hears ya havin' a good haul dis season. Gonna have 'nuff stamps to git the pogey?"

"No problem dere, bai. I got more stamps den one ah doze philly tellists. But it ain't easy, bai. The udder day I was gaffing a dogfish and I missed and drove da hook right trew me boat. Put one ugly lookin' hole in 'er. An' ya know I don't swim, eh? But neither duz dat dogfish anymar."

"Jeez, Duffy, ya gotta be careful, eh? Glad da hear you're gettin' lots of lobsters, but you're not keepin' any of doze tinkers now are ya, Duffer?"

"No way, Deekie, bai. Ya know its 'gainst the law da keep the small 'uns. I always trow 'em back, just like all the gang in Fundy Bay."

[just then Duffy bends down to empty one of his huge boots, causing a quart of water to spill out along with two small canner lobsters. Duffy feigns surprise, and pauses to allow laughter to die down]

"Deke, me son, ya shoudda seen the lobster I's hauled out ada Bay last week. It were a monster, it was, I'm a telling ya, bai. Musta been a twenty, thirty pounder!"

"Iszatso, Duffy? Whatcha do witda beastie?"

"Ah, I took 'er home to show Mildred, bai. Ya know, she's always sayin' ah can't so much as catch cold. And what does she spend 'er time doin'? Bangin' away on dat new pianie I bought 'er, makin' a terrible racket, she is. So I says to meself, 'I'll show, Mildred, I will.' So when she's outside hangin' up 'er bloomers on the line, I went and puts dis forty pound lobster on the top of 'er pianie, to get 'er 'tention, see?"

"I thought ya said it were a twenty pound lobster, Duffer ol' man?"

"My mistake, bai. Musta been all of forty pounds, or more. But what I'm wantin' to ask ya, Deekie, is have ya ever had a lobster on your pianie?"

"No, me son, but I've had plenty ah crabs on me organ!"

[pause to allow laughter to subside]

"Deke, I' been meanin' ta ask ya. What do ya think of me new hairdo?"

[removes his stained sou'wester to show off his hair, with one thick lock very purposefully curled on his forehead]

"Atwater Crawford cut it fer me the udder day. Kinda shows off me wavy hair, don't ya think? Mildred seems to like it. Says it looks very A-fected."

"Don't know 'bout that, Duffer, but by the looks of dem little green things crawlin' on your shoulder, I'm guessin' dollars to donuts that its problee IN-fested!"

[more laughter as Duffy looks down at his shoulder and snaps some imaginary bugs off onto the ground]

"Well, I got one for ya, Duff. Here I was the udder day, doing up me hay with Jeff Thackett's new baler, when all's a sudden, me false teeth feel out ontada ground, and den went rite inside the baler. I musta torn apart six bales of hay 'fore I found 'em. And just as I was rippin' into the last one, this green snake pops out and bites me on the hand. And wouldn't you know dat Gertrude Halfpenny would come along just at dat moment, expectin' me best manners and me usual million dollar smile."

"I doughno, bai, I've seen yer smile, and I wouldn't give ya a plug a tobaccie fer it!"

"Don't be a smart arse, ya old cod jigger. But has that ever happened to ya, Duff, having your falsies end up in the hay?"

"No, bai, but the reverend tells me dat it's happened to Ruby mor'en once."

[gasps, a collective "oh oh" from the crowd. Deke is laughing loudly, then after the crowd settles down, he suddenly and loudly breaks wind]

"Good golly, Miss Molly! Control yerself there, Deke!"

[Deke reaches down inside the front of his loose overalls, pretending to waft out the offensive fumes in an exaggerated manner. Meanwhile, Duffy all the while is contorting his face and rubbing his eyes, pretending to be stunned by the odour]

"Jeez, Deke, do you need a hand there, bai?"

"Thanks enaway, Duff, ol' man, but I think I can handle 'er."

"Yeah, Deekie, that's what I'm afraid of!"

[more laughter from the crowd as Deke removes his hand, looks at it, then rubs it under his armpit]

"I doughno, Duffy, its gettin' harder every day to make an honest livin'. If it ain't one ting, its the udder. Why, just the udder day, here I were mindin' me own business, when dis government inspector comes along, from da health department ya know, says he has to check me herd for wormies. I taut it was bad enough when each of me milkers got the finger treatment, but I really got hoppin' when he bent ME down and started ticklin' ma' piles!"

"By the liftin' Deekie, whatya do den, bai?"

"What could I do, Duffer, ol' man? I needed da piece of paper so I could sell me milk out in da Valley, eh? But I taut at least he couldda brought some grease and a second pair ah gloves!"

"Ah, well, ya gotta feel bad for doze poor government types, Deekie, ol' bai. All doze cutbacks, an' all. Its a cryin' shame.

[pause for a chorus of derisive comments from the crowd]

"And gloves ain't cheap, 'specially if ya gotta buy 'em at Anthony Brothers store. But I hear ya' talkin', Deke. And it kinda rings a bell in me mind. That government feller, he wouldn'da been a short, bald headed guy would 'e?"

"Don't know, Duffer, ah didn't get to see much of his face. But ah do remember he were wearing dese purple coloured gloves. Never seen anythin' like 'em."

"Ya, dat's the guy, Deekie! He came by me fish shack to poke at me and the lobsters too!"

It was probably due to their growing popularity in the community and their decaying reputation at school that they decided to drop out in grade eight to pursue a career in door to door sales for the Fowler brush company. Not having a car, they had to rely on their goodwill with the local community folk and became quite polished at explaining why the Fowler brushes were vastly superior to anything sold in the Anthony Brothers store. Since they were so well known and liked in Fundy Bay, they never had to worry about getting a door slammed in their face, and usually could count on a cup or two of tea from their host while they made their presentation. The twins found that these informal sales pitches were the perfect vehicle for some of their tried and true comedy routines, and the managed to blend the two successfully for quite some time, until everyone had all the brushes they could possible use in two lifetimes.

It was then that the twins decided to invest in a used car to widen their sales territory, not a move to be taken lightly when you are from a community with only a handful of automobiles. The brothers faced no competition for as far as a tank of gas would take them, so they established a sales territory within a fifty mile radius of Fundy Bay. Soon after the vehicle purchase, Fundy Bayers came to see very little of Peter and Jake, and of Deke and Duffy. Seems that they were heading out daily at about 5 am and didn't get home until about midnight. They were keeping fishermen hours, experienced much the same backache from lugging around the heavy suitcases of product, but got to wear fancy clothes and meet a variety of people. The folks they met in the neighbouring villages and towns proved to be a harder sell than Fundy Bayers, and apparently they weren't so awed by the boys' comedy routines. Nonetheless, the brothers managed to eke out a reasonable living, although it took its toll on them and their car.

Deke and Duffy stopped performing at the local community concerts, as Peter and Jake never seemed to be able to spare the time. Finally, on one of their trips, Peter met the girl of his dreams, Eleanor Riggs, and to everyone's dismay, most of all Jake's, Peter and Eleanor got married shortly thereafter. Eleanor's aging father owned a hardware store in Emmery, and soon Peter was working employed there as cashier, stockboy, assistant manager and delivery man. Peter sold his half interest in the car to his despondent brother, Jake, who gave up the Fuller brush business and started operating a taxi out of Fundy Bay. When that proved not to be lucrative, since Fundy Bayers had little reason and inclination to go anywhere they couldn't walk, Jake left Fundy Bay for good and headed his car to Saint John, where he managed to get by doing deliveries for grocery stores, part time taxi work, and even resurrected his Duffy character for some occasional on-air fill-in work at the local radio station doing live commercials for Brunswick Seafood.

Rollie's death in 1974 seemed to cast a long shadow over the entire Collins' family. All of the children seemed to lose a bit of spark, and their natural comedic gifts seemed to fade somewhat. It was observed by many that they were becoming more serious like their mother. Nonetheless, the Collins continued to be favourites in the community, and would listen patiently to their neighbours' well intended reminiscences about Rollie.

At the bottom of the hill from our house, bordered on two sides by the brook and the bay was the home of Dwight and Muriel Morgan. Dwight had been born in England in 1893. As an adult he served in the military there for over thirty five years, then retired to Fundy Bay in 1950. Dwight and Muriel lived quiet lives, perhaps because when they tried to strike up a conversation, very few of the local residents could understand what they were saying due to their heavy accents and the untrained ears of the Fundy Bayers. To the would-be linguists in the crowd, it was difficult to believe that the Morgans were speaking English at all; it sounded more like a Scandinavian dialect, with the occasional recognizable word thrown in to maintain their audience's interest. But they acted friendly towards everyone, smiling and waving a lot as they daily took long strolls around the community.

Not long after they settled in Fundy Bay, they were joined by their only son, Alvin, who at the age of 35 had himself decided to retire from his career of professional gambling and womanizing, a decision made easier by certain threats on his life by unpaid creditors and unamused husbands. Alvin took one look around Fundy Bay and realized that this was a community where he could feel right at home. Like a dog returning to its own vomit, Alvin soon rediscovered his former lifestyle, making it a regular pastime to fleece all would be takers amongst the male population while wooing their impressionable wives and girlfriends. Alvin was incorrigible, even taking time to flatter the most religious and bovinely of women. My mother would shake her head in mock disgust on the many occasions when Alvin would tell her how beautiful she was, usually when he was dropping by to ask Dad for a ride to town. Despite his many shenanigans, Alvin did possess a certain charm, and generally was able to calm the waters whenever he ruffled the wrong feathers. Being a heavy drinker and smoker, he could be seen at various hours of the day staggering around the streets of Fundy Bay in a much more disorderly fashion than his parents, never failing to doff his hat to the ladies or stopping to quaff any bottle of alcohol offered to him by his numerous drinking pals and fellow gamblers. It was as if Alvin was living according to his own rules, or perhaps no rules. As he always said, "life is a gamble, and if you're not willing to ante up, you're not in the game."

Living across the street from the Morgans, on the elevated side of the road and overlooking the bridge were the Goomar family, headed by Fergus and Otha. They lived in a small four room house with their fifteen children, nine boys and six girls. Despite the squalor in which they lived and the amount of alcohol consumed within those four walls, Fergus and Otha were not troublemakers in the community. They didn't attend church or any of the functions sponsored by these religious bodies, but neither did they harass or condemn anyone who did. They pretty went about their business, enjoying the amber nectar and various other liquid refreshments. And they were not selfish people. They believed in sharing whatever they had with their children. This was evident when one of their daughters, Freda, bragged at age ten that she had tasted every type of alcohol that any of us could name. Coming from families that fervently practised teetotalism, most of us could only draw on some names of beverages we had heard on the Saturday afternoon westerns on TV. Sure enough, with each mention of whisky, gin, tequila, bourbon, scotch, and sarsaparilla came a nod of the head, assuring us that she had not only tasted them, but managed to drink an entire glass in most cases. Of course, we had no way of verifying these claims, but something in the way she said it made us think that she was not lying.

Some of the well intended church going mothers used to comment on how sad it was that the Goomar children seemed to be so poorly dressed and fed, and therefore would usually try to pass along a sandwich or cookie or some used clothing to any of them who happened to drop by to play. I soon realized that rather than saving my leftover sandwiches from school for the neighbour's dog, I should give them to any of the Goomar boys looking longingly at my lunchbox of plenty on the daily bus ride home. The boys in the family seemed to feel totally at home in the great outdoors, and would quite unabashedly drop their pants at almost any open field, manure pile, or neighbour's lawn to rid themselves of their waste while their friends could only pause and stare in amazement. Once finished, they would just as quickly haul their pants back up and carry on with whatever activity they had previously been involved in, not ever missing or contemplating for a moment luxuries most of us took for granted, such as toilet paper and privacy. They were able to do their business with no more consideration than most of us would give to blowing our nose in public. With fourteen sisters and brothers in a small country shack, privacy was not an option even when performing the most basic of bodily functions. Their lack of cleanliness was not by choice but by circumstance. Without indoor plumbing, it was difficult to keep bodies or clothing clean in such cramped surroundings, and Otha and her daughters would have to haul the family laundry down to the brook to wash their clothes by hand, for all passersby to see.

Fergus did many odd jobs to help make ends meet, but relied quite heavily on a sizeable monthly family allowance cheque to maintain the lifestyle and vices to which he was accustomed. Somewhat later in life, after many of the children had moved away, Fergus bought a fishing boat and started to catch lobsters in sufficient quantities to enable him to expand and paint his house, install indoor plumbing and insulation, and even buy a brand new half ton truck. In a rather puzzling reflection on perhaps the nature of their upbringing and its differing effects on the psyches of the two sexes, all of the Goomar girls left Fundy Bay for good once they got married, whereas none of the Goomar boys ever left the community for more than six months, and none remained married for more than a year.

On the same side of the street as the Morgans, just east of the bridge lived the notorious Betts gang. Their one and a half storey house was actually quite solidly built, which was handy, since it housed seventeen Betts children and the two parents, Ennis and Beulah. Of the seventeen children, all but two were boys, which at least enabled the family to save money on clothes.

Ennis Betts always seemed to be busy, although he never seemed to stay with any one thing for very long. He worked away at farming a bit, he did some wood cutting, he even tried fishing for a spell. No one ever really questioned him on what he was up to, since he was known to have a short fuse. The family was too proud to accept handouts from their neighbours, and they never acted as if they were in need of anything. Perhaps they weren't. It was widely believed that the Betts family even refused to apply for any sort of disability pension.

Beulah Betts had been a very attractive young girl, local folklore had it, and had dated a lot of boys in the neighbouring village of West Appleton. One evening at a dance in the West Appleton community hall, a slightly drunk teenage Ennis Betts walked into the hall and instantly took a liking to the girl with the long black hair and plain white dress, Beulah Baker. Trouble was, Beulah was with Johnny Fardy, a West Appleton tough standing over six feet tall and with the disposition of a fighting cock. He rarely opened his mouth to speak; some of the locals used to say that Johnny Fardy's mouth was closed tighter than a bull's ass at flytime. Ennis, himself standing at least four inches shy of six feet, but giving away nothing in guts and gumption, walked right up to Beulah and asked her to dance. Beulah barely had time to give a startled and concerned glance toward Johnny, when Johnny reached over, shoved Ennis roughly, and said, "Get lost, punk. Get your own piece of ass." It was never clear whether Ennis was reacting to the shove, or if he simply wanted to defend Beulah's honor, but in a wink of an eye, before the chaperons had time to intervene, Ennis kicked Johnny Fardy in the stomach with a wicked force, and when Johnny doubled over, Ennis proceeded to pummel his head and face, holding nothing back. It took three adults to pull Ennis off, and by that time, Johnny was in need of immediate medical attention. He was rushed out of the hall to the home of a nurse who lived nearby, and Ennis and Beulah were kicked out of the dance hall. That night, Ennis walked Beulah home, and from that time forward, no one else ever dated Beulah again or even dared to ask her out.

The Betts children all proceeded to go through the school system until grade seven or eight, at which time they would quit to seek employment around Fundy Bay, hiring themselves out to any farmers or fishermen in need of a pair of strong arms or wanting to get in good with the Betts family.

No one in all of Fundy Bay or any of the surrounding villages would willingly cross any of the Betts clan. Their reputation as merciless brawlers was well entrenched. They may very well have been direct descendants of the berserkers. Yet they did have some honour: they would not initiate a fight with any of their neighbours. However, if one did somehow break out, the Betts boys would quickly end it. This made for some very interesting dynamics during the regular evening gatherings on the bridge or at the corner, when the Betts boys would be intermingling with their neighbours, the Goomars and Crawfords. It always seemed to the other Fundy Bayers that it was like a powder keg waiting to explode. It made the neighbours very nervous when they saw this large gathering of teenage boys with their unkempt appearance. People would purposely shy away from crossing the bridge or driving by the corner during these times and would detour down the poorly maintained shore road just to avoid any possible confrontation. If a car happened to come along as the gathering of clan teens was spread out across the road forming a bridgehead, the car would have to sit and wait until the boys moved of their own volition. If the driver dared to blow his horn, he might end up with a smashed in window, dents in the car, an earful of abuse, and threats to his person. The only persons in the community who were allowed to pass the bridge unchallenged during these times were members of their families, the preacher, or my father.

When the sounds accompanying these gatherings at the bridge or corner would filter up to our house, Mom would usually say, "Well, I guess the bohonks are out in full force tonight!" A bohonk was any rough and tough teenager out for trouble and a good time, engaging in countless nefarious activities. The church goers of the community did not seem to appreciate that these bohonks were restless and angry, feeling trapped by their economic debility, not knowing how to overcome. Many felt smothered by the claustrophobic boundaries of this sleepy community, while others revelled in it, enjoying being a recognized thug in small town Nova Scotia.

One thing all the bohonks had in common that the other members of the women's missionary group could never understand: they all had a raging fire down below, and wanted more than anything to share it with as many other like teenagers as they could. As soon as the bohonks hit teenage, and often before, they were very sexually active. The bohonks were perfecting the intricacies of fornication when most children their age and older were just coming to grips with masturbation. There is no doubt that incest was rampant in Fundy Bay, especially among the poorest of the poor with their large families who would be crammed into a small tar papered shack not fit for a barn animal. No one would discuss the subject openly, or ever consider contacting the proper authorities in the Valley when some child finally did get up the courage to tell a close friend about the atrocities being committed at home. The prim and proper of the community would simply shake their heads and dismiss further discussion with "isn't that terrible", quickly moving on to consider what overseas charity the women's missionary society should be supporting next year.

The bohonks also had in common an appetite for alcohol, or "licker" as the women in the church auxiliary pronounced it. The bohonk's dissipation was the source of much consternation amongst the women of the church auxiliary. They just couldn't understand why these teenagers wanted to get drunk and fight all the time. The concept of escapism and boredom didn't wash with the self contented of the community.

One Sunday morning while the bohonks were still asleep, a fed up or concerned anonymous person on route to church stopped at the corner to inscribe the following Bible quote in indelible ink along the length of the rail located on the northern side of the bridge:

"Being filled with all unrighteousness, fornication, wickedness, covetousness, maliciousness; full of envy, murder, debate, deceit, malignity; whisperers, backbiters, haters of God, despiteful, proud, boasters, inventors of evil things, disobedient to parents, without understanding, covenant breakers, without natural affection, implacable, unmerciful, who knowing the judgement of God, that they which commit such things are worthy of death, not only do the same, but have pleasure in them that do them —Romans 1:29-32."

This passing of judgement was undoubtedly intended to make the bohonks feel some remorse for their wicked ways, the anonymous scribe conveniently overlooking the next verse, "thou are inexcusable, O man, whosoever thou art that judgest: for wherein thou judgest another, thou condemnest thyself". Regardless of the scribe's intent, his actions had the opposite effect. Rather than becoming angry at this latest graffiti, the bohonks took it as a sign of recognition, a high honor, and it also provided them with the means to give credit where credit was due. The bohonks developed a rather elaborate system of apprenticeshipping whereby anyone wanting to call themselves a bohonk would have to demonstrate that they were guilty of committing at least five of these sins written out on the bridge rail. Five vices meant that you were a Level 1 bohonk. Those who aspired to a leadership role in the bohonks naturally had to commit a wider range of sins, everyone going up one level with each additional transgression. The attainment of the latest iniquity was noted by carving the initials of the bohonk member under the appropriate segment of the quote. The record keeping was made easier to follow when one of the bohonks, obviously a frustrated accountant, had the bright idea of drawing long vertical lines on both sides of each sin to sectionalize the quote, resulting in the widest wooden columnar ledger known to exist. And bohonks were only allowed to sit on those sections of the bridge rail where they their initials appeared, meaning that they had committed the sins described under their rear-ends. This in itself motivated the bohonks to continue to fill their sinful lists so they would be guaranteed a menu of places to sit that Friday evening. Any junior family member or visitor not yet initiated into the bohonks would only be allowed to stand and lean against the bridge railings. They were not permitted to sit. Even their harshest critics had to admit that the bohonks were demonstrating a much improved vocabulary since "the Romans incident", as it soon became known as.

To the citizens of Fundy Bay, it gave no one particular pleasure to see several sets of initials appearing under the "murder" section of the bridge ledger. The fewest initials appeared under "implacable" (none) since no one seemed to know what it meant, although it was suspected to mean having bad teeth. Timing and widespread acceptance of erroneous definitions played a major role. Those admitting to "malignity" found it difficult to achieve "fornication". However, those who confessed to "fornication" usually were seen despondently carving their initials under "malignity" within a matter of days, unnecessarily impugning their own character by acknowledging their newly acquired malignancy.

Only a few brave bohonk souls included their initials under "disobedient to parents", since that would usually result in them being on the receiving end of a vicious beating by their old man who would view this as a public affront to his authority and ability to kick the shit out of anyone under his roof. After administering the thrashing, the father, his dignity restored, would stroll down to the bridge with his hunting knife and demonstratively scrape his son's or daughter's initials off that section, then stop to admire the number of times his children's initials appeared in the other sections of the bridge.

Naturally, the fornication section was the first one to be filled, requiring the entire south side bridge rail to be devoted to this sin after the bohonks decided to also include the initials of the fornicatees. So if one bohonk was heard instructing another, "go sit on the fucking railing!", everyone knew that he was simply directing his peer to the south side rail.

The gatherings at the bridge and corner were especially explosive when teenage girls from or related to the Crawfords, Goomars, or Betts' would happen by. Most of their Fundy Bay relations were cut from the same cloth, so that any ready and willing females from the Ainsworth, Dicks, Caines, or Cobb families would also be welcomed. The male bohonks would vie for the attention of the girls, and none of them were good losers in love. The girls would usually stroll down to the bridge whenever they were in heat, knowing that they would be smothered with attention and possibilities. Quite often these sessions would end up in a shoving or shouting match, or with someone being dangled over the bridge by his ankles being forced to promise to mind their own business. This usually ended by the admonishment of the girl being disputed, who would say, "hey, why don't you grow up? Let him go", to the dominant male, althewhile being impressed with his raw strength and ferocity. The victorious male would comply, apologize to his humiliated foe, and proceed to stroll off with his prize to any darkened part of Fundy Bay, indoors or out, which would offer a soft resting place and some amount of privacy for twenty or thirty minutes.

Somehow, despite the fears of the neighbours, full scale fights amongst the dominant families were almost non-existent. The families would often resort to name calling: the Goomars were usually referred to as "Goomers" or "Gomers" during these times, the Crawfords would be called "Crawfish", and the Betts would be referred to as "Butts". The girls especially would get quite creative in their various putdowns and verbal exchanges. Almost every argument eventually degenerated into one of the girls telling the other to "kiss my red rosy ass", which would be met with a challenge to "produce it". The resulting statement would generally be, "yeah, you'd like that, you fruit", which would generate the come back "yeah, that's right. I'm a fruit. You wanna bite?" The repartee was not highly refined, but quite effective.

I went to school with many of the Betts children. Marjorie Betts was a year older than me, but due to failing grade three, was in my class, along with her brother, Luther. Luther was actually in my class from primary to grade eight and was a reasonably good student. Marjorie may not have been as promising a student, but she must have inherited good genes, since she was the only one in the entire elementary school who was able to read the eye chart in the gloomy hallways without making an error. Like most of the Betts family, Luther was quite short with a manic personality, and as a result of the family reputation and prowess, he had very little to worry about on the playground.

Luther actually was a fairly good student, and through our friendship, I was able to gain a better understanding of his family and be accepted or at least tolerated by them. None of us were ever invited into the Betts home on the corner, but we used to rendezvous with Luther at a neutral site. Luther would gladly take part in the various games we were preoccupied with, often forfeiting the chance to participate in bridge time swaggering. In later years, Luther even started to attend our United Baptist youth fellowship group, actively participating in our games, singing, and social times. He showed quite a lot of interest in spiritual matters, but when the biological clock struck sixteen, Luther dropped out of school and our church youth group.

We lost track of him for a couple of years as he moved to the Valley with one of his older brothers. During that time, he let his hair, which was always perfectly straight and dirty, grow to the middle of his back, and grew a beard as well. As rumour had it, he was walking into the grocery store in Glory one day when he brushed by an older, more conservative gentleman, who took one look at Luther and gasped, "Jesus!". Apparently Luther interpreted this not as an exclamation but rather a sign of recognition. Convinced that perhaps he did have some divine mission to perform, Luther started wearing knee ankle length ponchos with no underwear underneath, a headband, sandals, and carried a Bible around with him constantly. This phase lasted for about two months during the summer, after which he declared he would never eat locusts and honey again, at least not in combination. He promptly cut his hair to collar length, burned his rather worn poncho and headband, put on some briefs, acquired a green jumpsuit, and then got a job planting trees for the Forestry department.

Living just to the west of our house on the same side of the street were Merle and Ethel Newcomb, along with their two children, Freddie and Bonnie. I don't remember Merle ever working, although there was no denying his intelligence.

He had been a school teacher earlier in life, and had briefly served in the army, but somehow had settled into a lazy, sedentary existence in Fundy Bay. For a brief period he tried fishing with his brother Melvin, but gave up his half ownership in their small punt when he found that he got terribly seasick riding even the calmest of waters. Merle was a huge, barrel chested man who just seemed to get bigger year by year as he did nothing more than sit in his living room watching television and chewing tobacco. Ethel was a sweet, simple minded woman who weighed no more than ninety pounds at any point in her life. What Ethel lacked in looks and intelligence she made up for in industry and patience. While Merle chewed and spit, Ethel was always busy doing a laundry by hand, baking, tending to their nine cats, cleaning out Merle's spittoon, emptying the slop pail over the bluff overlooking the shore, carrying wood for the stove, scrubbing the floor boards, making meals for Merle, cleaning up after Merle then making meals for the rest of the family, and refereeing fights between her quarrelsome children.

Freddie obviously viewed his father as a suitable role model, as people often joked that all of Freddie's get up and go had gotten up and went. He daily redefined the term "slacker", doing as little as possible, making it his goal to avoid breaking into a sweat and being stung by any bee, hornet, or wasp. Freddie wanted to convince everyone that he really did sing like Elvis and hoped that someday he would lead the New Democratic Party to power in Ottawa after becoming wealthy, on that elusive day he often talked about, "when my ship comes in". Freddie changed hobbies as frequently as many Fundy Bayers did their underwear: once every week or so. One week it would be board games, the next would be listening to loud music on the radio, then stamp collecting, soon after it would be preaching to the lost souls of the community, followed by playing ground hockey, then rod fishing off the wharf, then reading historical novels, then sending away money for information on how to get rich quick, then back to board games.

Freddie befriended generations of children in Fundy Bay, usually accepting them into his circle when they reached age ten. At that age, the children thought Freddie, with all his silly jokes and mindless patter, was quite a wit. By the time they reached high school, they suspected they had only been half right. Freddie was known for his outbursts of uncontrollable rage, which his family and friends simply referred to as temper tantrums. These tantrums would usually be prompted by some cruel needling from a supposed friend, a humiliating loss in a game or competition, a rough bodycheck through the rickety shop door during a friendly game of full contact hockey, or frustration over being told he couldn't have something he wanted. During his rages, Freddie would appear to be demon possessed and would become very destructive, his eyes darting about looking for something he could pick up and destroy. It really didn't matter what it was. It might be his mother's new vase, her prized floor mop, his trusty badminton racket, or Bonnie's favourite cookbook. Whatever he seized at that moment, got smashed, chopped in two, twisted out of shape, or ripped into many pieces. It always took quite a while for Freddie to calm down when this rage would come over him. After destroying a piece of property on his right, he would turn to his left and search for a suitable target to vent his anger. These rages were very costly to a family which could not afford to buy many luxuries, let alone replace them. Other than this, Freddie was a true blue, reliable friend to generation after generation of Fundy Bay adolescent males, at least for those not interested in hanging out on the bridge, or sneaking sips from their father's beer bottle, or acting out their base fantasies with one of their pubescent cousins.

Freddie's sister Bonnie took after their mother in almost every respect, except for the gentleness. Both children had considerable cognitive and emotional problems, a fact some attributed at least partly to the sleeping pills they were fed regularly as infants so that they would not interrupt Merle's sleep. It apparently was essential that Merle get his rest so that he would be ready for another day of TV viewing. Freddie often told the story that he was quite normal until one day as a child when he fell out of my father's giant horse chestnut tree onto his head. We didn't believe the story, but it enabled Freddie to save face when word spread that his father was collecting a mental disability pension on his behalf, but not for Bonnie. Bonnie was harmless, enjoying nothing better than to play dolls with some of the children in the neighbourhood, while her contemporaries were out fornicating or studying for exams. Bonnie continued along in the school system for many years, undaunted by her multiple tries to get through each and every grade. Although she never learned even basics of the arts and sciences, Bonnie was a wizard at reading a cook book. She loved to borrow cook books from the school library or the bookmobile, scouring them for recipes which could be made with the few ingredients she would have on hand or could afford to by.

Despite her scholarly limitations, nonetheless Bonnie would eventually pass into the next grade. This was usually regarded as a reward for perseverance, rather than recognition that she had actually attained a fixed standard of knowledge. By the time she got into grade eleven, Bonnie was twenty-five years old, which simply made her somewhat of a celebrity in the Riverton high school since it was celebrating its twenty-fifth anniversary the same year. Bonnie did not pass that year, and decided that enough was enough and dropped out. Nonetheless, at least on paper she had attained a level of education few Fundy Bayers could match, and had bested Freddie by three whole grades.

Two hundred feet to the west of Donnie and Brenda Goomar's house lived the Reverend Fish Man, Melvin Newcomb, high on a hill overlooking the Edna Moore residence. In the winter of 1964, however, Melvin lost his house in a poker game to Eldon Cobb. Melvin had reportedly stopped by Eldon's trailer one Friday night to peddle some fish and discovered a poker game in process. In a classic case of bad company corrupting good character, Melvin pulled up a chair, slapped a fresh mackerel in the middle of the table, yelled "ante up", then proceeded to lose everything he owned within the next four hours, even including his fish bucket and leaky punt. Freddie Newcomb liked to tell a version of the story that his uncle Melvin, after hours of exhausting card playing and evangelizing in the smoke filled trailer, dropped a card on the floor, and when he bent down to pick it up he looked over at the feet of the bearded stranger who had been sitting next to him all night, only to discover that instead of feet he had cloven hooves. Uncle Melvin was so terrified at the revelation that he was in such devilish company that he ran out of the house screaming, leaving behind his house keys on the table and his fish bucket on the floor. As Freddie told the tale, Eldon Cobb negotiated with the stranger for the rights to the house in exchange for a lifetime of persecuting the Fundy Bay Sanctified Methodist church, where Freddie served as head usher. In any event, no matter the means, Eldon Cobb took possession of the house and Melvin Newcomb took up residence in the insane asylum in Riverton, a victim of his own internal conflicts.

Shortly after moving in, Eldon and his wife, Rita, renamed the house "Blind Man's Bluff", although it was uncertain what was being honoured, his pension generating disability, his renowned poker strategy, or the elevation of the land on which the house sat. In any event, the house on the hill did not seem to bring Eldon and Rita much happiness for the next eight years. During this time, they had two chimney fires and one house fire, the well water first became septic then dried up, their dog Tripper died mysteriously after digging in the back yard, Rita was diagnosed with cancer, and then Eldon truly started to lose his sight to the point where he could not distinguish the Jack of Diamonds from the Ace of Spades. Feeling that the writing was on the scorched kitchen wall, Eldon and Rita left Fundy Bay and moved to Saint John, New Brunswick, to be closer to family and the Legion. Eldon sold the house to Kenny and Ruth Peartree, a rather secretive couple hailing from somewhere in Alberta and heretofore unknown to the Fundy Bay crowd. Edna Moore would keep a watch on the

Peartrees while sitting in the rocking chair in her kitchen, but there was very little to report. as they seemed to come and go mostly at night.

After a while, Ruth Peartree, a tall, pale looking redhead, befriended Bonnie Newcomb, perhaps to get the lowdown on the neighbours from the most unsuspecting of sources. Kenny Peartree was a surly, slightly bent over man with a head covered in greasy black hair. It soon became suspected that Kenny was beating up Ruth on a regular basis, and she more or less confided this to Bonnie. During increasingly prolonged absences by Kenny, during which Ruth would be left with little food to feed her two small red haired waifish looking children, Ruth started socializing more with the neighbours, and would even accept an occasional invitation for tea and conversation. It was about this time that she met her next door neighbour's son, Ricky Plumb, a rather suave dark haired teenager who had just dropped out of school to seek his fortune working as a crewman on a trawler sailing out of Digby. Ricky was as strong as an ox, gentle as a lamb, and built like a stallion from the waist down. It wasn't too long before Ricky Plumb and Ruth Peartree started madly cross pollinating, lovers in a dangerous clime. Apparently Ruth was unable to keep her newfound affections for Ricky a secret, so on his next trip home, Kenny administered a terrible beating to her, without regard for the children watching and screaming from the next room or the sounds of the dogs barking from the front lawn. Kenny apparently thought of going to deliver similar punishment to Ricky, but he had caught a glimpse of him next door several days ago, shirtless and chopping wood, so thought better of it. Instead, he locked Ruth and the children in the house, and drove off to town to pick up some more beer. Rather than call the police, Ruth waited until Kenny had been gone for about twenty minutes, then managed to pry open the pantry window just enough to allow her and the children to crawl through. She threw a few items in a grocery bag, headed next door, and they rode off with Ricky in his car as fast as they could go. It was months before anyone heard from them, and even then their whereabouts were not confirmed, only that they were safe and sound somewhere in northern Ontario, leading fruitful lives. For his part,

Kenny decided that Fundy Bay was not the place for him, so he left his home locked in the middle of the night and never returned. The neighbours did not know what to do about the barking and sad wailing noises they heard coming from the house, since they were not sure if anyone was at or about to come home or not. By the time Edna Moore got up the courage to summon the police, they discovered two dead, emaciated dogs lying on the kitchen floor, in the midst of a carnage created by their vain attempts to free themselves. The house sat abandoned for many years after that while authorities tried to track down Kenny Peartree, a sad reminder of the turn in fortunes for this once happy home so proudly situated on its lofty perch with an unobstructed view of the Bay of Fundy.

Next to the Newcomb's house, across the street from the Reverend Fish Man, was our dear neighbour Edna Moore, in a house called "The Moorage". Her home was a grand structure by country standards, immaculately maintained, with its ten foot high ceilings, two large parlours, walk in pantry, and rap around veranda, and occupied a preferred position in the community, with an acre of land in the back gently sloping down to the edge of the bay. Born in 1886, Edna had lived a very interesting life, not at all provincial like most of the residents of Fundy Bay. Edna was a beautiful woman, with a heart nearly as big as her breasts. She always had a eye out for the men, and had many suitors in her day. Her first husband, Edward Beach, had been sent overseas in the midst of the first World War and was soon thereafter pronounced dead. Although widowed at a young age with an infant daughter, Honey, Edna was not wanting for male attention. Not too long after Edward's death, Edna fell in love with a dashing Fundy Bay farmer and beekeeper, Johnny Moore, and they married in 1918. Although Johnny was twenty years her senior, Edna and Johnny enjoyed almost thirty years of married life, working their farm, keeping bees, and raising Honey. Johnny supplied stores for miles around with his produce, which he sweetly named Honey's Honey. They made frequent trips to Florida and other parts of the United States to visit relatives and acquaintances. It was on one of these trips in 1939 that Honey, a stern looking woman with very little of Edna's natural charm and wit, met and eloped with an American insurance salesman from the Boston area, Samuel Pie, leaving her with the sweetest sounding name in all of Massachusetts. When Johnny died in 1947 from a single bee sting to which he was unknowingly allergic, Edna was left with only the farm and no one to help her work it. She therefore embarked on a part time career as a practical nurse, working throughout the United States for some of the elite of the day, including the sister in law of the great evangelist, D.L. Moody. Edna spent each summer in "the Moorage", returning to the States each fall to earn enough money to pay the bills. After nearly twelve years of this nomadic lifestyle, Edna returned to Fundy Bay for good in 1958, making ends meet by providing general nursing services to the locals as well as by selling the best doughnuts ever to come out of Fundy Bay.

Edna was the grand dame of Fundy Bay for many years, and welcomed young and old, rich and poor alike into her home with the greatest of enthusiasm and the warmest of embraces. She could disarm even the most hardened of teenagers with her effervescent personality and natural charm. Hanging on the wall in her front hall was a framed embroidery containing the words "Do not forget to entertain strangers, for by doing so some people have entertained angels without knowing it". Edna was the exception to the norm in Fundy Bay, never hiding behind convenient excuses of why she couldn't invite people in or couldn't afford to feed her neighbours, and never acting flustered when guests would arrive unannounced. The women of the community would just shake their heads in wonder when they would hear that Edna had fed and conversed for an hour with yet another of the community hooligans, a child that they personally would not even unlock their doors for, let alone welcome across the threshold. The truth was, Edna lived for all these social calls. With her there was no class system or generation gap. The only real distinguishing feature about folks was that some were there in her house at the moment, whereas the others were hopefully on the way. However, she couldn't hide an obvious fondness for anyone of the male persuasion and showed a particular weakness for good looking male evangelists and clergy.

Edna's front door was never locked, and in warm weather, it would always be opened wide, even if she was in the parlour having a nap, so as not to impede visitors even for a moment. Visitors to her home always left feeling uplifted and optimistic, in spite of their ofttimes desperate realities. It became somewhat of a joke around the community that you didn't dare drop by Edna's on a quick errand if you had other chores to do, since you knew she would keep you for a minimum one hour stay, feeding you her famous doughnuts and a hot cup of tea or coffee. Edna was never too busy to accept another visitor, the sitting room was never too crowded that another chair couldn't be added. And who could refuse to stay and enjoy the hospitality and Edna's storytelling which was accentuated by her sparking eyes and hearty laugh? Edna's home became a popular stopover for scores of people, many of whom had never even met her but had been sent by a friend of a friend who had once enjoyed an enchanting evening in Edna's parlour, sipping tea and marvelling at the beauty of the sun setting over the Bay of Fundy. No matter, Edna would welcome these newfound friends the same as she would her own family. Edna started a practice of having all of her visitors sign a guest book before departing, and she would proudly point to the volumes of such books that had become filled in a very short time. Edna was the envy of the many widows around Fundy Bay, not only for her popularity and seemingly inexhaustible love of life, but also because she freely confessed to having not an ache or a pain, even into her eighties. Her only ailment was a stiff right leg which required her to walk around with a cane in her later years, but which offered the advantage of always securing for her the front seat of any vehicle, a fact which always annoyed the sullen women who were forced to move to the back seat while Edna and their husbands laughed and conversed in the front.

Towards the end of her life, at Honey's insistence, Edna conceded to having a bathroom installed in her front hall, since it was too tiring for her to climb the long stairway to the upstairs loo. This bothered Edna greatly, since she was required to shut and lock the front door while she was using the downstairs bathroom, so as not to be caught mid session. She was always quick to reopen the front door when finished, a fact which allowed the neighbours to closely monitor her regularity. Despite not having a great deal of money, Edna was always dressed beautifully, and tastefully adorned her clothing, ears, hands, and wrists with the largest collection of broaches, earrings, rings, and bracelets of anyone in Fundy Bay.

The last five years of Edna's life were heart wrenching for all who loved her to watch, as Honey and Samuel during one of their annual summer pilgrimages to Fundy Bay, decided that Edna was no longer able to winter in Fundy Bay on her own. Despite her protestations, they found a small one room apartment for her located twelve miles away in Centretown in a home run by Mrs. Wiggins, a rather severe, bitter widow woman. For a woman used to entertaining in her own spacious home, being relegated to this small room crammed with the most precious of her belongings must have been a hard pill to swallow. Nonetheless, not one to dwell on such matters, Edna continued to receive hundreds of visitors all winter long in her small apartment, a fact which greatly annoyed the owner of the home, who rarely entertained at all. Each spring when Edna would be brought home by Honey and Samuel, it was as if her age rolled back another ten years. She would cram a full twelve months of entertaining into those precious six months, never pausing to catch her breath. This pace may have contributed to a decision made by Honey and Samuel in 1984 to install her fulltime at the Wiggins' apartment. There were few dry eyes in Fundy Bay that cold day in October when Honey and Samuel loaded Edna in the car for her final departure from her beloved home, the "For Sale" sign already on the front lawn. With no more hope for a future return to Fundy Bay, Edna's health rapidly deteriorated, and she died two years later just shy of her one hundreth birthday, a mere shadow of her former self. Edna had lived each day to the fullest of her ability, and had truly loved life and all those fortunate enough to share it with her. Nonetheless, despite her overwhelming and endearing popularity, Edna had been haunted right up until her death in 1986 by the whisperings within the community that her first husband, Edward Beach, had in fact come home alive from the First World War only to discover that his bride had remarried. Rumour had it that Edward faded into the background quietly, and lived out his days alone in a small two room abode in Mason's Cove, ten miles from Fundy Bay, never seeing his wife or baby girl again. In his old age, amidst the disjointed ramblings which ofttimes accompany senility, Edward would increasingly confide to humouring neighbours that he had once been married to a Fundy Bay beauty, and that he had fathered a little girl that he had named Honey, because she was the sweetest thing he had ever seen in his entire life.

△ △ △

CHAPTER SIX
The Squalor

Fundy Bay was viewed as an eyesore by many visitors, a curiosity to others, a quaint, picturesque village to still others, and home sweet home to those of us without either the means or inclination to leave. But no doubt about it: this was one poor village. Outsiders knew it. Fundy Bayers knew it.

A common statement expressed only partially in jest by certain parents was "we're so poor, if the boys don't wake up on Christmas morning with a hard-on they won't have anything to play with." And unfortunately, in a few of the Fundy Bay households that would pretty much leave the daughters with nothing to do also. There often wasn't much to distinguish the tar papered shacks in which many of the residents lived from the fish houses lining the shore road. About the only notable differences were that the fish houses were fronted by beach gravel rather than grass, and the homes were more crowded. The saying that the rich get richer and the poor have children may have had its origin in Fundy Bay. A little house on the prairie sounded idyllic to most of the locals. With the widespread squalor in Fundy Bay, your dwelling was more apt to be considered no more than a little shack on the seashore. Visitors to the area often mistook the unpainted homes for barns or fish houses, unable to comprehend that someone, let alone a family with membership into the double digits, could actually live in those conditions. These visitors usually did not return, at least not without their cameras.

Only a handful of homes in Fundy Bay were equipped with indoor plumbing, or "running water" as it was called by Fundy Bayers, and ours wasn't one of them.

This demographic wouldn't change significantly until the 1980s. Many homes did not even have a hand pump in their homes meaning that water retrieval was a daily chore for most households. You generally only saw running water in Fundy Bay when the poorly clad eldest son in the family would be rapidly retreating to the house on cold winter days with two buckets of drinking water just hauled from the outside well. Even for those homes fortunate enough to have a pump inside their home, often the source of water it was connected to was fit only for cooking and washing, meaning that someone still had to go on a daily trek to get drinking water. No one was ever really certain whether any of the water being consumed in Fundy Bay was fit for drinking, since only one or two homeowners ever bothered having their well water tested at the hospital lab in Centretown. Ironically, they were more apt to go to the hospital to have tests performed on the water discarded by their bodies than they were to test the water being poured into their bodies.

Usually every fourth or fifth year, the typical Fundy Bay homeowner would decide that it was time to clean out his well, since the water was starting to have a noticeable smell or taste. The problem was, none of the wells were securely capped or lined, so they would never really know what might have fallen inside. This was a concern since it was not uncommon to overhear a couple of teenagers walking by snickering about adding their two scents worth to the water level in the well.

As a slender, rather lissome youth with no history of claustrophobia, I was often called upon to make the descent into a neighbour's damp, musty well to do the necessary and overdue cleanup. A typical Fundy Bay well had a diameter of no more than four feet, a depth of between twelve and twenty feet, and a maximum water depth of six to ten feet. Bailing out a properly situated well was no small feat, as the water would continue to rush in almost as fast as I was able to pass the bucket up the line and receive it in return. Even working in the cool, damp interior, I couldn't help but work up a good sweat.

Eventually, after a lot of effort on everyone's part, mostly mine, I would get to the bottom of the well and usually discover at least one dead rat, some rusty nails, lots of mud and algae, sometimes a long lost toy, empty tin cans, and occasionally a snake or a salamander. I would be required to scoop out all the offending articles and then make some attempt to dig out as much muck as I could. Once this was done, I would ascend carefully past the heavily rusted pipes and retreat to solid ground above. The thankful neighbour would be satisfied that all the problems with his drinking water had been solved, and that night would enjoy many glasses of clean, purified water with his family while watching the Fundy Bay sunset and listening to rebroadcasts of classic Fibber McGee and Molly episodes on the radio.

At various times, certain individuals within Fundy Bay would decide that a reliable source of clean drinking water was a must have, so would hire Riverton Drilling to come over to drill a well for them. This almost always proved to be unsuccessful, however. This was because Riverton Drilling, in complying with a provincial government regulation that all drilled wells must be at least one hundred feet deep, hit salt water on every try. This was not surprising since all those living along the coastline of the Bay of Fundy were no more than sixty feet above sea level. This was particularly frustrating to the poor salt of the earth resident who couldn't really afford the $100 to hire Riverton Drilling in the first place. It was especially painful since he had almost been able to taste the cool, clear water when at fifty feet the drill operator announced that he had hit a huge seam of fresh water, only to see his jubilation sour as the drill continued its downward surge to the requisite briny depths. It was like having salt rubbed in your wounds, with the salt coming from your own well.

As a result, many of the residents with an indoor pump could only use it to bring salt water into the house, which was used for cooking and cleaning. It wasn't advisable to drink salt water, however, as it was rumoured that eventually it would make you go crazy. From the looks of many Fundy Bayers, you'd guess that they must already have had a few sips too many. It was one thing to have your conversation seasoned with salt, it was quite another to have your drinking water so tainted. Those who lived along the upper road leading up the mountain and out of Fundy Bay did not have this problem due to their elevation, and therefore, were expected to be neighbourly and provide drinking water to the masses sprawled out below them in the village centre.

With these question marks about the water supply, it was no wonder that so many of the community took to drinking beer and liquor to meet their needs for liquid intake. Mind you, the locally produced moonshine was made from local water, so likely was similarly contaminated.

Cleanliness aside, another complication with the water setup in Fundy Bay was the lack of pre-heated water. If you wanted hot water for cooking, washing dishes, doing the laundry, taking your weekly sponge bath, cleaning the floors, or whatever, it was necessary to heat all you needed on top of the wood stove. You would therefore never enter a Fundy Bay home without seeing at least one kettle on the kitchen wood stove. Often, the entire surface of the piping hot stove would be covered with metal pots and tubs, all containing water needed to do various tasks. A necessary item for most Fundy Bay homes was a wood stove with a hot water tank attached on the side. This tank would hold several gallons of water and meant that unless you got forgetful, you could count on having at least a head start for your Monday morning laundry. Of course, the down side of all of this water warming was the fact that in the heat of the summer, you had to keep the home fires burning just to get the required amount of hot water to do your daily chores. Unfortunately dirt didn't take a vacation in the summer months.

The cheapest way to do the laundry was to haul the family's dirty clothes down to the brook and wash them out by hand in the cool, bubbling water. By the time all the poorest in the community did this on Monday morning, the traditional wash time, the brook had a few more bubbles in it than usual.

The lack of indoor plumbing and sewage removal was most noticeable when it was time to exercise your bodily functions. Not having an indoor bathroom to toilet in meant that you had to consider other options. Many people had no toilets and simply used the woods, their neighbour's field, the nearest manure pile, lifted a floorboard, whatever. Most people did have an outhouse, but it was usually a two holer, although sometimes only a one holer. Our three holer was a luxury that most could never hope to achieve. Not only did it have room for company, it also was in a building attached to the house. This meant that you didn't have to go outside on a cold, blustery winter day. Of course, you still had to don your parka before heading out in the winter time, since there was no heat or insulation in the outbuilding.

Learning to defecate with a parka hitched up around your waist while your breath is crystallizing and your prized parts are getting frost bitten is an experience everyone, especially politicians, should try. No wonder each and every Fundy Bayer considered hemorrhoids to be like members of the family. You could truthfully say that hemorrhoids filled every seat in the house. The cold of winter did tend to minimize the likelihood of having any members of the arachnid family walk across your bare bottom while you strained to hurriedly "cast your ballot", to use the vernacular of the area.

Dad was careful to keep the toilet serviced with liberal doses of lime to keep the atmosphere bearable. Unfortunately few Fundy Bayers were as fastidious as Dad, so the thought of entering most of these johns left one hoping for a long lasting case of constipation. People who were not as frivolous as my Dad in the use of lime tried to compensate by making the toileting escapade a visual experience. Many papered their outhouses with pictures from last year's Sears catalogue. This proved to be rather convenient if the newspaper ran out as you could reach up and rip off the required pages of catalogue to finish your clean up. Toilet paper was for those with more money than brains, and for those who preferred the news over a cup of coffee rather than between their cheeks. And since no one could go home and soak in a nice warm bath, the headlines of the day from the toilet editions of the Riverton Times tended to stay with Fundy Bayers much longer than they did with the Valley gentry. Fundy Bayers became quite expert in being able to detect even slight changes in the type of ink used in the Riverton Times, not so much by sight but by feel, both while putting the news to good use and afterwards when the itching started. A popular joke in the community was told whenever a young person would be seen going by scratching their backside. One of the older folk would comment in a slow, country drawl, "well, I see young Harry must be on his way to the movies. He's pickin' his seat already".

Growing up in a family with a three holer toilet meant that when nature called, it was on a party line, and several people answered. It was very rare that you would find yourself in the outhouse alone, unless the liming was noticeably overdue. Therefore, when your innards started moving, you were usually in the midst of a conversation with persons on your left and right. This tended to break down all barriers and served to strengthen friendships. If you could without abashment chit chat with your seatmates while giving your regards to mother earth below, you pretty well were assured of being able to resolve any squabbles which might surface amongst you in fresher climes. The only time when you might feel slightly uncomfortable during one of these group bull sessions was when one or more of the seats were occupied by persons of the opposite gender. If nothing else, each of these occurrences could honestly be termed a "co-ed movement". Even then, the discomfort wasn't due to shyness, but rather from confusion about the obvious differences in anatomy that had somehow gone unexplained and perhaps unnoticed by your parents. A preference for segregation somehow overtook us, however, by the time we were seven or eight years old, mostly because we were becoming the butt of jokes being told by the older children who had themselves only recently graduated from communal toileting to discover the pleasures of more intimate interminglings.

Our home was similar to the other houses in Fundy Bay in another aspect as well: it had no insulation in the walls. This would not have been significant if the location of our home had been Montego Bay rather than Fundy Bay. However, living on the coast of the Bay of Fundy, when the nor'easters started blowing mid fall and winter, these seaside shanties proved to be colder than a tax collector's heart. Most homes were heated by a single wood stove located in the kitchen. A few homes had a second wood stove located in the living room. Even fewer came complete with a wood burning furnace. Fortunately for us, our house was one of those. There was probably only a handful of homes in all of Fundy Bay that were heated with an oil burning furnace. However, the owners of those dwellings never stopped complaining about the high cost of oil and winter visitors to their homes never stopped grumbling through chattering teeth about the chill in the air.

The provision of firewood was a reliable source of income to those able to afford a wood lot and some means of cartage. Dad was able to supply all of our own fuel needs from the Beck family farm over on the Porter road, and in fact for a time he even had a team of workers doing the wood cutting and peeling for him. Anyone with cords of newly cut wood on the side of the road waiting for it to dry could count on having a certain amount stolen before it was sold or carried inside. After all, those poorest of the community who could not afford their own wood lots or to pay the going rates for a sufficient quantity of firewood to get through the winter had to do what they could to provide heat for their family.

With a wood fire you obviously can't set the thermostat and relax for the evening. Therefore, usually by mid morning in the fall and winter months things would get pretty frosty around the house. The designated fire starters would have to steel themselves for the blast of cold air that would greet them when they peeled off their ten blankets and set their bare feet on the near frozen linoleum or bare floorboards. The rest of the family would stay covered until the fire was purring along nicely and its effects could be felt throughout the home. Strangely enough, very few of these shivering residents ever contracted a cold or the grippe.

Most of the homes in Fundy Bay could be counted on to have four, mostly solid wooden outer walls, often lacking shingles but instead covered with tar paper or plastic to impede the progress of the wind somewhat. None of the homes had brick or stone outer walls. Inner partitions defining and separating the rooms were often made of cardboard. Of course, those living in such houses would not complain since many of their neighbours had no partitions at all, and everything you said and did was in full view of at least several other people. Children were expected to sleep together, perhaps with six of them somehow sharing a single, well worn mattress thrown on the floor. No other arrangements were possible when you had a family of sixteen living in a one or two room shack. The parents might be the only ones to have a proper bed, meaning that in theory their conjugal activities would be performed at a safe elevation, out of view of the children huddled below, hopefully fast asleep. The advice often handed down in faraway urban centres from parent to child never to eat and shit in the same room could not be heeded in Fundy Bay because of the size and layout of the homes. With these widespread communal sleeping and toileting arrangements throughout Fundy Bay, it was no wonder that the residents had a very earthy sense of humour and rather voyeuristic tendencies regarding bodily functions.

The people of Fundy Bay generally were without many things persons in the outside world had undoubtedly taken for granted for decades. Things like electricity, refrigerators, telephones, paved roads, televisions, pasteurized milk, fluoride treated water, bathtubs, salaried jobs, and washing machines were by and large out of the reach of many of the residents of Fundy Bay all during the 1960s and into the late 1970s. The reliance on oil burning lamps for light during the evening only intensified the fire hazard that existed in these small shacks with their cardboard inner walls and red hot wood stoves. Those who did finally get hooked up to the electric power lines often got some untrained local to do all their wiring, resulting in their home becoming an even greater fire hazard than it had been before.

Having no fridge meant very little reliance on anything perishable. Meat being kept on hand was stored in a cool cellar, which wasn't a problem in winter when everything below ground level froze anyway. It would not be uncommon to see an adventurous dog or cat hauling away a piece of uncooked stew meat or roast from an unsuspecting neighbour's shed. In the summer months the lack of a refrigerator usually resulted in many residents complaining about recurring flu like symptoms, unwitting victims of mild food poisoning.

The typical diet of the Fundy Bayers would send shivers up a nutritionist's spine. Fried foods were a daily staple. The cheap, fatty, canned meats that were sold at the Anthony Brothers store were a treat that most tried to consume at least five times a week. These were especially popular fried along with some potatoes. Canned soup was also a favourite, although few would be able to afford anything more hearty than tomato. Many families had to endure countless meals consisting simply of butter sandwiches, potatoes, and some milk. The fishermen would spend all day pulling lobsters out of the water, but could not afford to eat a single one since they needed to accumulate all the poundage they could during the season to ensure they received an adequate supply of stamps to maximize their unemployment insurance cheque during the off season.

A typical Fundy Bayer would never get to see a green salad until they moved away from home, and if they had their way, they would never be so poor as to have to eat one again. Residents did eat some greenery, such as beet and dandelion greens, that is when they weren't using them to make wine. Most people tried to grow at least a modest garden, and those who didn't would not so secretly harvest their neighbour's produce after the sun went down. Most gardens were filled with fairly basic items, mostly potatoes, carrots, peas, and beans. Sometimes people grew lettuce so that it could be used as garnish around a bowl of potato salad, but rarely to be eaten.

My friend Gord Cobb used to tell that at least half of his weekly meals consisted of pancakes since they were filling, relatively inexpensive, and he could make them himself without disturbing his father's poker game or aggravating his mother's migraine.

Dad provided milk to all those in the community without their own dairy herd. Dad would deliver cool milk daily, so that the recipients would only have to worry about storing their bottles for a few hours. The milk wasn't pasteurized, but Dad took care to sterilize all his equipment used to separate the cream from the milk. Nonetheless, this was an imperfect process as each quart bottle of milk would generally be left with about three inches of cream on top. This didn't phase the area milk drinkers as they would simply put their thumb on top of the bottle cap and give the bottle several good shakes to mix the cream in with the milk. They would then pour themselves a nice glass of cool, refreshing milk with its 40% fat content. The residents became quite adept at recognizing changes in the diet of Dad's cows, for example, when the cows switched from hay to grass, since it would show up in the taste and colour of the milk.

The living conditions in much of Fundy Bay and the surrounding villages were responsible for certain health and hygiene problems. For one, every child knew what it was like to have worms. Parents who cared and could afford it always kept some worm medicine on hand. The others toughed it out, or perhaps more precisely, dug it out. Lice was certainly not uncommon in these parts, nor in people's private parts. The community myopes had a good chance of eventually being declared legally blind as they would go through life without getting their vision corrected. If you were born deaf, either fully or partially, this would go undetected and uncorrected through to adult life, by which time your learning problems had long ago been misdiagnosed as mental retardation and you were serving a life sentence at the Riverton adult residential centre.

Tooth decay, gingivitis, and halitosis were widespread, which generally made you wish that people's smiles weren't. Very few Fundy Bayers owned a toothbrush, and by the time they reached the age of twenty, most no longer had need of one. A pair of pliers and a steady set of hands was the most common solution to problems associated with poor dental hygiene. Whether or not you owned false teeth was pretty much the dividing line between some semblance of prosperity and destituteness. The hierarchy in this regard was basically the false teeth wearers at the top, followed by those with no teeth, who it could be argued were in the process of saving up for at least a top set, followed by those at the bottom of the barrel, persons with their own teeth intact. Having even some of your own teeth still anchored inside your mouth into adulthood was a give away that your family was either as poor as church mice or you didn't care one iota about your appearance. Emancipation from poverty and slovenliness was achieved on that glorious day when your nice, new shiny set of teeth arrived at the dentist's office. A set of upper teeth was about all even the most aristocratic Fundy Bayer could afford, and besides, that was all anyone really needed. Children grew up thinking that lower teeth were like virginity: both would be long gone before they reached the legal driving age.

When you heard someone referring to blackheads, it generally didn't concern hair colour. Ever present body odour wasn't so much an embarrassment as it was a means to ward off insects and small rodents. Changing your underwear meant that you turned them inside out, just to give the other side a chance to breathe. Baldness was extremely rare as few people ever washed their hair. If they had, perhaps it would have all fallen out at once in the sink. For many the only time their hair came in contact with water was when they went swimming in the brook, lake, or Bay of Fundy. All in all, it provided the county health nurse with enough horror stories to last a lifetime after one of her monthly visits to the local elementary school.

As bad as things were inside the home, things weren't much better outside. Fundy Bay's infrastructure was easy to define: there wasn't one. No paved roads, no libraries, no fire department, no health clinic, no waterworks, no garbage pickup, no sewage system. Fundy Bayers had to define their own rites de passage from adolescence into adulthood. Since almost no one owned a car, there could be no adolescent memories of making out with Bobby Sue in the back seat of a '59 Chevy. The closest Fundy Bayers could come to that was making out in the 5' x 4' cabin of one of the moored lobster boats illuminated by the pale moonlight, after which Bobby Sue would be picking fish scales off her backside for about a week.

Having no garbage pickup didn't do much for the looks or the smell of the community. Without having roadside pickup and with very few vehicles available to transport waste to the nearest dump in the Valley, people had to settle for disposing of their garbage over the nearest bluff, in the Bay of Fundy, in the woods, in a hole in the ground, by piling it up in the back yard, or by burning it. Dry garbage would be stuffed into a burlap bag and thrown in the shop, the attic, or under the veranda. This resulted in most garages and shops being nothing more than places where garbage accummulated and mice populated over a fifteen to twenty year period. A drive along the shore road would reveal the mess being tossed over the bluff. With no sewage system, people had the problem of disposing daily of their slop pail contents, so this generally also got thrown over the bluff, or perhaps would be poured down the toilet seat in the outhouse. This made for some very pungent aromas depending on which way the wind was blowing.

Fundy Bayers invariably felt the need to own a pet, and the poorer the family was, the more pets they had to have. This tendency never ceased to perplex those in the community who were actually able to afford three square meals a day. The pet owners didn't feed their animals, of course, since they were distracted trying to scrape together some scraps for their malnourished, anaemic looking children. These drawn out looking beasts, the four legged ones that is, would therefore roam the neighbourhood in search for some sustenance.

Those good providers in the neighbourhood who could actually afford to feed a pet generally did not acquire any, mostly because they had a steady procession of neighbourhood pets mixed in with the occasional children coming to their door throughout the day looking for handouts. These pathetic looking, unkempt dogs and cats would regularly go from one end of Fundy Bay to another, mating with any of their species in heat, fighting with any territorial mongrels, breaking into the neighbour's meat stores, dodging rocks and bullets coming from unwilling hosts or protective pet owners, swimming in the Bay of Fundy in hopes that the salt would perhaps kill some of their fleas, and occasionally enjoying the attention and strokes provided by the few genuine pet lovers in the community who could look beyond the shabby outer appearance of their visitors to see their inner beauty. These sad sack varmints would usually drag their tails back home at the end of a long day in case someone had actually missed them, perhaps now missing an eye, an ear, or a bit of semen.

Sometimes the half starving dogs would cluster together in packs and enter the woods looking for wild game, finding perhaps a deer and chasing it from its natural domain into the cold Bay of Fundy to its eventual death. Their owners experienced no remorse over such happenings, thinking of it instead as a perfectly natural call of the wild.

In the midst of all this squalor lived several families with money to burn. The retail success the Anthony brothers enjoyed translated into a comfortable lifestyle for them and their families. Gertrude Halfpenny always talked and dressed as if she was a woman of means, although people never really understood what was the source of her income. People would simply pass it off to having rich relatives somewhere in the States. Several homes clustered along the far end of the Crawford road were owned by the Baxter family, all of them well to do medical doctors living in the States and visiting Fundy Bay briefly each summer.

There was no question that the richest of the rich was Leopold Blunden, a locally born millionaire now living in the States. Leopold became rich manufacturing non breakable styrofoam cups and supplying these to restaurants and fast food outlets throughout the southern United States. Leopold's father, Isaiah, actually started the business years ago, but passed it on to Leopold at an early age so he could return to his beloved Mount Ruby home and enjoy the things that really made him happy, gardening, woodworking, and calling on my Aunt Melanie once she was widowed.

Leopold orchestrated many shrewd business deals right from the beginning and was responsible for tripling the size of the business within the first five years of his ownership. He married an American woman and decided to build a summer home in Mount Ruby so that he could come home regularly to visit his father and show off all the trappings of his growing wealth. Leopold built a three thousand square foot bungalow on a lot surrounded by seventy five acres of land at the highest point in Mount Ruby, and spared no expense doing so. The house, which he named Mount Olympis (sic), came complete with indoor pool, sauna, jacuzzi, solarium, exercise room, games room, four bedrooms, three skylights, a tennis court, and a five hundred square foot carpeted doghouse to be home to his wife's pet poodle, Pupsy. Even the outbuilding, which Leopold referred to as the boathouse, had solid marble floors and three bathrooms.

To show off the newly constructed boathouse to the community, Leopold organized a soiree for about one hundred persons from the area. He treated them to hors d'oeuvres, champagne, chips, and pop, then showed a movie which he had purchased for the occasion. Such an invitation could hardy be turned down by a group of people who had never been to a movie before or seen the inside of a boathouse, let alone one with marble floors and running water, hot and cold. As everyone sat in rows of seats watching the movie and eating the free food, the occasional whispered complaints could be heard, "you'd think at least he could have afforded a colour movie!", and "this wooden bench is going to make my piles flare up again". Apparently, the community have-nots were more concerned about butt knots. Personally, I was enthraled from the opening credits of "D.O.A.", and couldn't have wished for anything more thrilling or liberating, not caring for a second that the movie was in black and white or that my chips were stale.

It was no wonder that in the face of such opulence, the typical Fundy Bayer could only shake his head in amazement at Leopold and comment what a regular "typhoon" he was. The vocabular slip wasn't all that noticeable since Leopold was considered by most to be a big blowhard.

Not done yet, Leopold then built a three storey, twenty five hundred square foot "cabin" along the shore of Clay Lake, three miles to the west alongside the community of West Appleton. The cabin looked slightly out of place alongside the beat up buses and mobile homes that the other visitors relied on for lakeside accommodation. Leopold had a fifty foot wharf built beside his cabin, and imported generous amounts of white rocks and sand from Florida to give the area around his cabin that "havin' a great time, don't you wish you were here" look. Despite this rather obvious show of opulence in such a poor surrounding, no one disturbed the cabin or thought about burglarizing it for two reasons. First of all, Leopold paid an enormous sum of money to the provincial utility to run electric light lines back to Clay Lake so that he could have all the comforts of home while he was roughing it and getting back to nature. The power lines had not been extended beyond Mount Ruby up to this point, so Leopold's intervention and expense enabled all West Appleton residents to have the choice of having electric lines brought into their homes, if they could somehow afford the bimonthly charge. The second reason for the no vandalize policy was a rumour in wide circulation from Fundy Bay to Fenton to West Appleton: Leopold's cabin was apparently rigged with an alarm system which would be activated if any window or door was jimmied or opened. The alarm was supposedly so loud it would instantly deafen anyone within two hundred feet of the cabin at the time.

Nonetheless, it seemed odd that no one ever took up the challenge, since the worse thing that would have happened was they would have been legitimate claimants of a much sought after disability pension.

As his success back in the States continued to grow, Leopold had a large pond the size of an Olympic pool dug in the front lawn of his Mount Ruby home, right in front of the boathouse. The pond was stocked with fish, and it contained floating replicas of fishing boats, both past and present. Numerous statues of fishermen were placed inside the boats, and some of them were displayed casting and hauling nets into and out of the water. He even paid no small sum to buy realistic looking rubber fish to be put in the nets, although many were of the tropical variety. He then posted a sign for all the curious passersby that they were welcome to view the boats but not to disturb the fishermen or feed the fish. Many of these articles were put away in the fall, and brought out again in the summer. This display of eccentricity amused the locals who could easily go down to the shore and see the real thing when it came to fishing paraphernalia, vessels, and catch.

Although unadvertised, Mount Olympis proved to be a frequently visited tourist attraction for many years during the summer months when the boats and statues were on display. After about eight years, Leopold finally decided to sell all the replicas and statues and fill in the pond. The reasons were numerous; he had grown tired of having to get the bullet holes in the fishermen repaired each autumn, having to pay someone to haul out of the pond yet another drowned cat which had used up the last of its nine lives trying to catch one of the real fish swimming just below the water's surface, having to get someone to untangle from the nets all the dead fish and crabs that pranksters would leave behind on pre-dawn sorties, and worrying about pucks smashing his boathouse windows after receiving yet another telegram during the winter informing him that kids were playing hockey on his frozen pond again.

△ △ △

CHAPTER SEVEN
The Bootleggers

Fundy Bay was considered by many outsiders to be a God foresaken community of alcoholics, bootleggers, sexual deviants, uneducated plebians, and assorted reprobates. And that only described the women folk. Things really got hopeless when you factored in their no good Cro-Magnon husbands and the rest of the knuckle dragging populace. But of course, generalizations such as those by people who didn't live in Fundy Bay were unkind and usually way off the mark. For one thing, many of the couples weren't married. But certain notorious goings on in the community tended to taint the outsider view of an otherwise civilized village.

No doubt about it, Fundy Bay did have more that its share of interesting characters, many of them disreputable by Valley standards. Bootleggers were fairly well represented in the community fabric and demographics. These entrepreneurs would sell moonshine of their own making, or bottled beer at a minimum two hundred percent markup from the purchase price at the government run liquor commission in Riverton. Beer was the drink of choice for most Fundy Bayers, although some good hard stuff always went down easy. Not everyone drank to excess: some only had an occasional drink. Unfortunately, this generally meant that they would drink on each and every occasion.

One of the most notorious of the local bootleggers was "White Lightnin" Newcomb, "Lightnin" for short. Without question, "Lightnin" was just about as low on the evolutionary chain as a person could go. He had dropped out of school in grade 4 at age sixteen, after the teachers could no longer control his violent outbursts, his blatant thievery of his classmates' lunches, and his intimidation and bullying of all school students during each and every break.

"Lightnin" was quite unappealing to almost anyone with even impaired senses of smell or sight. He never took a bath, never washed his hair, never cleaned his few remaining teeth, and only changed his clothes when even he could no longer stand the aroma or when some relative died leaving him some new fourth hand duds. By the time "Lightnin" was sixteen, all that was left of the teeth in his mouth were black stubs, having rotted from years of neglect, an addiction to chewing tobacco, and assorted hereditary factors.

"Lightnin" was an embarrassment to his church going parents and younger brother, but his father, Slow Mo Newcomb, hadn't had the strength or quickness to catch and discipline his oldest son since being struck on the left side of his body by a lightning bolt one morning while seated at his kitchen table peeling an apple with his penknife. Slow Mo kicked "Lightnin" out of the house the same day he was kicked out of elementary school, having all he could take of his shenanigans and lack of industry. "Lightnin" regularly stole money from his parents to feed his drinking, chewing, and smoking habits, as well as to buy sexual favours from neighbourhood girls looking to make a quick buck to keep them in smokes. "Lightnin" was quite firm on expecting the biggest bang for his buck, so usually gave his business of the horizontal variety to Big Mama Goomar, a sixteen year old fellow school dropout who weighted over three hundred pounds soaking wet. Of course, "Lightnin" was lecherous with every teenage girl he met, which is why strolls taken by "Lightnin" along the community street were observed and tracked by a series of road watchers, and updates of his progress passed along by those who took up permanent residence on the party phone line. These snoopy residents ("concerned citizens" as they liked to call themselves) kept tabs on pretty well everyone and everything which moved in Fundy Bay, effectively creating the original neighbourhood watch.

"Lightnin" also turned out to be a threat to the local livestock, as he was sentenced in the county court to six months in jail for raping Gerry Crawford's prize hereford, Daisy. Damming evidence given by Crawford's neighbour and Big Mama's father, Norton Goomar, sealed "Lightnin's" fate, even though Norton's motives were called into question as possibly wanting to get back at "Lightnin" for having jilted his daughter and leaving her with no means of honest employment. Speculation around the community was that "Lightnin" would have gotten a much longer sentence if Daisy had only been in a position to present the judge with her mooooving tale. As it turned out, "Lightnin" enjoyed his time behind bars, being given clean clothes to wear and a regular bed to sleep in, so it was unlikely that his stay had any rehabilitative affect, seeming to him to be more like a reward for a job well done.

After being kicked out of his father's house, "Lightnin" erected on the outskirts of Fundy Bay a six foot by ten foot shack on a patch of wooded property rumoured to be owned by a pulp and paper company in Halifax. "Lightnin" bragged to customers about having stolen the lumber from his father's shed in the wee hours of the morning. His shack had one small door, no windows, no electricity, no insulation, a crudely constructed table and stool made from rough lumber, an oil lamp, and a small wood stove which vented through a hole in the wall and which was used to burn shore wood. A sign with a jagged, snapped off looking edge on its left side and with a white background and bright red letters stating "Welcome You" was hung above his doorway a few months after he moved in. Coincidentally, a similar looking sign saying "The Mailors Welcome You" which used to adorn the Mailor family's summer residence in Lamar's Cove disappeared at just about the same time. However, since the Mailors resided in Maine most of the year and rarely mingled with Fundy Bayers during their visits, they didn't investigate the matter, attributing the loss of half of the sign to the fierce winter winds blowing in off the Bay of Fundy. "Lightnin" would have had the perfect defence in any event: illiteracy.

Most of the floor space in "Lightnin's" shack was taken up with cases of beer and bottles of moonshine. "Lightnin" shared his shack with an assortment of snakes, rodents, and insects, which apparently left him alone while he was slept on the floor on a growing pile of clothing which had either been discarded over time by his neighbours or which he had stolen from their clothes lines on wash days. It was never clear what "Lightnin" ate, although most felt that his diet consisted mainly of white bread and molasses which he purchased from Anthony Brothers store, perhaps mixed in with some six legged protein.

No one really knew how "Lightnin" got the idea of becoming a bootlegger, but it gave everyone an excuse not to call him by his christened name, "Aloysius". It came as a shock to the adventuresome of the community to learn that "Lightnin" could whip up a pretty potent batch of moonshine. No one really knew what secret ingredients "Lightnin" included in his recipe, but it was noted by more than one person that "Lightnin" never drank his own concoction and that the population of vermin and pets in his shack never seemed to expand. It also surprised most to discover that he was quite adept at counting money and making change, proving that at least he wasn't colour blind and that he was fortunate not to be living across the American border.

"Lightnin" did a brisk business on weekends, especially amongst the teenage and pre-teen crowd who could count on not being asked for proof of age. People didn't linger long after the transaction was consummated, especially since any humorous interjection on their part would evoke a maniacal cackle from "Lightnin", exposing his mouth full of decaying stumps. Since "Lightnin's" residence was located on the edge of town, would be customers were able to approach the speakeasy without attracting attention from the teetotallers and concerned parents of the community, effectively dodging both of these groups of people. Some of the older customers, especially the bohonks, tended not to be intimidated by "Lightnin" or his reputation. These older rabble rousing teenagers, after receiving their order, would place themselves strategically around the interior of the shack, blow out the oil lamp, then start pounding their fists in the palm of their hands, effectively resulting in a one hundred percent discount in product price from a shaken "Lightnin". Other tricks were to have someone climb up the roof of "Lightnin's" shack while the others were inside transacting business. The person above would then start jumping up and down on the roof, creating a deafening racket inside, which would again prompt a nervous "Lightnin" to concede to major concessions to those left inside. Usually the deal would be concluded by the climber urinating over the top of the "Lightnin's" roof, as a reminder that they would be back.

In some cases, the thugs would even steal "Lightnin's" money roll, if they had any expensive habits that needing feeding, knowing that "Lightnin" could not go to the police. This thievery was possible because like most Fundy Bayers, "Lightnin" had no trust of banks or other financial institutions, so kept his money with him at all times. The disadvantage of not having a window was that "Lightnin" never knew who was at his door until it was opened. Of course, the bohonks were the only ones who won in these exercises, since "Lightnin" would simply turn around and hike the prices charged to the younger and more reputable customers. Despite the hazards, "Lightnin" managed to secure and maintain an enviable share of the bootleg market in Fundy Bay, although no one could figure out what he did with his money, or who he did it to.

Whereas "Lightnin" was located on the far western edge of Fundy Bay, Herne Crawford was the bootlegger everyone turned to when they didn't want to venture beyond the centre of the community and if they didn't particularly care who saw them going in for some liquid refreshment. Herne was a crafty old character who used to be Dad's sole competition for the taxiing business within the community. But while Herne continued to provide taxi service to the autoless of Fundy Bay, he discovered a more profitable use of time and gas was to shuttle cases of beer from the Riverton liquor commission to his house to be sold at a one hundred percent profit to needy souls. Herne had very little in common with "Lightnin" except for the income source. Herne was a family man, with seven children, all of them boys. He lived in an average size house, not far from Edna Moore's home. His home was often visited by members of the Riverton detachment of the Royal Canadian Mounted Police acting on tips from Herne's neighbours, in a search for the suspected bootlegging operation. But they rarely found anything more than a normal quantity of beer to suffice a couple of hardy drinkers for a few days, along with a few bemused looking neighbours sitting around Herne's kitchen table playing cards just for fun, not for money. Certainly nothing to build a case for bootlegging or any other nefarious pursuit. After yet another fruitless visit, the RCMP would usually head off to visit and hopefully surprise a few more of the known or suspected law breakers within the community.

What the RCMP didn't know and couldn't determine was that Herne had an elaborate series of tunnels, trapdoors, and removable wall panels running through and under the house, used to hide large quantities of beer, moonshine, and whatever else he wanted to keep a secret from the authorities. Also, Herne had on the dole a series of informants located strategically along both arteries leading into Fundy Bay. These scouts located at the extremities of the community would be paid to watch out for any sign of an RCMP vehicle heading to Fundy Bay, and then to phone Herne to give him time to hide all evidence of beer in bulk and the motherlode of all cash rolls. Herne himself was too tall to fit into the passageways which housed his stash of beer, so the youngest sons would be called upon in to retrieve or put away the cases of beer, often with little time to spare. During some visits by the RCMP, the sons would be trapped inside the walls or in other hiding places waiting until the coast was clear to move, cough, or sneeze. Unlike "Lightnin" who never seemed to project any outward signs of possessing money, Herne treated himself and his family well. His cars were never more than three years old, and when he traded in for a new one, he always paid for the difference in cash. Herne became somewhat of a folk hero around Fundy Bay to many of residents since he was able to successfully outwit the RCMP at every turn.

And then there was "Lightnin's" first cousin, Lazar Newcomb, who could outwit no one other than those living under his roof, and even then you had to exclude the family pooch. Lazar was an uneducated, uncouth brute who thought gene pool was something you played in your denim overalls. If you mentioned the word "oxymoron" to a Fundy Bayer, it would be assumed you were referring to Lazar. Nonetheless, he brazenly and successfully operated a bootlegging operation for many years from his home situated a mere stone's throw from the Sanctified Methodist church, on the lower east side of the community near the shore. Like his cousin "Lightnin", Lazar was able to concoct a pretty potent batch of home brew guaranteed to make you see visions and give your boat twenty miles to the gallon on the open seas. Lazar's brew was respectfully known as "rocket fuel" to the hardy locals. It was a well known fact that Lazar fermented his brew in a large tank sunk in the ground in the woods not far from his home. Legend had it that the bohonks and the wannabes would often drop by, remove the lid, and take turns urinating in the bubbling mixture, adding to the uniqueness of Lazar's recipe. This may have been why customers often commented that no two batches of Lazar's rocket fuel tasted the same. Rumors of product tampering and the lack of a quality control process didn't seem to phase in the least those faithful customers who gave new meaning to the term "diehards".

Lazar was often visited by the RCMP, but no real punishment ever seemed to follow, other than a quinquennial overnight stay in jail. Occassionally Lazar would lay low for a while, suspecting that the RCMP were planning a surprise raid, but after expiration of a grace period, he would be back in business full tilt.

Despite a striking resemblence to his primate cousin, "Lightnin", Lazar did manage to get married, to a plain looking, very promiscuous woman christened Lodema at birth, but known throughout the neighbourhood as "Scissors" because of her penchant towards opening and shutting her limbs to secure favours and satiation from locals and visitors alike. Some speculated that Scissors, having honed her skills, was responsible for Lazar being able to avoid arrest for bootlegging. Apparently Lazar not only approved of this extra marital activity but profited from it. As he often said, just as long as he had a harbour to moor his boat in he was happy, and it didn't matter to him how many others had dropped anchor there before he arrived. He just made sure Scissors collected docking fees.

Lazar and Scissors had three somewhat dimwitted sons, although it was anyone's guess as to their pedigree. They were about as varied in looks as batches of Lazar's brew were in taste. Nonetheless, some things they had in common with each other as they reached adolescence and with their second cousin "Lightnin" were a knack of negotiating sexual favours from local teenage girls and flogging cigarettes and booze to minors. The boys always had cash and their hands stuffed deep in their pockets as they roamed the neighbourhood streets looking to conduct business. Tragically, some of these girls had no sooner stopped playing with dolls when they learned to play for pay with the dolts. Although the Fundy Bay housewives and gossips often commented that "you can be certain that those hoodlums are up to no good!", the machinations of the Newcomb boys largely went unchallenged. But they were not completely unpunished. For one thing, none of them were ever invited to the crokinole parties or pie socials held in the homes of the Fundy Bay socialites. And secondly, the locals would generally refuse to do business with them when they came door to door selling produce from their father's garden.

The last noteworthy bootlegger in the community was Ennis Sullivan who lived on the Porter road. Ennis was different from all the other bootleggers in Fundy Bay in many respects. For one, he was a hardworking, gentleman farmer who had a loving wife and six attentive, industrious sons. Ennis also had a certain morale code, and would refuse to sell booze to anyone that he knew was underage. He had a very limited clientele as he only did business with those he knew and trusted. Ennis was not involved in making any home brew as he simply resold beer and hard stuff which he had purchased legally from the provincial liquor commission in Riverton. And the prices charged by Ennis were not unreasonable. He jacked the prices up just enough to pay for the gas he consumed driving back and forth to Riverton and to enable him to make a small profit. And unlike "Lightnin", Herne, or Lazar, Ennis would certainly not sell to any of the other community bootleggers who had underestimated demand and had themselves run out. Ennis was willing to be a retailer, but he drew the line at being a wholesaler.

The way most people looked at it, Ennis was simply providing a service to his friends, those who didn't have a vehicle to go to town to get their own supplies, those who lacked planning skills to quantify expected need, or those who didn't have enough willpower to make their own inventory last the weekend. In fact, very few people referred to Ennis as a bootlegger. He was simply someone who carried a larger than usual stock of booze and was kind enough to share it with persons in need for a negligible fee to help him defray expenses. The Sullivan house was further away from the Fundy Bay core than any of the competition, but those scrupled souls willing to put their thirst on hold just a bit longer would go the extra distance to enjoy a visit with Ennis and his family, perhaps sample some of Fay's homebaked rhubarb pie, help Ennis put some hay in the barn, play a hand or two of auction forty-fives with the boys, and avoid patronizing the true bootleggers who gave the profession a bad name.

△ △ △

CHAPTER EIGHT
The Superstitions

The people of Fundy Bay were simple folk, with basic values, many of them traditional, some of them unhealthy, others of them unmentionable. Nonetheless, each of the residents seemed to more or less follow by happenstance a fairly straight course throughout life, not pursuing any particular destination and taking very few left or right turns. That was too bad in some cases, since so many were deposited on the road to nowhere right from birth. Of course, going nowhere was not such a bad thing for those incapable of facing the obstacles and hazards lining more ambitious routes. Trying to chart one's course only had value when fishing on the high seas. Once back in dock, life went on in the recognizable and comforting rhythm of the Fundy Bay routine.

Symptomatic of persons who feel they lack influence over their own destiny, many of the people of Fundy Bay were natural born worriers. They worried about everything. They worried about whether or not it was ever going to rain. Then they worried if it was ever going to stop raining. They worried about not being able to afford anything worth owning. Then they worried about their neighbours breaking into their house and stealing the very belongings that they were eager to replace anyway.   They worried about what the doctor might discover when they went for their checkup in the Valley. Then they worried about what the doctor obviously wasn't telling them. They worried about not having a mean guard dog chained out front to protect their property. Then they worried about why no one ever came to visit. They worried about whether or not enough people would show up for the Friday night card party at the community hall. Then they worried if they would have enough tables to seat everyone who came. They worried about having too little food for their Christmas Day dinner guests. Then they worried that all the leftovers would go bad in the fridge. When they had nothing to worry about, they worried that things were too good and something awful was about to happen.

Mom was a world champion worrier. She worried about every minute facet of life. Mom felt it was normal for all concerned citizens to worry, especially with the communists controlling our weather patterns, contaminating our water supply, and spreading drugs and pornography to our impressionable young people. After all, as Mom often said, "mark my words, one day soon the unsuspecting west is going to wake up to find the hammer and sickle flying from every flagpole." Not that anyone would have noticed, since apparently they'd all be inside watching porno movies while in the midst of a drug induced state.

A shiny wooden sign hanging slightly crookedly on our front kitchen door said it all: "Today is the tomorrow you worried about yesterday." It was the first thing we all saw when we came down to the kitchen each morning for breakfast. It served as an inspirational reminder as we shuffled off to school each day, heads lowered, lunch pails dragging, somehow dreading the experience we were about to undergo. The plaque's message was not only Mom's motto, but also the principle shared by many of the adults in the community.

Life for many was just one big cesspool of worries and woes, and we were all swirling around hopelessly in a vortex leading down the big drain. Even the faithful churchgoers of the community declined the invitation to cast all their anxieties heavenward, preferring to keep them closer to ground level so they could mull them over in their daily "oh, my, you poor dear" sessions with their friends and neighbours. Retellings of the Martha and Mary story from the Gospel of Luke would draw disgusted looks from the church audience if the minister dared be so bold as to suggest that lazy Mary was to be commended for choosing to sit and listen to the Lord. In this crowd of Fundy Bay worrywarts, overworked Martha was the sympathetic figure, and was held in high esteem for her industrious nature even in the face of such unfair treatment. If a preacher wanted to strike a chord with his downcast congregation, all he had to do was start moaning and groaning during prayer time about all the hardships faced by God's flock here on earth. In that misery loves company, everyone went away feeling somewhat united and uplifted, reminded that their neighbour was just as down in the dumps and miserable as they were. The only time the gloom seemed to lift was when someone was telling about some genuinely horrible twist of fate that had befallen them or their family. This dramatic redefinition of the misery continuum tended for a while to appease the listeners and reaffirm that their reality was actually quite bearable. The next time someone would ask, "how are you doing?", they could respond with, "not bad", which was instantly viewed with suspicion by the puzzled and envious questioner.

People in Fundy Bay did not recognize themselves as worriers since all of their anxieties were legitimate. When someone could no longer stand up under all the pressures they faced, and just couldn't take it anymore, it was considered to be a case of "nerves" gone bad. Fundy Bay folk would often be heard saying, "its his nerves acting up, ya know", or "looks like poor Sadie is having a nervous breakdown". But there was hope for someone with a jangled set of nerves: nerve pills. These were prescribed by the Valley doctors to every second adult resident of Fundy Bay. Once on nerve pills, it was generally a lifetime commitment, since the thought of going off the pills really made the poor folk nervous. Those unable to get their nerves in check without some chemical assistance tended to go through nerve pills like shit through a goose. Prescriptions were usually open ended so that people very infrequently had to go back to the doctor to get approval for a refill. Fundy Bayers got to be quite proficient at diagnosing the symptoms of nerve breakdown, and in the true spirit of neighbourliness, would sometimes share their nerve pills with a first time user. These pills became so popular that parents might even give some to their nervous children at exam time or when they were shaking like a leaf at the thought of reciting their poem at the Christmas concert in the church.

Nerve pills were not considered to be drugs, but rather a necessary antidote for whatever ails you. One moment upstanding citizens of the community would be sitting around passing judgement on their alcoholic neighbours, while the next they would excuse themselves to get a glass of water so they could take their next nerve pill. Of course, hypocrisy wasn't restricted to the teetotallers. Many of the alcoholic parents in the community would allow their children to sample beer but wouldn't allow them to have a sip of coffee for fear they might get addicted.

The pervasive doom and gloom attitude did not wash with the farmers and fishermen who tended to be eternally optimistic. They kept on whistling as they went about their daily grind, obviously unaware of how unhappy they really were, or at least should be. Their happy go lucky nature was viewed as nothing more than ignorance and naivety by the more enlightened Fundy Bay naysayers and doomsday prophets.

Akin to worrisomeness came superstition. Being somewhat cutoff from the more civilized world had its share of advantages, but also its shortcomings. With limited understanding of and concern for many basic elemental truths, the people of the community tended to be a superstitious lot, although they would not necessarily own up to it. The fact that at various times up to four churches operated within Fundy Bay with its population of just over two hundred people was an indication that many wanted to hedge their bets in case those more serious worshippers with their downcast demeanour and long faces were on the right track.

The superstitions subscribed to by the Fundy Bayers were common knowledge passed along from generation to generation. The library at the elementary school in Lamar's Cove even had a hard covered book on rural superstitions that was required reading for anyone intending to graduate from grade five. Ironically, many superstitions held by the greater populace were largely disregarded by Fundy Bayers. For example, triskaidekaphobia was unheard of in an area where every other family had a thirteenth child which certainly had brought good luck and a little extra beer money by way of an increased family allowance cheque. The superstitions about black cats and walking under ladders were not ingrained in the community either, as black cats were just as good as any others in ridding the barns and houses of rodents, and things were not that congested in Fundy Bay that it would be necessary to walk under someone's ladder anyway.

A superstition held in high regard by the housewives was that if a boiling pot of potatoes ran dry, it meant it was going to rain. And of course, with no time limit on this prediction, it would invariably come true, if not that day, then sometime that month. A bird in the house was an especially bad sign and meant that someone was going to die. That generally came true also: unfortunately for the bird, it was usually him. This was not unlike the superstition which said that an owl hooting near the house was a sign of death there. Once again, the poor bird was unknowingly predicting his own demise as some cranky, light sleeping Fundy Bay farmer would take care of Mr. Hooter with a single bullet.

There were actually two different superstitions which predicted that someone was going to come and visit you that day: accidently dropping a dishcloth, and accidently dropping a potato and having it break. Apparently if they happened together it was good luck, not so much that you would cancel the prediction, but at least you could use the fallen dishcloth to clean up the mess left by the potato.

If the palm of your right hand itched, it meant that you were going to shake hands with a stranger. Again, without an expiration date, this generally came true, mostly because few persons were stranger than your very own Fundy Bay neighbours. If the itch moved to your groin, it generally meant you and the stranger had done more than merely shake hands.

A common superstition held in very high regard was that on New Year's Day, if the first person to cross the front door threshold was a man, it was a sign of good luck for the entire year for that household. However, if the first person to cross the threshold was a woman, it was a sign of bad luck. Certainly it was good luck for the man who visited first, as he would be treated to leftover Christmas fudge, kissed by the wife of his appreciative neighbour, and most likely have at least one child named after him that year. A woman daring to be the first to cross the threshold instantly was vilified and experienced nothing but bad fortune, as she was blamed by the household for every broken dish, cut finger, and episode of diarrhea for an entire year. New Year's Day was therefore not a time of relaxation in Fundy Bay: it was usually spend keeping a vigil at the front window, checking to make sure that no woman was so bold as to attempt an entry. This annual dilemma even convinced some that a telephone might be a worthwhile investment, so they could phone the nearest male to have him drop by early on New Year's Day to ensure their good fortune.

An overnight visit by a single member of the opposite sex at the home of a married couple was also cause for alarm and superstition. The basis for the superstition was that an unmarried person contained a certain, overpowering sexual allure that could be transmitted through their scent. According to local superstition, if an unmarried woman stayed overnight at the home of a married couple, and the single woman wasn't a member of the husband's immediate family, then it was critical for the married woman to take precautionary measures to ward off almost certain trouble. As soon as the single woman left, the married woman had to immediately strip the guest bed of its sheets and wash them, so as to remove the smell of the other woman from the bed. For every night following the single woman's departure that the sheets remained unchanged, it guaranteed one more infidelity on the part of the married man who would be overcome by the lingering scent of the single woman. That didn't mean that his infidelity would involve that particular single woman, of course. Her intoxicating scent simply spurred him to immoral action. The face and the name of the fellow perpetrator were rather unimportant as the husband couldn't be expected to control his hormones once fate had been tempted and was now involved. Curiously, the man of the household often tried to distract and keep his wife from her laundering duties following the departure of dear sister in law Suzie. The superstition was the same when a single man stayed overnight. In these cases the married man the following day often had a struggle trying to motivate his wife to get to it and change the sheets and sometimes even had to do it himself while his wife lazed around daydreaming. Oddly, in some cases apparently the curse kicked in a bit early and the husband or wife would inexplicably steal away to the guest bedroom during the night while their willpower was on holiday and be drawn uncontrollably into the waiting arms of the sexually charged guest. If the spouse happened to wake up and hear the sounds of a passionate encounter in the next room, all that could be done was to utter an obscenity about the damned curse before rolling over and returning to sleep.

The second part of the superstition was that if any member of the opposite sex actually slept in the same bed as the departed guest before the sheets were washed, it would mean certain divorce for married couples and a lifetime of lovelessness for unmarried persons. Because of the well known and accepted power embodied in this particular superstition, married couples coming to stay overnight would always be assured almost as soon as they walked in the door that the sheets on their bed were indeed clean. Guests unfamiliar with local customs and folklore who came to visit might pass off this guarantee of clean sheets as a by-product of fastidiousness but for the woman of the house to do otherwise would be to fail completely as a hostess.

A contraption which once commonly adorned the door frame leading to the master bedroom of every upscale Fundy Bay home was the portal piece. No one seemed to know how the superstition started, but it had a firm grip on many residents, at least those fortunate to have a master bedroom. The portal piece was an ornate metal device which was screwed onto the door frame of the master bedroom. Engraved somewhere on the portal piece would be the standard dire warning, "Record Your Presence or Suffer the Consequences". When you lifted up the clapper, underneath would be paper on which were recorded the names of all the occupants of the house, past and present. Observance of the superstition was widespread, so the portal piece diary served as a valuable log of house ownership and occupancy. Some people even added drawings or notations such as "happy Christian couple". It was considered very bad luck not to fill in the portal piece diary. As a minimum, it was expected that you would enter the names of the occupants, and the dates occupancy started and ended. It was not necessary to add the names of persons who visited the home; only those who lived there on a full-time basis had to be registered.

It was even worse luck to remove the portal piece. If a homeowner died suddenly, the person settling the estate would be expected to add a notation giving date of death and a respectful thought, such as "Gone to be With God".

By the 1970s, however, the portal piece superstition had all but faded into oblivion. In fact, by then, Edna Moore and Elma Anthony owned the only two houses in Fundy Bay which still had fully completed and up to date portal piece diaries hanging in place. All others had long ago stopped the practice. As the old diary paper became worn, fell from its place and became lost, the nervous homeowners noted that it really didn't cause their already bad luck to worsen, so the portal piece superstition was slowly demystified. The portal pieces became mere conversation pieces revered mostly for their decorative value and promise of becoming a sought after collectible in the future.

The number "3" seemed to pop up in several superstitions. The example which was most ingrained into the consciousness of the Fundy Bay populace was that deaths always came in groups of three. They might have to wait ten months for the defunct triumvirate to have its last member, but the citizens would say, "see, I told you that a third person was going to die!". Another superstition involving the number three was that if you broke something, you would break two more things in the near future, for a total of three. This prediction wasn't hard to complete, seeing as how most families fried at least two eggs each day for breakfast. A more obscure superstition invoking the number three dealt with the significance attached to the amount of times you sneezed in succession. The prediction was "a wish, a kiss, a disappointment" for one, two, and three sneezes. No one really knew what to expect if they sneezed more than three times; the poor person was in uncharted waters at that moment, and generally fell into a minor state of depression given the trend towards misfortune noted in the first three sneezes. From my experience, two and three sneezes really meant the same thing in practice. I used to eagerly await my kiss from even a moderately pretty girl at school, only to be disappointed when the kiss I received was from my own well intended mother once I got home from school.

Fundy Bayers learned to predict weather based on the signs in the sky and the aches in their limbs. This was not considered superstition, however, but rather a reputable form of meteorology. Such prognostications were essential to a populace relying on the cooperation of the weather to enable them to pursue their livelihood. And residents enjoyed a beautiful view of the sky and the heavens from Fundy Bay, with no tall buildings or bright lights blocking their vision. Fundy Bayers most appreciated their nightly view of the sun setting, seemingly disappearing into the Bay of Fundy over the horizon.

One of the most reliable signs related to sky watching was "mackerel sky, within 24 hours it won't be dry". Therefore, if the clouds formed a pattern akin to the skeletal outline of a mackerel, that meant to plan for rain. However, if there was enough blue in the sky to make a sailor a pair of pants, it was going to be clear. Now, it proved very difficult to apply this last one. Just how big was this sailor anyway? Therefore, the superstition was applied with great liberalism to avoid shelving it altogether. The nautical theme cropped up again in the forecast that "red sky at night, sailor's delight, red sky in the morning, sailors take warning". Of course, the delight of the sailors would be a fine day, whereas the warning referred to an impending storm. A slight variation of this rhyme also seemed to hold true, that is, when removing the word "sky" and replacing it with "eyes". This alteration recognized the rowdy nature of many of the fishermen, and served as a warning not to head out to sea if you were hung over from the night before. The cemetery was filled with gravestones containing the message "Lost at Sea" for all those who failed to heed the warning. The highest tides in the world were not to be taken lightly, even by the heartiest of sailors.

Fundy Bay experienced many magnificent thunderstorms during the warmer months. The view of the lightning flashing over the dark Fundy Bay waters was a spectacular sight that the trembling Fundy Bayers could not help but admire. In order to enable them to gauge how close they were to the centre of the storm, Fundy Bayers would count "1000, 2000, 3000, 4000" and so on, starting from the time they saw the lightning, and ending when they heard the next crash of thunder. If you got to "3000", it meant that the storm's centre was about three miles away. You felt relatively safe then, although Fundy Bay would invariably be without electricity due to a downed pole or blown transformer. At "3000", Mom would begrudgingly allow us to stand beside the kitchen window to look out at the lightning flashing over the purplish black, seething Bay of Fundy waters. However, if we only got to "1000", or even worse, could not even finish saying "1000" before thunder struck, Mom would force us to move away from the windows, say our prayers, and cross our fingers because the storm was directly over Fundy Bay.

Many buildings within Fundy Bay had been struck by lightning during their lifetime, and several families had lost their home as a result. Many of the farmers erected a lightning rod on their barns, so that in case of a strike, it would discharge to the ground without causing any major damage. Therefore, it was not unusual to see scorch marks all down one side of a farmer's barn. After years of anxiety whenever thunderstorms would pass over the area, the fishermen decided to follow the lead of their farming neighbours and erected a large rod on the wharf to entice the lightning away from their boats. During the next storm which passed directly over the area, a lightning bolt made a direct hit on the rod, splitting it from top to bottom and making such a racket that it was heard a mile away. Nonetheless, none of the ships had been damaged, so the experiment was a success. Residents went down to the shore the following day to pick up pieces of the shorn lightning rod, some chunks even being discovered in Edna Moore's field, a hundred feet away.

A final prognostication about the signs in the sky concerned the moon, when it was the first or last quarter of the moon. If the moon was tipped up so that it could hold water, it was considered a dry moon, and residents could expect dry weather for the next week. If, however, the quarter moon was tilted so that water would spill out of it, it was considered a wet moon, and everyone could count on getting a fair amount of rain during the upcoming week.

No doubt environmental science held all the answers linking these signs in the sky to particular weather patterns, but this was unnecessary detail for Fundy Bayers. It sufficed that these forecasts had come true time and time again. Also, the superstitions had proven their validity throughout the years, from generation to generation. Of course, no one would discuss how many times the forecasts or the superstitions had failed. To ask would run you the risk of being labelled a doubting Thomas or a know it all. That in itself was enough to silence the curious, as it carried an ominous sound of impending punishment from above, or perhaps from next door.

△ △ △

CHAPTER NINE
The Churches

Even though Fundy Bay rarely exceeded two hundred residents, no one could say that the inhabitants didn't have options when it came to choosing a place of worship. The oldest church was the United Baptist church located just outside the core area of Fundy Bay. The community forefathers had been somewhat optimistic about its relevance to the citizens as the church was built large enough to seat just over a hundred persons, representing half of the entire population of Fundy Bay. Just outside of Fundy Bay in the adjoining communities of Mount Ruby and Lamar's Cove were two other United Baptist churches, themselves built to seat approximately seventy and sixty persons respectively, not to mention Baptist churches located nearby in North Mountain communities of Port Heath, Fenton, Atlee, and Hurbertsville. Therefore, in an area of a few square miles comprising fewer than a thousand people, there was seating in Baptist churches sufficient to accommodate almost six hundred persons. By anyone's standard, the Baptist denomination was well represented in the area, perhaps due to an early century attempt to corner the market. The area residents therefore had a variety of choices for place to worship; the problem was, the product was pretty much the same in each place with similar packaging and promotion, or lack thereof.

In 1940, Jasper Parsons, a dynamic bachelor preacher from Boston, emigrated to Fundy Bay during a self imposed period of semi retirement from the ministry. Jasper was a huge barrel-chested man with a raspy voice and a full head of slicked back silver hair. He had served all over the world as a missionary for the Sanctified Methodist denomination, and having just turned fifty, decided it was time to settle down in a more civilized setting. Apparently he took a wrong turn somewhere since he ended up in Fundy Bay. When he first arrived, Jasper attended the Fundy Bay United Baptist church, but soon took notice of the long faces of the regulars, the dull delivery of the resident preacher, and the absence of any of the salt of the earth types he passed on walks along the Shore Road and the shiftless teens he saw hanging out near the bridge on weekend evenings. Jasper offered to assist in reaching out to these neglected wayward souls, but his offer was politely rebuffed by the elders of the church who seemed quite content within their own comfortable Sunday morning social club with its unwritten but nonetheless requisite white shirt and tie dress code for the menfolk and a trim knee length dress for the women.

After listening to the church elders' rather vague reasons for not wanting him engaged in reaching out to the impoverished of the community, Jasper's instincts to fulfil the great commission rose up inside of him, and he decided that his retirement had just concluded at that moment. That week, Jasper made it a point to visit the fishermen in their fish shacks, the farmers in their fields, and the teens on the bridge, to talk to each of them, befriend as many as he could, and to invite them to his home the next Sunday for a time of worship. He made one thing clear: there was no dress code. They should come dressed as they were when they were working or playing.

That Sunday, Jasper was heartened to welcome fifteen men, women, and children into his home. To his surprise, most of the men came wearing their best plaid shirt with their hair slicked back with whale oil. And the women wore clean, albeit simple dresses. Jasper was a jack of all trades at the service: he read scripture, he played the piano, he lead the singing, he sang a solo, he preached the sermon, and he declared the benediction. Throughout the service, he would address each of the visitors by name, making a point of personalizing his message in a way each person could relate to. Jasper didn't take up an offering that Sunday, feeling that those in attendance had no financial resources to spare, but instead started a tradition of leaving a brass collection plate by the front door in the hallway, so that anyone who wanted to leave some small pittance could do so anonymously on their way out. And if someone was especially in need that week and had to make a withdrawal from the plate, that would be alright too. Jasper was surprised to discover in the offering plate that first week a total of $1.21 all in pennies, nickels, and dimes, no small net amount considering the condition of those in attendance.

No one seemed to mind sharing the five old tattered hymn books which Jasper had provided that morning. Truth was, only two other people besides Jasper, both women, bothered to sing, not because the rest were shy, just they couldn't read. Jasper took note of this, and in following weeks asked them if they had any favourite hymns they would like to sing. Those that did volunteered their selections, and Jasper would invite persons to sing along by memory if they could, or to follow along in the hymnal, or to hum or whistle along if they wanted. Jasper had noted that the fishermen especially were world class whistlers, and these options allowed everyone to save face without having to show their own illiteracy. As Jasper pointed out, the idea was to make a joyful noise unto the Lord, anyway you could. Jasper also taught the people simple, short choruses that they could learn and sing without the need to follow a text.

As word circulated amongst the low and no income families within Fundy Bay about this new worship option, more and more persons started to attend, and fewer people were noted on Sunday mornings sitting down on the wharf or congregating on the bridge. The amount of money collected rose noticeably along with the numbers, and it was agreed by all to use the funds to get the piano tuned and to buy some workbooks for the numerous children who were now attending the Sunday School run by Jasper one hour prior to the Sunday morning church service. Various of the younger worshippers started to volunteer to sing solos and duets, and would practice during the week with Jasper playing piano. Word of all this activity amongst the great unwashed unsettled some of the staid members of the Baptist church. It was another variation on the story of the sacred message being taken to the unworthy Gentiles. The Baptists started to grumble and wonder about Jasper's credentials. After all, who really knew if he had ever been ordained, or if his schooling was recognized by the main denominational churches.

Perhaps unaware but in any event undaunted by this high brow elitism, Jasper Parsons carried on with his missionary work among the Fundy Bay natives, to the point where he was running Sunday School and church services Sunday morning, afternoon, and night, as well as a Wednesday night Bible study, all in his home. He was amazed at how spiritual these uneducated fishermen and farmers and unemployed persons were, after you got beyond their disdain for and distrust of religion and dealt with matters of true Christian faith. They seemed to be especially interested in hearing about his tales of missionary work around the globe, how he had witnessed hundreds of persons from all different races and cultures accept the simple message of Christianity.

Those attending the services always took time after the last hymn to walk around Jasper's living and dining rooms to admire the many souvenirs on display obtained during his worldwide adventures. The people were fascinated by the horns, swords, clocks, carvings, tapestries, ornaments, and furniture, the like of which they had never seen before. Regulars would usher their guests over to the items to show them the souvenirs on display and precisely recount the stories behind the treasures which they themselves had heard from Jasper weeks earlier. These simple country folk had never met anyone like Jasper who had been all over the world and spoke with such conviction and authority, and who displayed such genuine concern for their well being, both present and eternal. They marvelled that he had gone through life unmarried, a remarkable sign of self control that further convinced them of his fervour. And the uneducated lot were flattered to no end when Jasper asked them to vote on and accept positions within this new church as usher, treasurer, and secretary, as they had never before been entrusted with such a high position at any time during their life.

After the first four months of operation of this new worship group, Jasper performed his first baptisms, dunking Caleb and Fiona Goomar and their three teenage children in the chilly waters of the Bay of Fundy one clear August morning. This especially seemed to upset the Baptist members who couldn't remember the last time one of their members has gotten baptized, as they scoffed and commented, "Can you imagine? Getting baptized in that cold Bay of Fundy? I guess you'd never catch me doing that!"

It wasn't long before those meeting at the Parsons home started talking about building their own church building so they and their children would have a real place of their own to worship in, one where the youth wouldn't have to sit on the floor at their parents' feet. They also decided that Jasper should be paid some sort of stipend, so the treasurer held a vote one Sunday morning after the service had concluded and all present agreed that half of all future offerings should go directly to Jasper. Jasper was overwhelmed at their resolve, and wrote a letter to the headquarters of the Sanctified Methodist church in Minneapolis seeking financial assistance to erect a new church. To his surprise, a cheque did arrive in the mail, along with a letter of encouragement from the church executive. The cheque wasn't sizeable, but it was sufficient to buy a plot of land in Fundy Bay.

Jasper and his flock discussed numerous options for the church site. After many congenial exchanges of opinions over several weeks, one of the members offered to donate a plot of land he had been saving for his son. The location was perfect: near the head of the Crawford road, just up from the corner and the bridge, and situated on a high bluff overlooking the Fundy Bay harbour. It seemed too good to be true; it was just a stone's throw from the place of residence and employment for the vast majority of members. The impoverished members, despite their lack of funds, went ahead on faith as they were now learning to do, and soon found themselves recipients of numerous donations of lumber, cement, nails, paint, and old chairs. The members may have been poor, but there were certainly many capable carpenters and masons amongst the lot. Therefore, the crew set to work one bright April morning to break sod on the site, after a brief ceremony conducted by Jasper. As the days and weeks passed, the energy level of the crew grew and grew.

It seemed like all the members, young and old, men and women, stopped by to help in whatever way they could. Even those who had never attended the church couldn't help but stop and chat, and sometimes pitch in with some free labour and advice. When funds started to run low and the donated supplies were almost gone, anonymous donations from the United States or elsewhere in Canada would suddenly appear, enabling work to continue. Finally, six months after construction first began, the building was completed. The congregation was so proud of their new church, and why not? Scoffers had said it couldn't be done. Yet here it was, sitting proudly on top of the bluff. On the back of the church building, facing the harbour, was painted a ship's steering wheel with the message, "Jesus Saviour Pilot Me" printed in huge, bold letters for the benefit of the seafaring audience. The brown coloured building was very plain, not resembling a traditional church, looking more like a community hall. But nonetheless, it was functional, and it was all theirs.

That first Sunday service in the new building was a genuine, uplifting celebration of faith. People estimated that over half of the community were there filling up the pews and chairs. Even a few curious members of the Baptist church were spotted sitting slumped down in the back pew. No one could figure out how so many of the destitute church members had come up with fresh looking two piece suits and nice clean dresses. A children's choir enthusiastically if not harmoniously led the singing that morning, their clear, high pitched voices declaring to all in song that "the church's one foundation is Jesus Christ her Lord, she is his new creation, by water and the word". That morning, more than ever before, Jasper was filled with fire and brimstone, preaching a stirring evangelical message, ending with a call forward to the altar for all those who wanted to turn from their sins and profess their newfound faith in Jesus Christ. By the time the children's choir finished singing "Just as I am, Thou wilt receive, wilt welcome, pardon, cleanse, relieve; because thy promise I believe, O Lamb of

God, I come! I come!", there wasn't a dry eye in the place, and the membership of the Fundy Bay Sanctified Methodist church had increased by another twenty two persons.

Although it was difficult to sustain this enthusiasm and rapid growth, the Sanctified Methodist church nonetheless continued to be a vital part of the community, offering a unique, informal worship experience to the downtrodden of the community. Jasper started to take certain promising students under his wing to encourage them in their biblical studies and pursuit of a higher calling. Many of the young boys were engaged by Jasper to do chores around his house, to give them a sense of purpose and provide them with some much needed spending money, and to enable him to avoid aggravating his bad back and lame leg which he had been cursed with since a bad fall a few years ago in Nairobi.

As time went on, some of the parents of the community started to whisper about the goings on in Jasper's house when he would entertain his latest favourites amongst the church's young people. For one, he would often allow one of the young boys to stay the night, but as everyone knew, Jasper only had one bed in the entire house. Jasper himself would admit that they had shared a bed, but didn't see why this would be considered untoward. Certainly the young boys themselves never revealed any improprieties. Some of the comments from Jasper which certain of the young persons would reveal, however, tended to raise a few eyebrows. Most notably, word circulated that Jasper had been instructing the boys in the art of masturbation, as he viewed it as a necessary physical act as they entered their mid teens, and one which would keep them from following in the footsteps of the rutting bohonks and known insatiables like the Newcomb boys. This type of gossip did a lot to undermine Jasper's credibility in the community, and simply gave the Baptists another reason to feel smug.

The dynamic growth that the Sanctified Methodist church had enjoyed during its first year of operation petered out, with membership eventually stagnating at about fifty five, many of these attending sporadically. Many of the people who had given the church a try and had temporarily tried to understand and follow its teachings seemed relieved to go back to their former way of life, able once again to covet their neighbour's ass, or ogle it at the very least. Young boys were cautioned by their parents about going to Jasper's house without an explanation being given. Jasper undoubtedly heard the whispers and innuendos, but gave them no recognition, at least not in public.

Jasper Parsons continued on as pastor of the Fundy Bay Sanctified Methodist for another thirty years until 1971 when, at the age of eighty one, he finally retired for good due to declining health and an increasingly indifferent congregation looking for someone with a fresher, more dynamic delivery like those southern preachers you could hear on the radio on Sundays. He had also lost a lot of his enthusiasm for the ministry when his house burned to the ground during the winter of 1970 under suspicious circumstances. Tongues wagged all the more after that night when people heard about fourteen year old Calvin Goomar, wearing nothing but his loose white undershorts, rushing out of the burning house along with Jasper, himself wearing only his long nightshirt. Jasper and Calvin stood quietly side by side in the front yard, wrapped in blankets retrieved by a concerned neighbour, and watched along with a growing throng as the flames quickly consumed Jasper's house and all of its contents. The awesome inferno provided an intoxicating warmth to all gathered on that cold winter night in the front yard, causing them to feel rather sluggish from the heat and from having been woken mid dream. But not all of the neighbours were standing around mesmerized by the blaze. Many kept their eyes focused on Jasper and Calvin, and what they had only discussed previously within their own four walls was now being whispered to their receptive neighbours.

This public incident further smeared Jasper's character and credibility, so it was with almost a sigh of relief that Jasper finally gave up the ministry to concentrate on writing his memoirs. Unfortunately, Jasper never concluded this task, as he died in his sleep of a heart attack a year later, young Calvin Goomar at his side. Jasper didn't have many personal belongings to leave behind, most of them having perished in the house fire a year earlier, but those he did possess he gave to Calvin. Calvin seemed shaken up and confused by this turn of events, and would become enraged whenever teased about his close relationship with Jasper. Calvin, a rather striking, slim blond sixteen year old by this time, proceeded to prove his manhood by sleeping with as many of the teenaged girls and adult women in Fundy Bay as he could, being successful at seducing no small percentage of the female population. The teasing soon stopped as even the bohonks couldn't help but be impressed by Calvin's conquests, especially of the married church going women, one segment of the community the bohonks had always avoided. Even Calvin seemed to like his new nickname, Calvin Cool.

The Fundy Bay United Baptist church was the church attended by Mom, Johnny, and myself, along with all of our area relatives. It was the same church that Dad had attended years earlier with his parents and siblings. Mom had often attended the Fundy Bay church as a child as well, accompanied by her parents or relatives visiting from outside the province, and now served as the church organist. The Baptist church was a special place to me. I loved the big white structure, with the high steeple and the bell which deacon Rollie Collins would ring Sunday mornings. Rollie was the designated bell ringer, perhaps because he was the senior deacon, or maybe because his job as Fundy Bay lighthouse keeper had proven that he wasn't scared of heights or of scaling ladders. Every once and a while, Rollie would let Johnny and I or other young people follow him up to the belltower and pull the bell chord. The view of Fundy Bay from the bell tower was awe inspiring, at least to a ten year old kid.

The Fundy Bay United Baptist church was fronted by four long wooden steps which proved to be a struggle for the senior members to climb, until a handrail was finally installed. After making the climb up the stairs and going through the front door, you stepped into a small porch area, with swinging doors leading into the main sanctuary. The small area at the rear of the sanctuary was simply referred to as the "back of the church" by regulars, and it had a low ceiling with doors on either side, the door on the right leading to a storage area and the door on the left leading to a stairway accessing the balcony. Also at the back of the church was a small table and bookcase which housed the Sunday School supplies and the modest library of the church, containing a series of Danny Orlis books and a few others. As you stood at the back of the church and stared forward, you would be looking directly over the middle section of wooden pews to the elevated pulpit and the choir loft behind capable of seating twenty five persons. To the simple people of Fundy Bay, the solid oak pulpit and the three burgundy, felt covered, high backed chairs framing the pulpit looked very impressive and majestic. Out of respect and a godly fear, very few people other than those playing the organ or singing in the choir would ever climb onto the pulpit landing, and fewer still would contemplate sitting in one of the three front chairs. There were twelve rows of pews running along both sides of the church, with nine rows in the center section. Along both sides of the church sanctuary as well as in the choir loft were simple stained glass windows. The windows in the main sanctuary contained the shape of crosses made from a series of yellow glass panes. A narrow upper balcony stretched along the back of the church, resulting in the low ceiling for that part of the sanctuary, and was used to access the belltower and occasionally for Sunday School classes, but was never needed for overflow seating during church services.

Two rows of large lights hung from the church ceiling on six foot chains, and illuminated the few adornments within the church. These consisted of a very few wall hangings within the choir loft honouring the memory and words of those long forgotten. As children, we would stare at the plaques, and read and reread the words admonishing us to "look up not down, look out not in, and lend a helping hand" yet never fully grasp the meaning. In fact, we couldn't understand why someone would waste the time and money to engrave such a cryptic message on a marble slate, let along hang it in a place of solemn worship just to stymie future generations. We all thought a Christian should look inward to a person's true character and qualities, and not judge external appearances, yet this particular plaque seemed to contradict that belief. The true meaning of the large marble plaque didn't become clear until one summer day when the choir members all had their heads down buried in their hymnals, leading the congregation in discordant song. At just that moment, in the wink of an eye, the plaque came tumbling down, causing one alert, non singing church member to yell, "look out!", but it was too late. The heavy marble plaque hit Charlie Crawford, the only bass in the choir, squarely on the top of the head, opening a bloody wound and rendering him unconscious, at which point, about twenty parishioners surrounded him to offer assistance of varying effectiveness. Charlie eventually recovered but soon thereafter started singing as a baritone from the other side of the choir. And the plaque was cleaned off and remounted in the choir loft, this time secured with large bolts, its words now serving as a reminder of an incident which threatened to become nothing more than another folk legend.

The Fundy Bay Baptist church had a very static membership for as long as I can remember. Each Sunday you could expect to see the same twenty five to thirty persons wearing their Sunday best sitting in the pews, in the same spot that they sat in last week, last month, and last year. If an uninitiated newcomer came to worship and made the mistake of sitting in a pew designated for one of the regulars, they would likely get a very cool reception at the brief post service social time held at the back of the church, in the porch, and spilling out onto the front steps. And next week the displaced regulars would make it a point to arrive at the service fifteen minutes earlier to protect their turf before the upstarts formed any bad habits, making a point of staring victoriously at the scoundrels when they entered the sanctuary looking for a place to sit.

There were times when the Baptist church seemed to come alive, dispersing the mundane atmosphere which enveloped most services. One of these times was evangelical week held during the third week of August every year. During the hottest times of the summer, when the farmers were busiest tending to their haying, evangelical services would be held all week long each evening, featuring guest preachers who came from far and wide to lend their pulpit pounding talents and oratory skills to the cause. For that week, the church sanctuary would be packed to the gills with impressively attired men, women, and children. It was the place to be that week, the hottest ticket in town, and persons from various denominations and communities would attend, just because it was a happening in an otherwise dull, hazy summer. Farmers and fishermen would do all their chores early just to attend. Children were surprised to find that they could stay up later than usual just so they too could attend, even though it usually ended with them fast asleep leaning against their mother's arm.

The tone of these services was undeniable: we were all going to hell in a handbasket and had better do something right away, that very hour, to change our course. Even if you didn't appreciate or understand the message, you had to admire the delivery. These preachers were on fire with a story to tell. They may also have felt like they were in competition to win more converts than their predecessor had done the night before and more than their successors could achieve during the nights remaining. No matter, it made for interesting theatre. And these preachers didn't stick to the monotone delivery employed by our regular Sunday minister. They pounded the pulpit, paced all along the platform, occasionally hopping or doubling over for emphasis, hollered and screamed to accent certain key points, shook their fist and pointed a finger at the wide-eyed crowd, and waved their Bible around like it was a weapon to be used to strike sinners to their knees. Each service would conclude with the singing of the customary "Just As I Am", at which time all those petrified, earnest souls would stagger to the front to signal a turning away from their sins and the start of a new life of faith. Of course, some of those going forward did so every night, perhaps to get reenergized in a losing struggle against the forces of evil or to enjoy another brief moment in the spotlight in front of their cynical neighbours. In any event, these annual weekly evangelical services did much to boost the church membership and coffers.

The services used to attract a lot of down and out Fundy Bayers who took the words to "Just As I Am" to heart, showing up completely inebriated. This made for some interesting outbursts and retorts from the audience whenever the preacher would throw out some rhetorical questions mid sermon. If the preacher made the mistake of waiving his finger at the crowd while asking, "what do you think you'll say on judgement day when you stand before your maker after a lifetime of sin and debauchery?", he might be interrupted by a response yelled somewhere from the back pews, "pleased to meet ya! Mind if I come in?", which would be met with a mixture of "shame shame!" and half stifled guffaws. Or if the preacher was not as dynamic as those on previous nights or those on the bill later in the week, some local might stand up in the midst of an alcohol induced hallucination and shout, "we want to hear Reverend Moore!" At this point, the unflappable reverend of the moment would calmly reply, "all in good time, friend, all in good time."

As a child, I would drift in and out of consciousness during these prolonged services. I recall one occasion when my ears perked up as the preacher told a tale of a person entering a darkened room and turning on the light switch. He then posed the question, "what do you suppose happened?" Now, I wasn't sure if this was one of those rhetoric questions, so I sat back and waited. Ledwin Goomar, an elementary school dropout but a trained albeit unemployed electrician, felt he finally had a test he could pass and thereby vindicate himself in front of his neighbours, so he yelled out "the lights came on!" To Ledwin's dismay and complete mortification, the preacher said with a slight smile on his face, "no, the lights didn't come on. Can anyone else guess what happened?" As a shaken Ledwin was being noticeably reprimanded by his disgraced and unimpressed wife, a hush fell over the audience. No one was willing to fall into the minister's trap. Well, to me the answer was obvious, even if I was only seven years old. Here was my chance to prove to everyone in the community what I was made of. So I yelled out proudly from my back pew seat, "the lights went off!". At that, the minister and the entire congregation broke into gales of laughter, but from the smiles being offered I suspected that it was all good natured and not mean spirited, recognition of the impetuousness of youth. Nonetheless, like Ledwin, I felt rather humiliated. As the minister chuckled, saying, "no, no, the lights didn't go out", I was at a loss to know where I went wrong, since if the lights didn't do on, they must have gone off, somehow forgetting the detail about the darkened room. With no other takers, the preacher revealed that "nothing happened", going on to relate this in some inane way to the sharing of the gospel. I rapidly lost interest in the scenario and took solace and shelter in my mother's hug, determined never again to participate in these public question and answer type sessions.

Summer was also the time for vacation Bible school for those children attending the Baptist church. This was highly anticipated by the young people of the church, as it was a week filled with crafts, games, and understandable Bible teachings. We usually had as leaders many of the teachers who normally conducted Sunday School throughout the year, but in addition we would have smiley, loving ladies from the community or former residents visiting Fundy Bay that summer. These new leaders really added spice to the whole experience, as they would come with different skills and ideas.

We especially loved it when we had as our teacher Preston or Daphne Allison. The Allisons were regular summer visitors to Fundy Bay, usually staying with Edna Moore. Daphne was a sister to Deacon John Grady, and was as loving and kind a woman as you could find anywhere on the face of the earth. Being silver haired and in her late fifties did nothing to dim her beauty and charm in the eyes of we preteen boys as we were all smitten. Daphne was a sincere Christian woman who would explain the daily lesson with such clarity and conviction that several of us were led to publicly declare our faith right then and there. For his part, Preston was without peer regarding his engaging personality and ability to make others smile. He was a master magician who would continuously confound his entranced audience, always concluding his slight of hand tricks with a hearty laugh and his eyes noticeably twinkling behind his glasses, knowing that he had fooled us all, hook, line, and sinker. Preston was the son of a Boston area preacher, and although he himself had not felt the calling to the ministry, he nonetheless was an effective and credible messenger of the good news.

Living next to Edna Moore, Johnny and I would avail ourselves of each and every opportunity to visit whenever Preston and Daphne were staying next door. It was always uplifting to the soul to be in the presence of three persons who derived so much pleasure from life and so gifted at passing along a ray of sunshine to whomever they met. All the young people would flock to Preston whenever he was spotted outside, and he never hesitated to comply with our requests for "just one more trick". His forte and our favourite was his trick of seemingly putting an object such as a coin in his shirt of pants pocket, or even throwing it away, then magically pulling it out of our ear. We somehow suspected that Preston's many card tricks were learnable, but it did not lessen our willingness to be deceived. Even as we became teenagers, Preston and Daphne's charm did not diminish, and we would thoroughly enjoy sitting in a rocking chair in Edna's living room chatting with Daphne, or lolling around on the wharf with Preston on hot summer days fishing for harbour pollack and smelt. Becoming seasoned rod fishermen at a very young age, we thought we knew all the tricks, but even we were dumbfounded when Preston predicted one afternoon that there would be a fish on the end of his line when he reeled it in, and sure enough, there was. His reputation reached mythical proportions at this point, as we had taken careful notice of the fact that his fishing rod was not bending or even quivering when he made his bold prediction, but seconds later, he had a good sized pollack with lots of fight on the end of his line.

Preston and Daphne Allison, and adults like them, added a lot to the effectiveness of the annual vacation Bible schools held in the Fundy Bay United Baptist church. Even children of adults who never attended the church would show up religiously for vacation Bible school each summer, often their one and only exposure to the church all year. The vacation Bible school would end with a concert on the final morning, and we were generally quite proud of the skits we were able to perform with very little preparation and in front of such a large and appreciative audience of smiling family and neighbours. For years people of the community were still chuckling about the time little Norville Goomar, then only seven years old and looking adorable with his straight black hair slicked back and wearing a bow tie and high water pants, stood on the pulpit platform of the church yelling out in a loud voice a prayer to close the concert, concluding by saying, "and now, to the Father, the Son, and the Holy Smokes, eh-MEN!".

The Baptist church also had a fairly well attended Sunday School through the years, often comprising five or six separate classes for the various ages. Of course, in some classes there were only two children, but no matter, the Sunday School offered different learning opportunities for all the young people. At various times attempts were made to hold an adult class, but these usually failed after a season of halfhearted attendance and enthusiasm. The Sunday School was held each Sunday morning at ten o'clock, one hour before the church service, and lasted forty five minutes. Since the church did not have a basement or any other usable rooms other than the church sanctuary, there was no possibility of holding Sunday School at the same time as the adult church service. Therefore, it made a fairly long morning for the children of church attending parents, since they would be expected to sit through the hour long church service after waving goodbye to Sunday School colleagues whose parents avoided the church experience.

Sunday School would begin with an assembly of all age groups seated in the front pews as the church superintendent, Leticia Grady, would lead us all in prayer and song, and would share a story intended to be on topic with the day's Bible theme. Unfortunately, the true meaning of the story would often be lost amid the joking, heckling, and commotion caused by the older children who were trying to impress their peers and the younger, more impressionable young children with their rather dull wit and repartee. But Leticia was a very good natured, unflappable woman who would simply laugh and say, "now come on, boys, keep the noise down to a dull roar", forging ahead to conclude her story despite the unrelenting din. After this exercise in futility was completed, we would all be dismissed to our classes, the smaller children almost getting trampled by the stampede of pushy students charging through the narrow aisles to their designated class area.

The church actually did not have any proper classrooms, as the church sanctuary was completely open without usable walled in areas. Therefore, four classes were held in the corners of the sanctuary itself, and two classes had their class area on opposite ends of the upper balcony overlooking the sanctuary. This open classroom concept required the Sunday School teachers to be adept at keeping the bedlam to a minimum, but nonetheless there were frequent outbreaks of pandemonium within certain classes which tended to spread like wildfire until Leticia would request everyone, in her loudest possible voice, to please pipe down. The different classes varied in depth of Biblical teachings depending on the age group involved. For the youngest, things never really progressed beyond colouring some pictures representing famous people and events from the Bible while the teacher droned on about the day's lesson. The older children were tested in scripture memory and expected to answer a variety of questions in their workbooks, followed by a discussion in the group of the deeper truths of the Bible passages in question. Those who successfully spouted without hesitation or error and with proper references the required Bible verses would be awarded with another coloured star on their official looking preprinted certificate. It was a proud day when children would attain the last star, garnering them a hug or handshake from their proud teacher, and enabling them to finally rush home with the completed certificate to show to their indifferent, half asleep parents still hung over from their Saturday night bender.

Despite all the commotion throughout the Sunday School time, things generally settled down around 10:40 am out of respect for Deacon Rollie Collins who would quietly saunter into the sanctuary, climb the stairs to the balcony, and up to the belltower to ring the bell announcing the eleven o'clock church service to commence in fifteen minutes. At this point the children in the balcony classrooms would invariably try to get dismissed a few minutes early so they could peek into the belltower room and perhaps go up with Rollie to actually ring the bell. Before classes would be dismissed, everyone would receive their Sunday School paper for the week, which was a four page booklet representing in cartoon format the latest instalment of an ongoing Old or New Testament saga.

The Sunday School Christmas concerts were an annual event sure to pack the church with proud parents and curious neighbours. It was a magical time for all the children, and we liked to think for all those adults in attendance as well. Usually during the first Sunday in December rehearsals began for the upcoming concert, as the children from each class were given some role to play, perhaps simply a member of a choir, a part in one of the acts to be presented, or to deliver a recitation of varying lengths and complexity. For these sorts of concerts, you could count on being served up some turkey, along with plenty of ham. The hyper, extroverted children eagerly hoped for and sought after the large solo parts, while the more withdrawn children hoped to be able to hide in the back row of their class choir. For the first two Sundays in December, it would appear unlikely to most observers and participants that the ensemble would ever be able to put on a cohesive presentation and celebration of the Christmas story. But slowly and patiently the Sunday school teachers worked with their class, encouraging them in their efforts, and gently suggesting ways to improve their delivery and stage presence.

A ten foot high Christmas tree would be erected two weeks before Christmas, and all the children would be tasked with making and hanging decorations. This is when everyone started getting serious and occasionally terrified about the upcoming production. Children stopped being so giddy and disruptive during rehearsals. Seeing the tree made them realize that in two short weeks their restless parents would be sitting out in the crowd somewhere waiting for their award winning performance, althewhile shifting uncomfortably in their seats from having to wear those confounded dress up clothes once again this year and almost being overcome from the smell of moth balls which filled the air.

The children no longer had to be asked to pay attention, they longed for some clear direction and some help in getting their part just right. During these stress filled weeks, children often broke down and cried or threatened to quit when they just couldn't get their lines right when rehearsing in front of the entire Sunday School. The teachers would have to come to the rescue with some workable remedy or suggestion, sometimes being a major edit of the material, a resequencing of the acts, rewriting solo parts to become ensemble pieces, or just plain telling those children in the audience awaiting their turn to rehearse to please be quiet and stop laughing. The tension was eased somewhat by the drawing of names for the gift exchange to be held at the concert. The name drawing usually went without incident, other than the occasional groan of "oh, no, not him!" and persons trying to return the name they had chosen to the hat, or to trade it to their gullible seatmate.

The dress rehearsal was held the morning of the evening concert. The children never really thought about where all these dressup clothes had come from and the effort that had gone into making them; their teachers just appeared that morning bearing the outfits, and magically most of them seemed to fit just right. Those that didn't were noted by the teachers, and promises were made that before the evening concert, alterations would be made. It was then that the presentation finally began to make sense to most of the children. Before then, the acts had appeared to be a hodge podge of unrelated material, and who could believe that little Calvin Goomar would make a believable wise man? A wise ass maybe, but not a wise man. But once everyone donned their costumes, you could suddenly see the children losing their own personalities and taking on the characteristics of the figures they were portraying. And you would feel amazed at how the teachers had made such a good choice in selecting little Calvin to play one of the wise men. He was so right for the part, not missing a step and holding his head high like royalty.

The final skill for the children to get down pat was how to curtsey and bow, a talent not practised since last year's concert. This usually was good for a few laughs as at least one confused boy would accidently curtsey instead of bowing, a fact which he would be reminded of by his side slapping friends repeatedly over the next few months. Also, some boys were so enthusiastic that they would take the bow to new depths and at breathtaking speeds, almost giving themselves whiplash and usually sending their headpiece flying into the cackling crowd. When they straightened back up, they would be momentarily dizzy from the rush of blood to and from their head, sometimes leading them to fall off the platform, again to the delight of the howling audience. The girls seemed to have less trouble with their curtseys, although there was great variation in the speed at which they were performed. Some of the girls did them so rapidly that you might have mistaken their movement for a buckling of the knees caused by their obvious nervousness. Others took more time to complete their curtsey than had been required earlier to sing the entire chorus of "The First Noel".

The night of the Sunday School concert was pure magic. The children were expected to show up early and congregate upstairs in the balcony, hidden from view by some strategically placed blankets. For the first time during the season, the Christmas tree was aglow with such beautiful twinkling lights, its branches covered to the point of saturation with long icicles. This was a sight to behold for the children, as so many of them came from homes too poor or cynical to decorate a tree at Christmastime. As the parents and guests started to arrive, more than one child would have a case of stage fright and suddenly forget their name and purpose in life, let alone their recitation. The teachers had to be masters of psychology at this point, pumping up the troops and assuring them that they would do just fine. It was at this point when the children would often come to the realization for the first time that their teacher's reputation was at stake in this production, so word would circulate to "let's do it for Mrs. Grady" mixed in with similar rallying cries. And suddenly, someone would announce to all the children huddled in the balcony, "hey, look at all the presents under the tree!" And sure enough. All the presents that had been passed over to the teachers that morning were now piled under the tree, along with many others that had appeared. The excitement of getting a present usually calmed the nerves considerably as the concert suddenly was put in perspective. It was but a prelude to the gift giving.

As the sanctuary filled to capacity, the organist started playing an assortment of Christmas songs to set the tone for the night's program. When it reached the top of the hour, Leticia Grady would stand up in front of the crowd, motion them to be quiet, and a hush would come over the entire church. The lights hovering above the congregation would noticeably dim, adding to the allure of the Christmas tree and people's ability to focus on the illuminated stage area. Leticia would then give her perfectly rehearsed introduction to the night's program, thanking everyone for coming and assuring them that the children and teachers had put a lot of effort into the upcoming production. This usually elicited a round of applause, which calmed a lot of nerves of those waiting in the balcony. Althewhile, little Anna Crawford was making her way down the stairs to wait at the back of the church for her call to start the concert. Once Leticia said "okay now, let's get started with Anna Crawford from our grade one class who is going to say a little recitation". Heads would crane to see this dear golden haired little angel making her way up the aisle, resplendent in her pure white costume and halo which had slipped sideways on her head. As she curtsied to the crowd, a grin could be seen on every face, and as she blurted out her brief part in record speed but perfect meter, concluded by another curtsey, the entire crowd broke into spontaneous applause and head nodding, punctuated by numerous expressions of "isn't she sweet?" and attempts to catch the eye of her beaming parents.

Buoyed on by Anna's reception, each group and individual would proceed to present their part of the concert, whether by way of song, play, or recitation. Inevitably certain of the children would freeze once on stage, totally forgetting their opening line and frantically searching for the familiar face of their teacher then struggling to read her lips to understand her prompts. But even at these times when everything fell apart leaving behind a flustered child wondering how he had gone so wrong, the crowd was forgiving and would acknowledge completion of his effort by the same applause that was given to more polished presentations. As the evening wore on, those who had completed their segments would have a mixture of relief and regret, having surprisingly enjoyed their moment in the spotlight and basked in the warmth of the ovation. After the porcelain baby Jesus made his annual appearance, the program would conclude with a singing of "Silent Night" by the entire Sunday School.

Leticia Grady would then instruct all the children to be seated with their parents, where many of them would be greeted with a congratulatory hug or squeeze on the arm from their family. Leticia would then proceed to call out the names of the Sunday School children to come forward and get their gift. The wrapped present would sometimes be no more than a new scribbler for school or maybe a few crayons, but at the first sign of disappointment the child's mother would quickly remind him that whoever gave the present probably couldn't afford even that much. This usually left the children more curious than ever wondering who had drawn their names. But no matter, in addition to the gift, the children would be thrilled to receive a treat bag consisting of a juicy orange, a turkish delight, a cream candy, a piece of ribbon candy, a large candy cane, some hardtack, a wax stick, and two chocolates. We couldn't wait to get back to our seat to devour at least one selection, parents permitting. For many of those children, these would be the only gifts they would receive that Christmas and in fact that year, making it all the more special of an occasion.

After every child received their treat bag and present, Leticia would proceed to hand out presents to the Sunday School teachers, then would distribute the left over treat bags to all those wide-eyed children in the audience who did not attend Sunday School but who were seen looking longingly toward the bags of treasure the like of which they had never seen and didn't even dare hope to receive on Christmas morning. After the singing of a dismissal carol by the entire congregation, the sleepy eyed children would be taken home by their parents to be put to bed, to dream of wonders to come and of blessings which sometimes do come to those who believe in miracles.

Although Christmas was the most celebrated event of the year within the church, it was not the only time when the sanctuary took on a festive look. The other time was Thanksgiving, a time when we were to show and express our heartfelt appreciation to our maker for all the good things that had happened to us during the past year. To the aging congregation, the main blessing was simply to be still drawing breath. The tradition in the Fundy Bay United Baptist church was for the congregation to present the minister, usually a single man in his mid twenties, with a portion of the harvest which those in the church had reaped that fall. This was done with a certain amount of ceremony, as the ladies of the church would decorate all the church windows and the table at the back of the church with branches from hardwood trees, the leaves a splendid mixture of reds, oranges, and yellow. On the window sills and table top, amongst the leaves, would be placed various vegetables and fruit, along with numerous jars of preserves. The church always looked so magnificent and colourful for the Thanksgiving Sunday morning service, and put everyone in the proper mood for the occasion. Following the sermon in which the minister had emphasised how the area farmers and fishermen were dependent on God for good weather and a sizeable harvest, Deacon John Grady would saunter up to the front of the church unannounced and would present the puzzled minister with an envelope of money from the members. After expressing his sincere thanks to all those present for the generous gifts of food and money, the minister would lead us all in a rousing rendition of "Come Ye Thankful People Come". This gathering of primary producers and their families would pour out with heartfelt emotion and celebration the words,"all is safely gathered in, ere the winter storms begin, God our Maker doth provide, for our wants to be supplied". After the customary handshaking at the back of the church, the foliage would be collected and discarded in the deep grass behind the church, and the donations would be gathered up and carted by a chosen group up the road a few hundred feet to the parsonage.

The normal Sunday morning church services offered very little variety from week to week. Mom had learned long ago not to try out any unfamiliar hymns on this crowd, so pretty much drew from a repertoire of twenty or thirty proven favourites. Deacon John Grady could generally be counted on to step down from the choir mid service to sing a decent baritone solo, occasionally opting to perform a duet with one of the female choir members. Deaconess Lily Miller would often usually read the scripture and play the organ during Deacon Grady's musical number. Unlike in the Sunday School when the children were expected to fill the front pews to be close to the superintendent leading the proceedings, those attending the church service week after week opted to fill the very back pews, creating a twenty five foot barrier between the minister and the congregation. No matter how earnestly a new preacher would urge the people to move forward, the regulars would not budge from their comfy pews for which they had long ago been accorded squatter's rights. Johnny and I were rather akin to gypsies as we had no particular preference for seats, and since Mom was always seated on the organ bench and Dad never attended church, we were relatively free to choose whatever seat we wanted, just as long as it wasn't reserved for one of the regulars. Eventually as we got older we pretty much settled on the very back pew on the south side of the church. We were soon joined by our teenaged friends who preferred to sit at the back with us than take their place in the pew reserved for their own family. It wasn't considered to be a desirable location since it backed onto a narrow area housing the coat rod, and you could count on being disturbed and having your seat jostled by those putting away their overcoats and hats while you sat waiting for the service to begin.

During the winter, the bulky winter coats hung on the rod would spill over into the back pew, further compounding its undesirability. Nonetheless, it enabled us to have a back pew like the elder church stalwarts, a status symbol not to be taken lightly. As we got older, it also put us in perfect position to torment Slow Mo Newcomb, who would faithfully come to church every Sunday and sit in the pew directly in front of us. Slow Mo had long ago given up on trying to get his wayward son "Lightnin" to attend the services, but he did have success in getting his youngest son "Holt the Dolt" to come along. Holt was about fifteen years older than us, but was really only slightly brighter than his delinquent brother, although morally he was certainly on much more solid ground than "Lightnin". Slow Mo always wore a gentleman's wool hat to church and would place it at his side on the pew. For whatever reason possesses teenagers to make a nuisance of themselves all in the name of harmless fun and jocularity, we teenagers got a neverending sense of amusement from positioning Slow Mo's prized hat underneath him whenever he slowly rose to sing a hymn. And of course, when he slowly eased himself back into his pew, being a large man he would thoroughly crush his hat. It would then take a superior effort on his part to ease his tired body off the hat enough to pull it to safety. After he managed to get the hat back into its intended shape, he would replace the hat on the pew. From the minister's opening remarks to the closing benediction, we looked for opportunities to slide Slow Mo's hat in the path of his rearend. We always kept an innocent look on our faces whenever Slow Mo would turn around slowly to glare at us, hoping that he would conclude that he must have misjudged his direction on his descent back to the pew, and accidently shifted his body to the right and onto his hat. After about the second or third landing on his hat, Slow Mo would place the hat on his knee or lap for the remainder of the service, our fun now reduced to trying to catch and de-wing the flies buzzing around in the window alongside our pew. Despite all the times we pulled the hat stunt, Slow Mo never once reprimanded us. Perhaps he reasoned that since Dad was kind enough to drive him to and from church each Sunday he shouldn't complain about our shenanigans.

Even though Dad never attended church, he chauffeured many of the elderly in the community to and from the services each week, sometimes requiring him to make three separate trips. This throwback to his taxiing days seemed to suit Dad, and since Mom didn't drive and preferred not to walk the half mile to church, it made Dad's service invaluable. Dad would also have to come pick us up after the service, never once in all those years keeping us waiting in the church yard for him to show. On those extremely rare occasions when Mom was able to shame Dad into attending a service, she would usually end up being mortified to look down from her lofty vantage point behind the organ and see Dad slumped over, mouth wide open sawing wood. At these times, Mom would give us a look and a shake of the head which we knew meant to wake Dad up. Dad would respond to our elbow in the ribs with a groan, then would momentarily sit upright, only to fall back into deep sleep bliss a few minutes later.

An early example of the 80:20 rule, the Fundy Bay Baptist church relied on a handful of faithful members to do most of the work, and without them, the doors would have been closed a long time ago. Those twenty percent doing eighty percent of the work consisted of Deacon John Grady, Minnie Grady (John's wife), Deacon Rollie Collins, Deacon Hume Goomar, Lavetta Goomar (Hume's wife), Deaconess Lily Miller (referred to lovingly as "the Lily of the Mountain" by those within the church because of her inner beauty, sincere faith, and genuine concern for others), Aunt Marion and Uncle Harlan Reeves, Leticia Grady (John's daughter in law), Eben Rhind, and my mother. These persons took responsibility for everything from searching for and hiring new ministers, to arranging and playing the music, to fund raising, to bill paying, to maintaining the church roll, to visitation of shut-ins and the sick, to making arrangements for the monthly celebration of communion, to cleaning the church sanctuary, to mowing the lawn, to making sure the furnace was started each week two hours before commencement of Sunday School and turned off right after the church service ended and everyone had left. Nothing happened in the church without at least some of these people being involved. The ministers, mostly students who would stay no more than two or three years at the Fundy Bay church, very early on learned that these people were the power brokers, the ones to get in thick with for job security reasons. These people all had their own strengths, mixed in with many human weaknesses, but overall served the church and the community well instead of sitting back like the majority, waiting to be served.

Any minister taking on the pastoral role for the Fundy Bay United Baptist church actually had a very large field to cover. The reason was that for economical reasons, the Baptist churches in Fundy Bay and Fenton both contributed equally to the minister's salary so he had a responsibility to conduct services in both communities each Sunday. This generally meant working a rotational schedule whereby for six months the hour long services would alternate between 9:30 and 11:00 am starts in the two churches, and in the warmer summer months the services would rotate between 10:00 am and 7:00 pm starts. The Baptist churches in Mount Ruby and Lamar's Cove had just too few members to be able to afford their own pastor, so they by necessity became closely affiliated with the Fundy Bay and Fenton churches respectively. Once every four weeks during the summer months, the regularly scheduled Fundy Bay church service would be held in the Mount Ruby church building, and likewise, a Fenton service would be held in the Lamar's Cove church. These once proud churches in Mount Ruby and Lamar's Cove therefore only got to open their doors to worshippers three or four times a year, a sad reflection on the changing demographics of the communities in which they were situated and the shifting priorities of the residents therein. Nonetheless, proving that absence indeed makes the heart grow fonder, church services in either of these two small buildings generally drew twice the number of worshippers who attended the regular services in the two larger communities. Occasionally the Mount Ruby and Lamar's Cove churches would be opened to host a wedding of two non-church going residents eager to exchange in a proper church setting their vows to "love and honour", "for better for worse", "in sickness and in health", "as long as we both shall live", and "til boredom do us part".

There was a brief period during the mid 1970s when the Fundy Bay Baptist church services fell belatedly under the influence of the charismatic movement more closely associated with those southern Baptist churches. Many of us enjoyed the less formal atmosphere, and delighted in the surprises that each new week would bring. Undoubtedly the impetus for the change was the unparalleled success story of a non-denominational church in Glory, a small Valley community just a few miles from the North Mountain. Fact was, the church really wasn't a church. It was a stable owned by Olaf and Marjeta Gosta, a Scandinavian farm couple who emigrated to Canada a few years earlier and who had become fervent born again Christians following a Billy Graham crusade in Toronto, Ontario. Olaf and Marjeta set out to make a difference in this small Valley community, and by the sweat of their brows and with the help of their six sons, they cleaned the main body of the stable and installed pews and a pulpit, and made room for overflow seating in the hay loft. They then printed up a hundred leaflets announcing the inaugural service and inviting people to come out to the "Say Amen Stable". All the family members walked around the community that week, dropping off and tacking up leaflets, taking time to visit with their neighbours and pass along their regards. That first Sunday, even the eternal optimist Olaf was surprised to see a full stable of curious worshippers. Everyone had to admit that it was one of the most moving services they had ever been to, and so many young people in attendance! These Valley farm folk felt right at home in this rough stable with a faint trace of horse manure in the air, and as Olaf pointed out, Jesus himself came into the world in a place like this. Olaf and Marjeta proved to be capable singers, and the Gosta family choir was a special treat, their voices blending together very nicely. Olaf may have not received formal training to be a minister, but he preached from the heart, with sincerity. As someone later pointed out in response to a criticism that Olaf was preaching without accreditation, "hey, if everyone had an attitude like that, Jesus himself would be unemployed if he came back to earth since he couldn't get a preaching job if he didn't have the right piece of paper".

The Say Amen Stable enjoyed a period of tremendous popularity within the entire Valley, as it soon became a drawing card for young and old alike throughout the neighbouring towns, for all those tired of the old, stuffy church services and dying for an alternative. Olaf and Marjeta punctuated every other sentence with "Amen!" or "Hallelujah!", and encouraged people to shout out their praises whenever the spirit moved them to do so. Also, mid service they allowed an extended period of time for sharing of personal testimonies. People would be free to stand up and share in front of all present their struggles, their prayer requests, and their victories achieved through faith. This was unlike anything ever seen in the area.

Olaf and Marjeta had no interest in undermining the work performed by the mainstream churches, and often attended their services to meet the ministers and offer whatever support they could on joint venture evangelical initiatives. The success of the Say Amen Stable had a huge impact on how the mainstream churches arranged their order of service as the others were envious of the huge crowds which flocked to the Say Amen Stable week after week, for the morning, afternoon, and evening services. Most impressive was the percentage of young people in attendance, children whose had long ago stopped going to the established churches. The Gosta family kept renovating the stable as best they could to make more room for the growing number of worshippers, even installing a sound system to reach the overflow crowd seated outside in lawn chairs and on the ground. Slowly but surely, in an attempt to corner some of this newfound market, the traditional area churches started to borrow some of the techniques which were a regular staple at the stable, most noticeably the open time for personal testimonies.

One summer, the young student minister at the Fundy Bay United Baptist church fell under the influence of the Say Amen Stable form of worship, and decided to institute a time for personal testimonies in our staid services. This made many of the church regulars uncomfortable, and for the first couple of weeks, the only ones offering up their personal testimonies were the minister himself, Deaconess Lily Miller, and any of the Gosta family members who happened to be in attendance to show their support for our young preacher. However, eventually the entertainment possibilities started to surface, and once they did, there was no turning back. It all started when twenty two year old Rory Crawford, nicknamed Dorey Plug because of his diminutive size and intelligence, got up one Sunday and gave a rather convoluted testimony about how he had been living in sin for years, couldn't get a job, was being beaten by his parents, but was trying to do the right thing. The part about being beaten generated the most discussion afterwards as many people pooh-poohed it, saying that it was just another case of Rory trying to get attention. After all, this was the same Rory with his simian features and hygiene that Fundy Bay children immortalized in their daily games of tag, saying "Rory's disease, keys!" when they would tag someone who would become the infected one looking to pass it along. Rory had long ago learned the fine art of playing to people's emotions, and jumped from church to church whenever the initial attention he received as a new member started to wane. No matter which church he was attending, he would respond to each and every altar call from preachers looking for new converts to the faith. At the mid summer evangelical services in the Fundy Bay church, Rory would go forward each night.

But to the young people of the church, Rory's testimony was very entertaining, almost lurid. Nothing like we were accustomed to hearing from the others volunteering their testimonies. One thing for sure, we wouldn't miss the service next week. Sure enough, that summer Rory proceeded to present more sensational testimony each week. One week he admitted that he had been a homosexual for two years, but with divine help, had put it all behind him. Apparently possessing a limited memory or assuming that we did, Rory the following week stood up and announced that he had been a homosexual for two and a half years, but had given it up. In another two weeks, the confession had changed to three years. Someone dubbed this Rory's testicular testimony time since he always seemed to dominate the floor telling of things sexual. We couldn't determine if his new found faith was improving his sense of inner peace, but it sure looked like it was doing wonders for his sex life or at least his recollective abilities thereof.

No one wanted to discourage these shocking testimonies, since with each passing week, as Rory's testimonies became more and more outrageous, the crowds grew and grew, with persons waiting impatiently for the singing and praying to end so they could hear Rory's testimony. When the minister would finally ask if there were any personal testimonies, everyone would nudge their friends to wake them up and sit up straight in their pews, since the eagerly anticipated moment was at hand. Feeling the eyes of the congregation upon him, Rory wouldn't disappoint, jumping up right after Deaconess Lily Miller had finished giving thanks for her many blessings. After Rory had completed his unbelievable tale of woe and discredited yet another member of his family or the community, many of the satisfied Johnny-come-lately types in attendance would quickly compose themselves, then get up and leave so they wouldn't have to sit through the sermon. The minister soon cottoned onto this, so placed the personal testimony time at the conclusion of the service, realizing that he was simply the opening act and Rory was the main attraction. Even though the newcomers didn't particularly like this change, they nonetheless kept coming out, bringing more of their friends each week. Soon the Baptist Sunday worship service was the hottest ticket in town, even drawing many of the regulars from the Sanctified Methodist church curious to see what the fuss was all about.

If Rory had been the only one taking part in this sensational testimony time, interest may have started to wane. But Holt (the Dolt) Newcomb, Slow Mo's thirty-five year old son, started to get in on the act, perhaps envious of Rory's notoriety. Holt had earlier caused a sensation in the church when he purchased a lawn tractor for general transportation purposes, and started driving it the mile and a half to church each week, parking it proudly alongside the Chevys and the Chryslers. The fact that he could have gotten to church faster by walking didn't phase Holt. He was the proud owner of a vehicle and he revelled in it. That feeling didn't last long, however, as the RCMP, acting on an anonymous tip, waited outside the church one day until Holt pulled out in high gear to start his drive home, then put on their lights and siren, pulling a startled Holt over and giving him a ticket for driving an unlicensed four wheeled vehicle on the main highway.

With the testimonies, Holt took things to a new level. Unlike Rory, he didn't even try to work any expression of faith into his mad ramblings. He simply got up and started slandering various members of the community who had done him wrong the past week, saying how he was going to seek his revenge. We all got to hear in intimate detail how Ruben Crawford had poured turpentine all over Holt's once luscious vegetable garden, how Tedman Betts had stolen wood from Holt's pile in back of his shed, and how Holt was going to marry fifteen year old Erlina Goomar since she was pregnant with his child, even though Ruben Crawford was telling everybody its was his. The minister would just keep a stunned look on his face throughout Holt's testimony, sometimes trying to break in to suggest that Holt come and see him afterwards to discuss the matter rather than talk about it now in front of everyone. This had no effect on Holt who would always finish his piece before taking his seat.

Soon the drawing power of these testimonials started to get downright inconvenient. With the crush of people now descending on the church each Sunday, you had to arrive half an hour early just to make sure you got your usual seat. But that was a small price to pay to witness such high comedy. Neither Rory nor Holt knew a damn thing about mathematics, but they certainly knew how to appeal to the lowest common denominator of public taste. The testimonies would be rehashed all week long, people arguing about whether it was Rory or Holt who had delivered the most startling and amusing revelation. Finally, the elders of the church came to their senses, and although they hated to lose the crowds and revert to the customary twenty faithful, they convinced the minister to pull the plug on the testimonial time. Besides, they reasoned that all those extra people were doing little more than putting their two cents worth into the service and the collection plate anyway, and we were running the risk of becoming the laughing stock at the annual convention. Despite being so stifled, Holt continued to come to church each Sunday, now presenting his claims outside the church to those mingling about on the front step rather than during the service to the entire congregation. Rory didn't take as kindly to this attempt to silence him, so he took his act on the road, playing various area churches each Sunday until they too ran short on tolerance. When that happened, he would simply continue to other churches on the circuit.

As we reached our teenage years, Sunday School became somewhat of an eye opening experience which we eagerly anticipated each week. It probably wasn't so much to do with our newfound insight into the deeper meaning of biblical truths as it was attributable to having Harman Dicks as our teacher. Now Harman was a lifelong bachelor and Fundy Bay's only self proclaimed non-practising homosexual. We teens assumed this meant he no longer needed to practice since he had it all down pat. Harman was a likeable fellow, very thin with pointy facial features, antiseptic smelling, and possessing a rather maniacal laugh. He good naturedly listened to all the Patrick Fitzgerald and Gerald Fitzpatrick type jokes and the teasing about his last name without ever complaining about harassment.

Harman was also a sympathetic character to many in the community, since he was constantly on pain killers to help him deal with a severe leg injury suffered while he was in the military, leaving him with one leg longer than the other and having to rely on a cane to assist him when walking. He was an expert marksman with a wide assortment of guns hanging over all his doorways inside the house. Harman's door was always open to any of the young people who wanted to come in and visit, challenge his supremacy at croquet, or admire his extensive stamp and coin collection. People in Fundy Bay did not feel bothered by Harman at all. He was accepted for what he was, a harmless down on his luck, fully pensioned ex-military man. And besides, many Fundy Bayers assumed that homosexuality was a curable condition afflicting those who couldn't get a date with someone of the opposite sex. In the scheme of things to the typical Fundy Bayer, the real citizens of concern were "Lightnin" Newcomb who had done time for doing Daisy, and Alphonso Menz, a hermit originally from Austria now living in a tiny shack in Lamar's Cove. Reportedly Alphonso used to catch squirrels, castrate them, and hang their testicles on a string from his ceiling. No one knew why he did this or particularly wanted to ask.

About the only thing concerning most Fundy Bayers was not Harman's sexual orientation but a fear that a tragic accident might occur whenever Harman allowed his young impressionable visitors to go outside to shoot target practice with real bullets. Of course, more worldly visitors to Fundy Bay who maintained summer homes in the community took a different, more cautious view of Harman, not allowing their young sons to go anywhere near his property. The real Fundy Bayers shrugged this off as big city paranoia, having yet more evidence of how urban life destroys a person's faith in their fellow human beings.

As teenagers, we never really thought much about Harman's method of teaching Sunday School, but occasionally even we would have to admit that it was unorthodox. The entire class was comprised of boys aged thirteen to fifteen. Harman occasionally tried to pass along some relevant Biblical teaching, so would offer a twenty-five cent reward to the first person to answer each of the workbook questions or find and read out selected text. While we may not have come any closer to understanding the true meaning of the lesson, we certainly got cutthroat when it came to competing for those quarters, often ending in an exchange of punches which Harman had to settle by giving quarters to both of the hotheaded parties.

While Harman proceeded to speed read the day's lesson, we would be busy none to discretely looking at nude girlie pictures someone had cut out of their father's discarded skin mags. Harman would then move on to relate to us various stories about his life, for example how he had become a homosexual. The story of how his betrothed had jilted him at the altar made us feel terribly sorry for the guy and we gained a glimmer of understanding of why he had turned to homosexuality: out of spite, to teach his girlfriend a lesson or two. While the other classes were methodically working away to complete their workbook and memorize scripture, Harman would tell us stories about parties in Fundy Bay he had gone to, not that long ago, where several of the men ended up undressed and in compromising situations. He wouldn't tell us who these closeted men were but he said it would surprise us if we knew. The way he looked at us with a glint in his eyes somehow made us momentarily suspect our own fathers, wondering if it could possibly by true. Naw, but it might be our best friend's father.

Harman liked to tell the tale of a Fundy Bay party he was at where an unnamed person was bragging about the length of his manhood, only to have another person call his bluff. As the story went, bets were placed as to how many quarters, lined up end on end, the braggart could swipe off the table with one flick of his flaccid lance. We all became instantly green with envy when Harman concluded that the braggart broke the bank that day, successfully swiping twelve quarters off the table. As we all sat in Sunday School in silence, contemplating this masterful stroke and trying to calculate in our heads how many quarters we could have displaced, Harman mused aloud, "what do you suppose you'd do if you had a tool that big? I guess you'd have to stick it up through your belt!". Well, that was an option we hadn't considered, and it left us momentarily stunned, as Harman simply laughed his maniacal laugh and went on to another story about those stretching the anatomical envelope. If Harman was in a really good mood, we could usually talk him into concluding the day's lesson with our favourite trick of his at the back of the church, where he would stand upright, take his double jointed leg and hook his foot around behind his neck. This would draw a lot of stares from the other classes situated in the three remaining corners of the sanctuary, as they struggled to imagine what lesson we must be studying.

Occasionally we would share these stories with our mothers when they would ask us what we had learned in Sunday School that day. About the only response we would get was, "why, that's terrible. Harman shouldn't be talking about those things in Sunday School!". But nothing further would be done since the church was low on volunteers, and after all, Harman did have a good rapport with the boys. So next Sunday we would pick up where we had left off the previous week.

Every so often, not too frequently in the winter but occasionally during the summer, visitors would attend our Sunday morning worship services. If these guests included any teenage girls, all us boys would be unable to concentrate for the rest of the service, the adrenaline pumping as we did our best to act cool and create enough of a commotion to get the new girl to turn around and take notice. This generally meant that we had to act more smart alecky than usual, testing the patience of our elders with our disturbing outbursts of forced snickering meant to create speculation about our witticisms and actions. Generally all we succeeded in doing was convincing the guest parents that we were complete cretins, not worthy of another glance from their much more sophisticated daughter.

While we occasionally enjoyed such visits during the Sunday morning church service, it was extremely rare to get such newcomers in Sunday School, unless a cousin of one of the regulars happened to be visiting that Sunday and decided to come along for the experience. One Sunday morning when I was fourteen, sitting in the church waiting for Sunday school to commence, still feeling half groggy from sitting up late the night before to watch the hockey game on television, my eyes suddenly opened up wide as I spotted a beautiful angel walking through the doors in the company of my first cousin Justine Reeves. I couldn't take my eyes off her: she was the most beautiful girl I had ever seen in my entire life. I am sure my mouth dropped open as I stared at her long, crimped golden hair, her slender physique, her perfect features, her beautiful smile. My cousin and classmate, Logan Reeves, must have seen something in my mesmerized stare, informing me, "that's Cassandra Miller, Lily Miller's thirteen year old granddaughter and Harman's niece. She lives in Dartmouth, but she's down for the weekend. She stayed at our place last night."

Whoa now, Paul. I tried desperately to compose myself and act nonchalant. But inside I was burning up with envy that Logan knew this city girl. He had actually spent the night under the same roof as her. He could actually look directly into her eyes and carry on a conversation with her without fear of rejection or provoking repulsion on her part. And I hated him because of it, for having a scarless face that so many girls seemed to find pleasing. As Cassandra walked by, she said in a melodic voice, "hi, Logan. Hope you have a good time in class.

See you later.", and took a seat two rows in front of us alongside Justine. Try as I might, I couldn't take my eyes off the back of Cassandra's head. Telepathically I urged her to turn sideways, even briefly, so I could get a glimpse of her perfect profile one more time, althewhile conscious that I couldn't allow myself to be seen by her. All of a sudden, I felt so self conscious of my appearance that I wanted to run and hide, in fear that she might be repulsed by my looks and I would never have a chance to win her affection.

When we were dismissed to class, I allowed myself only fleeting glances in her direction, nonetheless keeping accurate moment by moment tabs on her movements. As she ascended to the balcony, my sweet Juliette, I went over in my mind time and time again each characteristic of her face, each word I had overheard her speak, each toss of her head. That morning I didn't care when I failed to win a single quarter playing "look up the verse". As Sunday School faded into church, I kept my distance from Cassandra, fearing a sideways glance from her that might reveal my deformity. I felt that the entire morning was going by much too fast, and yet at the same time, much too slow. I wanted to soak up her beauty, but at the same time, I was terrified that I might be spotted. I wouldn't be able to bear it if she was like the others and gave me the piteous looks I often saw in the eyes of the well intended strangers I would meet. Not her. Not Cassandra.

As the church service finally concluded, my mother proceeded to stroll over to Cassandra's parents to carry on an extended conversation, apparently looking around for Johnny and I to do introductions. I had bolted out the door and was watching the proceedings like a hawk from a safe distance. I recorded in my mind every smile Cassandra offered in response to my mother's comments. Finally, when Mom led Cassandra and her parents outside, I retreated to the back seat of the car, exchanging small talk with Dad who was too busy rolling a cigarette to notice this vision of loveliness not more than thirty feet from where we were sitting. On the way home I was very interested to discover that Mom had taught Cassandra's father for several years back in her teaching days. That morning, once we got home, I used ever trick in the book to slyly and nonchalantly get Mom to spill everything she knew about Cassandra and her family. All the while I was imagining what Cassandra and Logan might be up to at that very minute, hoping that she had at least noticed me in church, then hoping she hadn't, and wondering to myself if I would ever see her beautiful face again.

P. B. Russell

△ △ △

CHAPTER TEN
The Hospital: A Stiff Upper Lip

It is undoubtedly hard for many people to pinpoint with any certainty their earliest memory. In my case, it was aided somewhat by a rather traumatic experience, a series of prolonged stays at the children's hospital without parental escort and 100 miles from home. Being born with a cleft palate, more commonly referred to by that heinous term "harelip", I was soon scheduled for numerous bouts of corrective surgery to be performed in the years leading up to kindergarten. Throughout my later childhood, while I couldn't talk to my mother or father about my condition, I would turn to the dictionary to gain some small understanding of what it meant to have a cleft palate. Unfortunately, Webster's had very little to say, except to point out that it was a congenital fissure of the roof of the mouth. Not too enlightened by that definition, I would gird up my loins and flip to the definition of "harelip". That added a bit more clarity, noting that it was a congenital deformity in which the upper lip is split like that of a hare. I then turned to our two volume Columbia Viking Desk Encyclopedia, hoping for some real insight. Once I got over the annoyed feeling of finding no reference to "cleft palate", I would turn to the "H" section and read that harelip was a congenital cleft or split of the upper lip which occurs most often with an associated cleft palate. Hmmmm, that was interesting. It seemed to suggest that "harelip" and "cleft palate" were two distinct conditions. Strange. After pondering that for a while, I continued reading. The entry went on to note that it is a disfigurement, with speech and eating problems present, and then concluded by noting that it is correctible by early surgery. Yeah, now that just about described the package I had received. After being satisfied with that lesson in biology, I would quickly turn my attention to other subjects, returning to my research to look up the definitions of sex, vagina, and intercourse.

As the most amplified definition of "harelip" noted, it was a condition which could be corrected by early surgery. However, this was not an option to be entered into lightly by a simple country farmer struggling to feed a family of four in a time before universal healthcare and without the benefit of a private health plan. But being poor did nothing to dull Dad and Mom's sense of love for and obligation to their newborn son, the one with the split lip and flattened, almost non-existent nose. In later years Mom often recalled how when the doctor first held me up to her for viewing, she burst into tears, saddened by the thought of the obstacles and torment that this little life would face. It is a sobering thought to know that at that magical moment when you are first introduced to the world, you brought sorrow to the hearts of your parents and evoked pity in others. Not exactly the image that most children have of their own birth. Not really a good lead in to the rah rah "you can be anything you want to be" speech. It is also humbling to realize that in some cultures and at certain times in history I would have been flung over the nearest cliff once born, as this obvious weakness would have been a sign from the gods that they found disfavour with me.

Mom often told me though that everyone who came to see me commented on how bright I looked, because of the glint in my eye. Now, I wasn't sure if this was simply a matter of people searching to say something kind, or if they really meant it. Also, this emphasis on how bright I looked seemed rather insulting, as if people assumed that with the facial deformity automatically came some degree of mental disability: "the kid is harelipped, so it follows that he must be harebrained".

Mom usually recounted during these sessions that she had been very sick during most of the time she was pregnant with me, reassuring me that therefore it wouldn't be passed on to my children. As was her custom on most issues, however, Mom would hedge her bet and note that Aunt Melanie, one of the family historians, had told her that she recalled hearing that one of our ancestors reportedly had a cleft palate also.

In any event, life being what it is, things go on with or without answers to the "why" questions so often posed, those usually cast heavenward while contemplating a hellish future. So Mom and Dad agreed that little Eddie, as I was known at birth, would have the necessary surgery, to better enable him to lead that elusive normal life. For many, normalcy would undoubtedly sound like a rather uninspired, mundane aspiration for one's child. However, in my situation, attaining average was a goal worth striving for.

So, during my first five years of life, I endured six different facial operations. The good Lord only knows where the money came from. Mom and Dad did not anguish over it for long, but of course, such is the essence of faith. Apparently Great Aunt Gracienne helped pay some of the initial costs with money she saved when she plucked the dentures out of her deceased Aunt Muriel's mouth and discovered that they were a perfect fit. When people said Great Aunt Gracienne had her Aunt Muriel's smile, they weren't joking. Or come to think of it, perhaps they were. In any event, Great Aunt Gracienne's charity proved to be short lived when she and Mom got in an argument about a silly matter. Seems that Great Aunt Gracienne wanted to pass along some used blankets to Mom to be used on my bed. Now everyone knows that you don't offer used bedding to a prideful family, no matter how clean and well embroidered the blankets are. Of course, to the woman with the second hand grin and the one who quilted the items in question, this reeked of snobbery and impracticality, and what better way to make the point that to withdraw further contributions to the charity case? Besides, how necessary was the surgery anyway?

I am not sure what was worse; the prolonged stays at the hospital or the drive to the hospital. The problem was, Dad was no good at confrontation, and Mom would get emotional at the most innocuous of occasions, so neither of them would ever inform me when it was time to go to the hospital for another operation. Come to think of it, no one ever explained to me why I needed to go to the hospital.

Cosmetic surgery is very hard to explain to a child. Obviously, the child does not feel sick, so it seems ridiculous to suggest that you need to go to the hospital. As well, as a toddler I had no appreciation for the fact that I looked different from other children. Vanity hadn't set in yet at that stage. I think I rarely ever looked in a mirror, and when I did, all I saw was a bright eyed boy looking back at me. Also, I hadn't encountered anyone yet that had made me feel odd. Hell, in Fundy Bay, every other person seemed to be "unique".

In any event, the day for going to the hospital was invariable a Sunday, and it would commence like any other Sunday, except that I soon noted how quiet everyone was, and how Mom seemed to be perpetually daubing her eyes with a kleenex. Hey, not a good sign here. Also, there was never any talk about going to church. Now that was weird. Mom never let us get out of going to church. Mom always made us get up early on a Sunday, which didn't seem right. After all, if God got to rest on the sabbath, why couldn't we? But on these hospital trip days, I noted that the usual Sunday wake up time somehow got ignored. Another weird thing was that I would see Mom packing a small suitcase. This was another bad sign. I knew Mom and Dad couldn't be going anywhere since in their entire married life, they had only slept away from home once, and that was on their honeymoon.

Meanwhile, in the midst of all the obvious preparations, in true journalistic style, I would pose a penetrating question, such as "Are we going somewhere?". Mom would respond without looking in my direction, "Yes, honey, we are going on a trip to Halifax today.". Well, not all was lost. We did sometimes make the four hour trek to visit Mom's sister, Aunt Allie. My brother was very skilful at sidestepping any questioning about our destination, since he was obviously awaiting his reward for honouring the silence. Since no one was volunteering anything, I usually went back to my playing, although I had a sinking feeling deep inside that I couldn't attribute to anything in particular.

Being a rather long drive, made longer by the expectation of one or two flat tires along the journey, we would set out before lunch. Mom always packed a great lunch for us to eat in the car along the way, and that was something to look forward to. Our family always took Sunday drives since it was the only way that we spent time together as a family all week, excluding meal times. Although Dad was a workaholic farmer, even he could not stand up to Mom's "thou shalt rest on the Sabbath" lectures. So, with great resignation, Dad would minimize his Sunday chores to the milking of the cows, which was conveniently scheduled precisely at church time, and the bottling of the milk. The rest of the day belonged to the family. So a Sunday drive to Halifax did not seem overly suspicious. Some cause for concern, but nothing to get alarmed at yet. As the drive wore on, the sombre mood of the carload would start to clear the planks out of my eyes. In the back seat, my brother seemed to keep his eyes fixed on something outside the window, rarely looking in my direction. Mom's usual incessant humming seemed to be replaced by a litany of small talk and chatter, of the type that didn't need a response.

Before too long, reality would come crashing in on me. Almost always, it would take a question from me to get the issue out on the table.

"Are we going to the hospital", I would ask, in that deploring tone that melts a parent's heart.

At that moment, Mom would no longer avoid the issue.

"Yes, dear, we have to go to the hospital. But you won't be there long. Your operation is on Tuesday, and the doctor says that you should be able to come home next Saturday."

Invariably my eyes would well up with tears, and being despondent, I would either stare at the floor, or look at my brother for solace. Or perhaps for protection.

"Are you going to stay with me?"

"No, dear, we can't. Dad has to look after the cows."

"Can Johnny stay with me?"

"No, honey, Johnny has to come home with us. There wouldn't be any place for him to stay. But we'll phone you while you're in the hospital. And you know the nurses. They always treat you nicely. And Veronica will be there."

Now Veronica Collins was a cousin of ours who used to live across the road from us in Fundy Bay. She was a tall, thin, gentle, beautiful woman, who oozed charm and sophistication. She visited our house a lot, and Mom knew how much Johnny and I liked her and her entire family. She was now a nurse at the children's hospital, and knowing that she was there was comforting somehow. A familiar face, someone who would look out for me. Johnny and I agreed that we would like to marry Veronica when we got older, if she was still available. Trouble is, we also had thoughts of marrying our cousin Erica Reeves from Fundy Bay. Of course, she was only five years older than my brother, and not nearly as mature as Veronica.

I almost never questioned the reasons why I had to go to the hospital. It had something to do with my mouth, but I couldn't understand the explanation anyway, so why bother. The remainder of the drive usually consisted of Mom daubing her eyes incessantly while wondering as she did with every Halifax trip if Dad would remember to take that left hand turn off Robie Street, Dad clearing his throat periodically, and my brother now assuring me that "hey, Paul, it's going to be alright. I'll be there to get you next week. And Mom says that we can buy you a present for when you get home."

With that, I usually slumped into a morass of self pity and amazement that I hadn't been able to read the signs before. Why was it always me that had to go to the hospital? Why didn't Johnny have to go? Was this going to hurt? Who would I play with? I always hoped that Dad would somehow forget to take that left off Robie, but never fail, he would make it first try every time, after which Mom would compliment him on his ability. As far as I was concerned, damn that fire station on the corner, since I knew without that landmark, I had a chance to get lost with the family and miss my date with Doctor faceless.

Once we arrived at the hospital, everything would become a blur of Dad looking for a parking spot, Mom admonishing him for parking too far away, going through door after door, being hit with that familiar smell once inside, filling out of papers, checking into some antiseptic room with no charm but plenty of heat and other children, althewhile escorted by some hospital employee who would smile at you while your parents were there but who you knew would forget your name once you were alone.

Once in the room, Mom would do her best to get me settled, showing me all the nice toys, colouring books, and crayons that she would be leaving with me. Johnny would usually hop on the bed and explain to me how comfortable it was. Dad would be looking out the window trying to figure out which way was North. Mom would also be saying "Hi" to all the other kids and their parents, hoping she could establish some friendships for me before they had to leave.

It is true that misery loves company, since these parents seemed to become instant best of friends, talking outwardly about how nice and bright the hospital was, while telepathically or otherwise sending off notes about how heartbroken they felt to have to leave their little children alone in this strange place. I was always glad that my big brother was there, to let these little terrors know that if they were mean to me, a day of reckoning would come. Nothing spoken, of course, just a few subtle messages.

"Johnny, you're coming up to get me next Saturday, right?", I would question in a slightly louder than normal voice.

Once reassured, I would usually cast a glance at my soon to be roommates, to see if they were suitably shaken. After what seemed like many awkward minutes of superficial chatting about the benefits of crank-up beds, hospital food, and the lovely view of the city from fifteen floors up, it was time for the family to go.

About this time Dad would usually start fumbling through his wallet to leave behind some spending money, or start searching through the hospital for a place where he could buy me some ice cream to leave in the small kitchen down the hallway. Johnny would usually hug me and pat me on the back and again reassure me.

"You'll be alright. I'll see you next week. Take care of yourself, little bro".

Mom would then smother me in hugs and kisses, and would start crying, despite all her earlier attempt to be brave for me. I would reciprocate, tears running down my cheeks, while I hugged her with all my might. I didn't want to let go, because I knew when I did, they would leave, and I would be alone, in this building housing hundreds of children, all like me, scared and alone. I was afraid that maybe they wouldn't come back for me, since I didn't really know why they were abandoning me anyway. Maybe they were lying about coming back.

"I want to come home", I sobbed.

"You'll be fine, dear,", Mom said vainly, trying to convince herself as much as me.

"Stop shaking. We love you very much. We'll be thinking about you all the time. The nurses will take care of you. Veronica will drop by to see you tonight. We have to go, now."

At that, Dad usually would pat me on the back and say "see you later", in that unconvincing, somewhat dismissing tone used by cashiers whom you don't even know after they give you your change and you start to walk away.

Then off they went. I could tell by the quick deliberate steps that Mom was taking that she was upset. Dad was no good with words, so he would not be able to comfort her. She would have to work it out herself. No one looked back, except Johnny, to give me one last wave.

When they disappeared into the elevator, I turned around and saw all the children and parents looking at me, all with that understanding, sympathetic look, but with no ability to help. I would then walk to the window, to have some privacy as I wiped away my tears, and to hope for one last glance at my family. It was then that a feeling of being disconnected from the ground swept over me; being from the country, this was the only time I ever got into a building higher than two floors. In fact, I felt disconnected from every reference point in my life. And as I watched the unrecognizable dots move around on the streets below, I became numb with fear of whatever lay ahead.

The children's hospital in Halifax wasn't that bad as hospitals go. Clean. Hot. A place for everything, and everything in its place. Bright lights. Lots of nurses. Ice cream two times a week. Wide halls. White walls. White floors. White uniforms. Come to think of it, everything seemed to be white, except for the cleaning staff. They were easily recognizable not only by their blue uniforms, but also since they were the only ones who seemed to enjoy their jobs, and who would take time to smile at the children.

I was in the oral surgery dormitory, along with others who were having similar cosmetic makeovers. This wasn't particularly bad, except at night time. Most of the children were pre-school age, and many like myself did not have the luxury of daily visits from loved ones to remain connected to the outside world. At night, the anguish of the children seemed to surface, even though they had seemingly been fairly well adjusted during the day. In many cases, it was the pain associated with stitches which seemed to pick the nighttime to tighten, and of surgery which these fragile ones were being asked to bear without complaint. For others, it was remorse over a favourite toy which had mysteriously vanished from their night stand or locker during the day.

Some were dealing with the sorrow of realizing that they were away from home, a fact reinforced by an unexpected nocturnal phone call from Ma and Pa and little Sis, which brought many tears but seldom cheer. These phone calls invariably came at night, just when the children were settling down for bed, preparing to be left alone with their thoughts and fears in the dark cave of a room, hoping for sleep, and at a time when the nurses would scold and soon after threaten anyone keeping the others awake by crying.

I remember such a call from my family. Honestly, once you have been at the hospital alone for several days, being such a young age, you soon start to forget that you even have a family. If you do think of them, it is in distant, somewhat uncertain terms, such as when you are contemplating Santa Claus or the Easter Bunny. I even would forget what they looked like. For some reason, they never thought to leave me a family photo for any of my hospital trips. That would at least have kept them alive in my mind and heart, and given me a sense of connection to something out there.

One night Nurse Curly Hair informed me that I was to come to the phone, as someone wanted to talk to me. I very gingerly took the huge receiver in my hand, and quietly, almost in a whisper, asked "hello?".

"Hi, dear, it's Mom. How are you?"

"Mom?", I asked disbelieving.

Did I have a Mom? What did she look like? All of a sudden, my head felt like it was going to explode. A rush of images and memories filled my mind, and I realized at that moment that I had a home and this wasn't it.

"Where are you? Can I come home?"

"Soon dear. We all love you very much. We hope your operation goes well tomorrow. Johnny wants to talk with you. Hold on."

I then tried to hold back this wave of self pity and sorrow that was rapidly enveloping me.

"Hi, Paul!" I heard Johnny say in his big brother tone. I couldn't contain my composure much longer.

"Is Dad there? I want to speak with Dad."

"Dad's in the barn doing chores", Johnny answered, "how are you doing?"

I wouldn't be distracted. I had to hear Dad's voice.

"I want to talk to Dad. Can you get Dad?"

It was then that I started to cry.

"I want to talk to Dad!" I sobbed.

I don't know why I wanted to talk to Dad. Perhaps it was to complete the family circle. Perhaps because Dad represented my best chance at a rescue. Maybe I just needed reassurance from my father that I would be OK. Realizing that things had irreparably deteriorated, Johnny passed the phone to Mom who tried in vain to calm me down.

"It's OK, honey. Dad is in the barn. He will talk to you next time. We all love you. Don't cry. Everything will be OK. We are looking forward to seeing you. The doctor says you can come home on Saturday if everything goes well."

What did this mean to me? I didn't even know when Saturday was. All I knew was, my family hadn't forgotten about me, but neither were they with me. I didn't belong in this hospital. This wasn't my bed afterall. I wanted to talk to Dad.

Seeing that I was beyond comfort, Nurse Curly Hair took the phone from me, and spoke a few dismissing words to Mom, then led me back to this cell she kept calling my room, althewhile trying to sooth me with false and empty words. That night I sobbed while I lay in bed, being comforted periodically by my cellmate in the next bed, another faceless child in a heartless world.

For others, the nighttime sadness and crying were nothing more than a fear of the dark, especially of the half dark in which unfamiliar shapes and shadows abound. I remember trying to comfort a boy lying in the bed next to me. I couldn't raise up to see him, or him me, but I guessed he was about my age, no more than three. His sobbing was interrupted only by a few brief phrases.

"My mouth hurts"; "I want my mummy!".

I tried to help, while reminding him, "Don't make noise or the nurse will come in and get mad".

I remember saying repeating several times, "It's okay, it's okay", althewhile myself sinking into a sea of doubt.

I didn't know why, but I felt myself getting sad, not only for my roommate, but also for myself. It's a delicate balancing act in an institution such as a hospital. As long as everyone seems to act calm and moderately well adjusted, you feel that things were alright. It couldn't be that bad if no one else was complaining. However, as soon as someone breaks down and says any of the forbidden words ("Mummy", "Daddy", and "Home"), then the scales seemed to fall from everyone's eyes and we could no longer be duped. Then widescale self pity sets in and the nurses have a lot of rationalizing to do to assure us that everyone is okay after all. In this instance, my comforting was to no avail as Nurse Crooked Nose came into the room, and as I had warned, scolded my friend, telling him that he was a big boy and shouldn't cry like a baby. If he didn't stop she was going to have to turn out all the lights. Now this didn't appeal to me a great deal, so I chimed in "he's sad because he misses his Mummy and Daddy".

This was an ill advised move since Nurse Crooked Nose turned her attention to me.

"Have you been picking at your stitches? I'm going to have to tie your hands."

"No", I said, "I haven't picked my stitches!"

"Well, maybe you didn't mean to, but it looks like you picked at them during your sleep."

Now this hadn't occurred to me. How could I know if I was guilty of this crime or not? I didn't even know what stitches were, let alone know what I might have been doing to them during those forgotten times when I actually slept. Nonetheless, I assured Nurse Crooked Nose,"I won't pick my stitches while I sleep, I promise."

I must have gotten the nurse at a good moment, or maybe it was my roommate's ongoing crying, but she turned away from me and simply told him, "Now that's enough. No more of that. You're just going to make yourself sick".

Somehow, this overwhelming display of humanity and compassion seemed to appease my roommate, to the point where he was left with only a few sniffles, and intermittent gasps for air.

A hospital can seem like a scary place at night, even if the door is left open, when you are lying in an oversized bed, with your arms strapped to the bedrails so that you will not pick at your stitches during the night. The sound of heels hitting the well polished hall floors invariably interrupt the few moments of silence when elevator doors are not opening or shutting, conversations are being muted, children's groans are silenced, and there is a lull in the monotone announcements being made over the P.A. system.

The morning always brought new, albeit often unpleasant surprises. Such as, what happened to your friend who was in the bed beside you when you went to sleep? Questions like these generally were unsatisfactorily answered by the nameless nursing staff, since after all, you were not one of the family and did not have an inherent right to know. You couldn't help feeling that maybe he was being punished in some other room because he had shed more than his allotted number of tears the night before. Or you might discover that today was your day, and you were the one being wheeled off for more surgery, a fact that had been explained to you by some doctor yesterday, but which you had forgotten by lunch time. Doctors always seemed overly familiar for someone you had never met and didn't trust. The fact that they knew your name was of little comfort. Anyone with a grade 3 education could read your name from the chart at the foot of your bed. Why would you trust someone who rarely looked up from his pad of paper while he talked to you? And when he did, it was simply to pry your mouth open with his oversized fingers, or to test the elasticity of your upper lip.

The day of the operation usually found me in a resigned mood. The nurses and doctors had been prepping me for this moment for some time, perhaps trying to make up for the rather abrupt manner in which Mom and Dad dropped me off in this place.

It is hard to say which was the worst part of the operation day; it may very well have been that moment when a good humoured, no nonsense orderly arrived at the bedside, transferring me quickly and effortlessly to a bed on wheels, and then started the ride to the operating room. It was then that I knew the gig was up. At this stage, it did no good to complain. I had no rights. No one was going to save me from what lay ahead.

As the orderly chatted aimlessly about how "they" were waiting for me down in room 2A, I simply felt mesmerized by the blur of florescent lights and chrome whirring by. The trip on the elevator was the first exercise in humiliation this day, as the nervous passengers now had something interesting to stare at, saving them from having to simply watch the light move amongst the floor numbers in sequence. At these moments, I always wished that the orderly would do the humane thing and allow me to cover my face with a sheet or towel, so that the curious onlookers would have to go home unsatisfied. Nonetheless, that trip was soon over, and I was being whisked along a corridor of a much more noticeably antiseptic smelling section of the hospital. Soon, I was pushed through a last section of doors, into a room where all of sudden, everyone was my best friend.

"Hello, Paul, how are you today?"

"We've been waiting for you, Paul", another masked stranger would offer.

Being in a hospital, hearing your name being spoken was something to be dreaded, rather than enjoyed. It was not like hearing "under the B, 16" when you could yell "BINGO" victoriously, or hearing your name when the roll is called up yonder. It was more the feeling you get when your name is called when you are cooling your heels in the waiting room at the dentist's office. You knew it meant that you had just been singled out of the lineup for some tortuous procedure or discipline.

Looking around the operating room, it was a nightmarish scene. Everything looked very stark and futuristic, covered in chrome and reflecting bright lights. The masked crowd then usually started some inane chit chat amongst themselves, no doubt to give the impression that they perform this operation with no more attention or effort than would be required to change a light bulb, or to drive to the office every day. At that moment someone who appeared to be the chief honcho bent over me and said, "Hi, remember me?".

I had to assume that it was the same quack who visited me in my room the day before, Doctor Jawbreaker, although you could never be certain since like everyone else, he had a mask covering most of his face. What was there to like about this guy, anyway? To begin with, had anyone checked his credentials? I mean, after all, the reason I had to keep coming back to this hell hole is because he couldn't seem to get it right. Why couldn't I get a doctor who could do the surgery properly the first time, to save me from all these repeat efforts? However, since all my rights were suspended once I had been abandoned at this place, it wasn't much good raising a ruckus now. Might as well simply nod complacently, give a few obligatory "Ah, ha's" as they chattered while slipping a large mask over my face, make a few last minute mental notes of the surroundings, and hope that awful ether smell would soon dissipate. My final thoughts were usually wondering why these masked persons were laughing when the person who clamped the mask on my face responded to my complaints with a laugh, telling me to simply blow the smell away. Only later did it occur to me that I was being duped into achieving his end goal.

When one is three years old, alone in a hospital without any visitors for weeks on end, time really becomes a lost concept. You could be there for three days or three weeks. It really doesn't matter. The only distinguishing parts of the day are meal times, play time, and when day passes into night. Everything else is a blur of sameness, day after day, week after week. Even the operations seemed to be the same for each hospital trip.

Play time was usually fairly enjoyable. At least we were excused from our stuffy rooms, and free to mingle with our peers. On the way to the play room we would all predictably glance into the two rooms down the hall, where all the burn victims were housed. These children got sympathy from everyone, including us. Hell, at least we could walk around, and go play. Daily one of our troupe would ask "are they going to be OK?", as we passed the burn unit rooms, a question inspired by the constant and unmistakable groans coming from those horribly scarred children confined to their beds. Sometimes, however, during these play times, something so awful or humiliating would happen that you would actually ask one of the nurses if you could go back to your room.

One such incident happened to me one day when, in the midst of my playing, I realized that I needed to pee very badly. As I looked around, I noticed at that moment that there was no adult in attendance. This was trouble, since I had no idea where the bathroom was. Being three years old, I had no desire to pee myself, but I could feel my ability to hold back the flood diminishing. Just at that moment, Nurse Fat Butt popped her head into the room. I rushed over and exclaimed, "I need to pee!". Underestimating my need, she said, "OK, just wait a minute", as she darted across the room to break up a tug of war that had started over one of the favourite trucks. By the time she got back, I was desperate, beyond words.

"I need to pee really bad!", I exclaimed, the exclamation point being the way I had my legs tightly crossed.

She then led me to the bathroom only to discover that someone else was inside. "Just wait a minute", she told me. After what seemed like an eternity, the bathroom door opened and a boy I didn't recognize came out. By this time, my teeth were practically floating. Nurse Fat Butt started to help me take off my pants, struggling to bend down that far, but it was no good. I couldn't hold it any longer. I lost all control of my bladder, and the pee just gushed out, all over the floor and all over Nurse Fat Butt's stocking and shoes. This was greeted with outrage on her part. She tried to reposition my body so that I could hit the toilet, with only minimal success.

I didn't need to be scolded, since I felt terrible. After all, I was three years old and had been toilet trained since I was one and a half. Nonetheless, once the downpour had subsided, Nurse Fat Butt had to deal with the problem of a humble child whose clothes were all soaked, not to mention the soiled room and her own damp clothing. I'm not sure if it was done to further humiliate me or simply to solve a problem, but she stripped all my clothes off, dried me with some paper towel, then told me to wait in the room for a moment. I felt fairly certain that she was going to get me a change of clothes, so that I could retreat to my room with at least some dignity intact. When she came back, she said, "here, this will do for now", and produced a large sized diaper for me to wear.

I was horrified.

"I don't wear diapers anymore. They're for babies!"

"Well", she remarked, "big boys don't usually pee their pants, do they? And besides, this is all I could find. You can change into your clothes when we get to your room."

There was obviously no arguing with her, as she quickly wrapped the diaper around my bottom, leaving the rest of my body bare. With that, she flung open the bathroom door, grabbed my hand, and led me out into the room where all eyes suddenly were on me. The laughter was spontaneous, the sight of this three year old boy in nothing but a tight fitting diaper, holding Nurse Fat Butt's hand, obviously tickling the funny bones of all age groups. The walk to the far end of the hospital had to be the longest I had ever experienced. For one thing, I was cold. The hard floors felt cool on my bare feet. Everyone we met either laughed out loud, pointed, or snickered. I was so humiliated that I decided to stare at the floor, being practically dragged along by a noticeably perturbed nurse. I then wondered if anything could ever be this bad again. I was never so happy to see my sauna bath of a room, with my familiar bed and slippers to the side. I decided then and there that I would never speak to Nurse Fat Butt again.

For me, being an optimistic little sod, I eagerly awaited each meal and each play time, hoping that something great would happen. It didn't have to be stupendous, just something to indulge my senses. More specifically, I couldn't wait for snack time each morning in the play room. That was the highlight. Sure, the toys were okay too, but invariably, just when I started to enjoy playing with a toy, some pushy kid or peace loving nurse would take it from me all in the name of sharing. This generally left me to figure out once again how to propel the patrol car with two wheels missing.

As far as I was concerned, snack time was like an oasis in the middle of a parched dessert of sensory deprivation. And it wasn't the dry cookies that I waited for.

No, it was the liquid refreshment. Cold chocolate milk, right out of the fridge. Now this was living. I never got chocolate milk at home, since all our milk came from our own cows and they all seemed to be the single flavour breed. I cherished my little cup of chocolate milk. If nothing else good happened all day, it didn't matter. The chocolate milk coated my stomach and my consciousness for 24 hours until the next serving.

There was one major threat on the horizon, however, one which I had to face every morning. It came in the form of apple juice. I hated apple juice. It was sour and thin. It was vile beyond all comprehension. Why would anyone drink apple juice when they could have chocolate milk, ambrosia of the gods? The problem I was faced with was that when Nurse Snack Time brought out the tray of liquid refreshments each morning, if contained an equal number of apple juices and chocolate milks, all poured in the same size Dixie cups. Nurse Snack Time seemed to have a back problem as she would only bend over slightly, lowering the tray only enough so that the bottom of the cups were at eye level. I would always pause, trying to gauge which cups seemed to hold the darker substance, surmising that chocolate milk obviously was darker than apple juice.

Hedging my bet, I would usually say, "chocolate milk, please". Trouble is, Nurse Snack Time always seemed to be in hurry, and didn't appreciate my reasons for lingering over this decision, while I inspected the tray of cups. Ignoring my specific request, she would say daily "Hurry up and pick one", sometimes punctuated with "do you want a drink or not?". In all fairness to her, she did have both of her hands full carrying the massive tray with drinks enough for a small army, so I can concede the fact that she couldn't have handed me the requested ambrosia. Therefore, faced with imperfect information and a non-obliging nurse, I would have to go with my gut instinct and the results of my shade test. I can still feel the bitter disappointment and despondency that would come over me when I would lower the cup from its lofty perch and discover that once again, I had selected the apple juice. My attempts to trade it for a chocolate milk were always misunderstood as an attempt to get two drinks, and were usually rebuffed with "you chose that one, now drink it, it's good for you", or "you've already got one. Move along", or "I haven't got time to play games. If you don't want a drink, don't take one next time".

I would be left with no other choice but to let someone else have my drink, or try to leave it on the floor in some quiet part of the play room, envious of all those mocking children who were licking chocolate milk from their perfect lips. I would then vow that tomorrow it would be different, that I would make a more intelligent choice tomorrow, and hope that perhaps I would grow a few inches taller overnight.

One of the few moments in the hospital when I would truly feel peaceful was on Sunday morning when I would go to the chapel along with a handful of children and nurses. I don't recall how Nurse Sunday knew to come to get me, since most of the roommates opted for playtime rather than church time. I never really understood what the minister was saying, but something about the way he said it made me feel warm inside. As I sat there on the plain bench, with my feet dangling over the side, sitting next to Nurse Sunday, I felt as if I was going to be alright, and that God cared for me. I felt like there was someone or something bigger than all of us, keeping watch over us all. There was something soothing about listening to the people warbling to the hymns, as the pianist valiantly played on despite missing note after note. No one seemed to mind, and even though I couldn't read the words, I would hum along as best I could. And sometimes, if I concentrated hard enough, I could almost imagine myself sitting in the back pew at the Fundy Bay Baptist church, sitting next to my brother as the minister droned on. The picture of Jesus on the wall even looked a lot like the one hanging in the Baptist church back in Fundy Bay. After being away from home for what seemed like an eternity, any familiar object, no matter how inconsequential, was capable of delivering a great psychological boost. All the grown ups seemed to take a special interest in the children who attended, and they would ask us how we were doing, why we were in the hospital, and if we had had our operation yet. I would usually pray a silent prayer that God would allow me to go home soon, and for the first time, despite all the earlier guarantees given by family, doctors, and nurses, I would actually allow myself to believe that it might happen.

I don't recall how or why it happened, but there were many moments during the day when I was allowed simply to roam the corridors, chatting with my fellow inmates, peeking inside rooms, and generally trying to satisfy my inquisitive mind. It usually was not a solo effort: you would join up with another would-be explorer and head off into the unchartered territory. You never knew when there might be a big, cantankerous nurse lurking around the next corner, waiting to swat small children like us. It was hard to get exercise in the hospital, a fact not lost on a child like myself who was used to the wide open space of Fundy Bay to satisfy my need for running room. When I could stand it no longer, I would initiate a game of tag with my new best friend, and we would chase each other around the treacherous hallways, so slippery and polished that you could see your refection in them. We would usually disregard the warnings of the cleaning staff, as their blue uniforms betrayed their lack of authority. It was not until someone in white grabbed us by the collars or hollered at us that we would slow down to a gallop.

The two things which stand out most about my section of the hospital on the upper floor are the laundry chute and the kitchen. I don't know why, but the laundry chute fascinated me. It took many hospital visits for me to fully understand what it was. I learned to walk around the halls in an orderly fashion, so as to go almost unnoticed while I purposefully followed the cart of soiled linen to the laundry chute. When the man opened up the chute and started throwing the laundry inside, I would rush up and ask if I could watch. The man always smiled brightly and was willing to oblige, obviously ticked that this child would take so much interest in a job that had brought him so much ridicule in the adult world. So he would let me look down inside, so I could see the linen tumble down the chute, around the corner and out of sight. I would always listen for a sound that the linen's journey had ended, but to no avail. I didn't know if it was because of the lack of weight of the linen, or because the chute went on and on for miles. Whenever I asked the man, he would simply smile and say that the linen had gone to the basement, to the laundry room.

Since I was on the fifteenth floor, the thought of the being able to slide all the way to the laundry room filled me with wonder, with a healthy dose of fear. Some days, when I was feeling sad, I would go to the laundry chute, open it up, and stare down. I would wonder what it would be like to jump in, and what adventure would await me. I was sure that I could escape the nurses this way. I might even find a whole new world. I couldn't imagine what a laundry room would look like. What were the people like who worked there? Were they mean? Would they give me chocolate milk? Sometimes I would yell, "hello down there", down the chute, marvelling at the beautiful echoing sound it produced. I spent many moments looking down the chute, usually stopping only when some concerned, agitated person in white, such as Nurse Yells-A-Lot would rush up, asking "What do you think you're doing? Get away from there before you hurt yourself!" I sometimes tried to enlist my best friend for the day in my adventure, the trip down the chute to the magical basement, where we could do whatever we wanted, and from where we could go home. However, very few children found the laundry chute as fascinating as me, so no one was up for the ride. Nonetheless, I never ceased wondering what waited down around the corner of that silver laundry chute, offering the possibility of taking me away from all this.

The kitchen area was another matter. It wasn't really a kitchen. Simply a small room with a sink, a refrigerator, a hotplate, a small table, and cupboards. The fridge was the main attraction, as visitors would leave cold treats for their loved ones before they left. Trouble is, usually the treats had vanished by the time the loved one came down looking for relief from a parched throat or to satisfy that special craving that the family had so thoughtfully provided for. Of course, to the inmates, this was not surprising. All of our favourite toys also routinely disappeared from our night tables, usually no later than 48 hours into your stay. But of course, these disappearances of toys, food, and other personal belongings were always blamed on the cleaning staff. It made one wonder if the primary purpose of the cleaning staff was to clean the hospital or to serve as a convenient scapegoat for the closet kleptomaniacs amongst the higher salaried nursing staff. Nonetheless, gone is gone to a child. It becomes somewhat irrelevant who took your favourite TONKA, popsicle, or your $5 bill given to you lovingly by your father.

As children, we often checked inside the fridge when it was unattended, to see if any of our lost treats had mysteriously reappeared. I remember one such day. After a succession of thefts which had left me with little more than my Johnny shirt and chewed piece of bubble gum, I was walking by the kitchen area when I decided to check out inside the fridge. Low and behold, inside to my amazement was the exact single serving size tub of chocolate ice cream that my father had bought for me a week ago, and which I hadn't seen since. I looked around, hardly able to believe my good fortune. I loved chocolate ice cream almost as much as chocolate milk. I was quite sure they must be members of the same food group, the chocolate stuff group. Not being one to look a gift horse in the mouth, I seized the moment and the ice cream. I practically floated back to my room, slowly savouring each dab of ice cream that I would shovel into my mouth with that thin wooden spoon.

In the midst of my bliss, Nurse Black Moustache suddenly appeared in front of me, shouting, "Where did you get that ice cream?!"

Quite startled and not wanting to appear opportunistic, I simply said "From the fridge".

Well, that set her off on a tirade.

"That ice cream belongs to Johnny. His parents bought it for him this afternoon when they visited. See, it has his name written on the side of it."

Well, she had me there. So it did. Boy, did I feel rotten. As I stood there, caught redhanded, looking into her scrunched up face, I could feel the ice cream turning sour in my stomach.

"I..I.. I thought it was mine!" was all I could muster.

"That was a bad thing you did, stealing Johnny's ice cream. You are going to pay for that from your own money."

Hah! The joke's on her. My money was stolen days ago.

Nonetheless, I knew that some unpleasant reckoning was ahead of me. To my amazement, from somewhere in my room Nurse Black Moustache found some money which she said was mine, and she handed it over to Johnny, while I was forced to apologize for eating his ice cream. This furore came to be known as the ice cream incident in our family, a tale not relayed by me but rather by Veronica Collins who heard of it at the nurse's station the next day.

Despite all the assurances by my mother that I would see the lovely Veronica Collins during my staff, I rarely did. Strangely, though, whenever I would get home, Mom would have all sorts of stories about what I had done while I was at the hospital, the names of kids I had been friendly with, trouble I had gotten into, all tales brought homeward by Veronica. I started to wonder if she was spying on me the entire time. On the rare occasions that I did see her, I would not recognize her until she stopped me and introduced herself. It was quite a shock to discover that Nurse Long Legs was actually Veronica. It seemed odd how even the most recognizable persons and things become alien to you when they are in the midst of an unfamiliar landscape. I somehow felt duped again that I had actually taken some comfort from the guarantee of frequent visits from Veronica, when in fact, she was a no-show as far as I could tell.

Eventually, despite all indications that I might be in for the long haul, the day would come when it was time for me to go home. This was never announced in advance, which was probably just as well. It was usually sprung on me the morning of my parole, most often by Nurse Smiley Face. And then, a whirlwind of activity was scheduled for me. I started to wonder if the day had taken the staff by surprise.

Check out day was always accompanied by the removal of the stitches. For most times, this would seem painful and a must to avoid, but on parole day, it didn't seem to hurt at all. The stitches were never taken out by the doctor I had seen in the operating room, since the eyes were definitely different. This doctor seemed pleasant, very upbeat, and spoke encouraging about how well the scars had healed. He worked quickly and seemed to understand my enthusiasm about going home. Truth was, I couldn't really remember what home looked like, or who lived there with you, but hey, take a chance, go anyway. Had to be better than this place, right? Then, after what seemed like hours of rummaging through the room to find all my belongings, my family would arrive, totally unannounced.

At the sight of my family, I would be filled with a pure, uncontrollable joy. Everything that I had forgotten was remembered. There was Johnny, looking just as happy to be reunited with me, as I was to be with him again. Mom was able to smile and laugh genuinely now, knowing that there was no bad news to be hidden away. Dad would usually be in the background, with a noticeable smile on his face, obviously looking forward to settling in again on the farm knowing that all of his family were safe and sound under his roof. Every hospital stay seemed to end the same way, with Mom wondering what had become of all the toys they had left me, followed by Dad's expressions of "For heaven's sake" when he was told that I never got the money or ice cream he had left.

Mom and Dad would discuss whether they should go see the nurse, while I was busy introducing Johnny to my soon to be ex-best friends. I always felt somewhat guilty on parole day, since I knew what it was like to be lying in bed, seeing someone else's smiling family come in to pick up their child and leave you behind. So, I usually tried to leave my friends with the same hollow assurances that my family had left me with when they had dropped me off. Then, after Nurse Smiley Face agreed with Mom that it was terrible that you could not leave things in a night table drawer without having them stolen, Dad would grab my suitcase, and we would head to the elevator.

It was amazing to me how pleasant the hospital was the day of my departure. It was as if the entire staff had worked overtime to redecorate the place. It was interesting to discover that Nurse Black Moustache did have teeth after all, and as she told me that all the nurses would miss me, I had an odd feeling of leaving behind something familiar, something that perhaps hadn't been so terrible. As we walked the corridors, I pointed out every nook and cranny to Johnny, being somehow proud that I could serve as such a knowledgeable tour guide. When I paused at the laundry chute for Johnny to peer inside, Mom would move us along, saying "Don't look in there, dear, it's dangerous." Oh, well, it was only a laundry chute after all.

Once I got outside, I would be delirious at the great expanse that was the outdoors. No walls holding me in. I would usually want to race Johnny to the car. Once inside, Johnny would start telling me about the surprise gifts that were waiting for me at home. After telling me how good my lip looked, Mom would commence her four hours of chatter at Dad. Dad would take one look at the map, remind Mom that they had to be careful not to miss that right turn on Robie, and off we would go. Despite the slight tightness in my upper lip, I don't think I stopped smiling all the way home.

△ △ △

Made in the USA
Middletown, DE
17 June 2018